The Secret Recipe for Moving On

Karen Bischer

Swoon Reads
New York

A Swoon Reads Book

An imprint of Feiwel and Friends and Macmillan Publishing Group, LLC

120 Broadway, New York, NY 10271

The Secret Recipe for Moving On. Copyright © 2021 by Karen Bischer. All rights reserved. Printed in the United States of America.

Utensils pattern by Kashtal/Shutterstock

Our books may be purchased in bulk for promotional, educational, or business use. Please contact your local bookseller or the Macmillan Corporate and Premium Sales Department at (800) 221-7945 ext. 5442 or by email at MacmillanSpecialMarkets@macmillan.com.

Library of Congress Control Number: 2020911197

ISBN 978-1-250-24230-3 (hardcover)

Book design by Trisha Previte

First edition, 2021

10 9 8 7 6 5 4 3 2 1

swoonreads.com

FOR MOM AND DAD
LOVE, BRAT

CHAPTER 1

Some of my best decisions have been the spur-of-the-moment kind:

* Stopping at Kenny's Ice Cream Palace between work and home and being the ten thousandth customer and getting free cones for the rest of the summer.

* Not getting on that Six Flags roller coaster just before it got stuck and no one could get off for two hours.

* Going to that college fair and meeting my boyfriend.

* Finally sleeping with him.

Well, okay, in three weeks, anyway.

I just made *that* decision while sitting on the beach next to Lake Newman, and feel very secure in it.

Now I just have to tell my boyfriend.

We're surrounded by friends, so I need to get him alone. Unfortunately, Hunter and his friend Steve are listening intently to Steve's phone, trying to pick out new songs that will fit in their a cappella group's repertoire.

But maybe Hunter isn't concentrating too hard, because he was just kind of weirdly staring at Brynn Potts as she slathered sunscreen on her arms and legs.

Earlier, when I'd swum across the lake and stopped to catch my breath, I'd turned just in time to see him pick up a squealing Brynn and toss her in the lake, which wouldn't have been a big deal if 1) Brynn wasn't wearing a skimpy bikini and 2) Brynn hadn't popped out of the water and chased after Hunter, the two of them giggling like crazy.

A nagging feeling of what I assume is some kind of biological "Hey, that's my man" territorialism suddenly forced me to think about whether I was finally ready for condom-purchasing and the ensuing nakedness after all.

So I stride over to Hunter, sticking my shoulders back, and hope I look just as hypnotizing in my purple-striped one-piece.

"Hey," I say, putting a hand on his shoulder.

"What's up, babe?" he asks, his eyes closed. He's "feeling the music," as he likes to say.

"Want to join me for a walk?"

"Uh, maybe in a few minutes," he says.

But in a few minutes, Brynn will probably be sitting on his lap, and even the idea of that sends a weird spasm of urgency up my spine, so I squeeze his shoulder, a silent way of letting him know I need to talk to him.

But he doesn't get it. I feel like Hunter and I haven't been in sync much lately, mostly because we've barely seen each other the past couple of weeks.

"I'd really like to talk to you about something," I say, and that seems to catch Brynn's attention, because she turns around, shades her eyes, and gives me a smile.

"Uh, okay," Hunter finally says as he takes the earbud out of his ear.

I wait for him to pull on his sneakers and T-shirt and try not to be bothered that he seems a little annoyed by this interruption. I comfort myself by thinking about how excited he'll be when I tell him I'm finally ready to sleep with him. The possibility of sex kind of trumps music at this point.

We follow the path away from the beach to the top of the small cliff overlooking the lake. He's silent for most of the walk until we get to the top of the cliff, when he asks, "So, what's up?"

My palms start to sweat. "Is everything okay between us?"

Hunter cocks his head. "Okay? What do you mean?"

You're imagining the weirdness. Awesome, Mary Ellen. But I plow on. "I just feel like you've been a little distant the last week or so."

Hunter rolls his eyes and puts his hands on my shoulders. "I've been so wrapped up in getting the Ringtones' setlist together, I've been ignoring you, haven't I?"

"So we're cool?"

"Yes, and I'm sorry. And I want to find a way to make it up to you."

Relief floods me and I smile. "Well, I've been thinking. You know how our camping trip is coming up?"

Hunter slaps his hand to his forehead. "Oh, crap, I still have to buy a tent."

I try not to seem ruffled by this. "They're on sale at The Sporting Zone. Maybe we can go there later this week."

He nods. "Yeah, sure."

That's when Steve and some of the others on the beach start yelling up at us, "Jump! Jump! Jump!"

Even if my priority weren't to drop this sex bombshell on my boyfriend, I'd still have no desire to jump right now. For one thing, I'm wearing my shoes, and my biggest pet peeve is having wet feet and not being able to take your shoes off. Second, I'm wearing the semi-pricey eyeglasses that I accidently tried on before seeing how much they cost, but my mom insisted on paying for ("You've worked so hard this summer and they look great on you; let me treat you," she'd said), even though I think she's had to bring lunch to work for the last three weeks as a result. I felt guilty enough letting her buy them given our family's current financial state—I don't even want to know how I'd feel if I lost them by jackknifing into Lake Newman.

Hunter just waves at everyone like he's a politician or something.

I can't hold it in anymore. "I think we should do it that night."

"What night? I've got rehearsal every day this week."

He still thinks we're talking about The Sporting Zone.

"No, I mean *do it*. When we're camping. Have sex."

Hunter looks confused. "In the tent?"

Now, I'm a little thrown. I was expecting him to smile dazzlingly and be like, "No way!" like the time his parents surprised him with Devils tickets. I mean, he doesn't even like hockey, but he's wanted to sleep with me for at least eight months now.

I try to force a laugh. "Of course in the tent!"

Hunter sticks his hands in his pockets and stares at the ground. "Oh . . . I just . . . because you were so . . ."

I know he wants to say "picky."

". . . cautious before, I didn't think you'd want to do it, like, in the woods."

I can't help it when a feeling of angst swells inside me. When I'd put off all of his previous attempts at having sex, I'd stopped because it didn't feel right doing it in his sweaty-sock-smelling room with his gerbils watching us from their cage. My room wasn't an option because I have a really narrow twin bed. It didn't feel right doing it in our parents' beds because that's gross. And the backseat of a car just isn't romantic. But most of all, I knew once you had sex you couldn't undo it.

All those times I'd said no, I didn't feel guilty because my mother, *Teen Vogue*, health class teachers were always like, "Wait until you're ready." It felt okay saying no. But when it feels like every other girl is saying yes and your boyfriend is aware of that?

Yeah, there are times when it feels like I'm in some remedial sex zone, like I've been left back three grades and everyone else is on the AP track, graduating early and with full sex honors.

"I think it will be romantic," I finally say. "No one around except us, nature, and the elements."

This seems to bring him back into the moment. "You'd better use those forecasting skills of yours and pray it doesn't rain," he says, smiling.

"That might be even more romantic! Rain tapping on the tent . . ." Okay, probably not, but he's not giving me much to work with here.

"Not if we're getting washed away in a mudslide." He reaches an arm out. "Come here."

I snuggle into his chest and breathe in the smell of sunscreen on his T-shirt. I'm still getting used to his harder and more defined pecs, the result of all his excessive working out of late. In the last few months, ever since his a cappella group, the Ringtones, won the Ringvale Heights High School talent show, he'd gone from mocking our school's gym rats to weight-lifting in his basement on a daily basis. I'm not complaining. He looks amazing.

"If you're sure . . ."

"More than you know."

". . . then three weeks from now it is." He kisses me on the top of my head, but before I can reach up for full-frontal lip contact, he lets go of me, tears off his shirt, and runs for the edge of the cliff, yelling, "Cannonball!"

Hunter obviously does not have a problem with wet feet in wet shoes.

His jump is followed by cheers and chanting, "Panz! Panz! Panz!" (short for his last name, Panzic) from our friends on the beach below. I see him pumping his fist as he emerges from the water. I'm not sure if he's feeling victorious because of his jump or because he's finally going to lose his virginity.

I stand there awkwardly, watching Hunter swim back to shore. I always thought deciding to have sex would feel like something momentous, not end with my normally soft-spoken boyfriend shouting and cannonballing to get away from me.

I peer down at everyone on the beach, where no one seems aware of me, except Alisha Desai, who's wading in knee-deep water. She gives me a big smile and a wave. I wave back, but stay put. It's hot, but I'm not done enjoying the view of the treetops and endless stretch of New Jersey sky, where cumulonimbus clouds are starting to gather in the west.

"Ellie Agresti!" Steve screams, startling me. "Jump on down here!"

I give a faint smile. I think of my best friend, Jodie, who wants to be a TV writer someday. We play a game called "If this were a bad TV show . . ." and fill in situations with television clichés. Like, right now, if this were a bad TV show, I'd jump off the cliff, which would represent me 1) leaping into the sexual unknown and 2) proving that I'd grown as a person, overcoming my fears of growing up or something equally "barfy," as Jodie likes to say.

I sigh as I turn my back on the beautiful scenery, grab Hunter's shirt, and head down toward the beach. When I rejoin our friends, Hunter's shaking his dark brown hair like a dog, spraying water all over Kim Darrett and Brynn, who squeal and giggle. Well, Brynn giggles—she and Hunter have been best friends since second grade, and she thinks everything he does is hilarious—but Kim pulls her black hair into a bun and flops over on her beach towel and onto her stomach.

"Sorry, Kim," Hunter says, fighting a grin.

"Whatever," Kim huffs.

I just smile, not wanting anyone to think I'm taking sides.

See, *our* friends are mostly *Hunter's* friends, since he's known them longer. When I transferred to Ringvale Heights in January, I met Hunter right away, and we started dating soon after that, so his social circle became mine. And while I do like a few of them, some can be a bit . . . ridiculously stuck-up.

Like, I can tell the wheels are turning in Kim's head when I see her eyeing Alisha's reading material on the towel next to her.

Alisha, who may be the sweetest person in the senior class, let alone our group, has pulled from her bag *Prom of the Undead*, a current best-selling book about high school zombies and the girls who love them. Kim rolls her eyes at Brynn when she sees this, and I pray Alisha doesn't notice.

"How is that?" I ask.

Her eyes light up. "It's amazing. Amazingly cheesy, but I love it."

That's when Kim lets out a seriously condescending snort. "I don't get why everyone loves that book so much. Don't people realize there are better things to read?"

I bite my tongue, not wanting to say what I'm thinking, which is that there has to be a better way for Kim to express her opinion without tromping on Alisha's.

Alisha shrugs and blows a strand of dark hair out of her face, not seeming bothered. "It's nice to have something fun to read before delving into the school reading list."

Brynn takes this moment to jump in. "I read the first ten pages and had to put it down. It was so ridiculous. But I guess *tweens* like that sort of thing."

"It's escapism," I say, forcing a laugh so I didn't come off as combative. Because, I mean, Alisha is in all honors classes and is obviously not a tween. "It doesn't have to be great literature."

That's when Kim pulls out her book, *Crime and Punishment*, and tilts her head, as if daring me to say something.

Alisha smiles, opening her book. "To each her own."

I move over to where Hunter is, trying to ignore the feeling of annoyance bubbling up inside me. He and Steve are sharing a pair of earbuds again, listening to something on Hunter's phone.

Hunter smiles at me. "It's a song we could do as a group." He hands me his earbud. "What do you think?"

Ever since the Ringtones won the spring talent show with my song idea—Bruno Mars's "Grenade"—Hunter likes to bounce possibilities off me.

Just as I'm about to put the earbud in my ear, Brynn stands up and walks over. "As the Ringtones manager, I get veto privileges." She snatches Steve's earbud from him and scoots between him and Hunter.

Brynn asked if she could manage the Ringtones after they won the talent show and group members had girls throwing themselves at them and asking when their next gig would be. Brynn wants to be a publicist someday, so she viewed this as her first big job, and has since scored them a couple of gigs singing around the area. If you consider nursing homes and the local farmers' market "gigs," that is.

I put the earbud in and try not to be bothered that Brynn, with her revealing aqua-color bikini, is practically sitting on my boyfriend's lap. I remind myself that they've been friends forever and probably think of each other like siblings at this point.

"Ed Sheeran," I say as the music fills my ear. "You guys will kill with this."

"I know, right? You always get it and I love that," Hunter says, beaming. Then he looks around. "Did anyone bring food? I'm starving."

"I brought cookies," I say, reaching for my bag.

"Oh no!" Steve cries. "I don't want anything you've baked. I'm still remembering your chocolate chip cookies!"

I give him a dirty look and toss a package of Oreos at him. "How many times do I have to tell you? My dad keeps the sugar and kosher salt in unmarked containers. It was an honest mistake."

Hunter laughs and I want to push him into the lake. He knows my chef father doesn't label everything in the pantry, and I even showed him the salt to let him see just how much it looks like sugar. At the time, he agreed it could have happened to anyone.

"It's not like I see you guys baking up a storm," I mutter under my breath.

"Chill, Ellie," Hunter says with a grin, and my face flames knowing he heard me. "We're all taking home ec for a reason."

"Yeah, an easy A," Brynn says.

Hunter laughs. "Well, that, too."

Brynn, Hunter, Steve, and I signed up for home ec as our elective for senior year. Actually, the class is called Applicable Life Skills for Young Adults, but from what I hear, it mostly involves cooking.

Alisha stands up. "I've got to get home for a family barbecue. If anyone wants a ride with me, speak now."

"Ooh, I'd love a ride," Brynn says. "We're having my sister's birthday dinner tonight."

I glance at Hunter, since we got a ride with Steve, but he's watching Brynn. "Diana's home?"

Brynn nods. "Yeah, you should stop by later, she'd love to see you. You're, like, family."

I get a twinge in my stomach when Brynn says that. I know Hunter's known her family longer, but he's closer to them than I think he'll ever be to mine. Granted, I don't bring Hunter around to my house that much because I could tell there was a mutual dislike between him and my mom when they met. Hunter was all, "Does your mom really read tarot cards?" and not in a fascinated way, and Mom was like, "That Hunter seems pretty aloof," and not in a "but that's okay" sort of way.

Hunter looks at me. "We should probably go. Cool?"

I nod, since I don't really want to be here without him.

Kim makes a face. "I'm going to stick around." She turns to me. "Hey, Weathergirl, is it going to rain? I need to put the top up on my car if so."

To her credit, Kim sounds like she may be trying to be friendly when she says this. But I think several of my friends seem to think it's funny that I want to be a meteorologist, like I'll be some bimbo pointing out smiley-faced sunshines on a big map of the United States. I tell them all the time that I want to do research on weather, not broadcast it, but no one seems to listen. I glance to the west, where the storm clouds were forming before. They're getting closer now.

"Nope, not that I know of," I say, plastering a smile on my face.

It's not like the rain will kill her or anything. Maybe just make for a mildewy smell in her BMW convertible. We'll call it my revenge for her ripping on Alisha's book.

I feel a little guilty thinking like this because of Hunter—he obviously cares about his friends, but sometimes I can't deal with how cluelessly snotty they are.

But when we walk toward the car with Alisha and Brynn, I try to make an effort. "Alisha, will there be a broadcast tomorrow morning?"

Hunter's walking ahead of me, but I hear him snort. He thinks everyone at our school's TV station takes it way too seriously . . . even though he's just as intense about the Ringtones.

"Yep," Alisha says, either not hearing Hunter or choosing to ignore him. "I went in yesterday to cover football practice."

It's only then that I notice Brynn has increased her pace, then gets in the back seat with Hunter before I can get to the car. I realize I'll be getting dropped off last, since I live closest to Alisha—and me being in the front seat makes sense—but it almost feels like Brynn was racing me. I bite my lip as I buckle my seat belt and Alisha starts the car.

We turn out of the woods and onto the road leading to Brynn and Hunter's neighborhood. I gaze wistfully out the window as we pass all the gorgeous old mansions and their manicured lawns on either side of the road. While Brynn and Hunter's parents don't own houses like this, they are definitely upper-middle-class. They live in the new section of Ringvale Heights, in the big brick-and-stucco homes that were built in the last ten years, complete with gourmet kitchens and three-car garages. Alisha and I are in the older section of town, where the houses are far less opulent. Most of them don't even have garages, let alone ones for three cars.

"Damn it," Hunter groans. "I got a mosquito bite on the bottom of my foot."

I peek behind me and Hunter is studying his bare foot in his lap. I notice Brynn's sitting closer to Hunter than to her actual seat. They're shoulder to shoulder and she touches his foot as she examines it for a bugbite.

I chew the inside of my cheek as if to keep myself from spitting out the snarly "Can you move to your own damn seat please, Brynn," that's bubbling up in my throat. The last thing I want is to look like a psycho possessive girlfriend, so I stare straight ahead and silently will my sex deadline to get here quickly.

There's something vaguely terrifying about coming home after deciding to have sex and having both your parents sitting on the porch as if they can read your mind and are waiting for you just to be all, "You're going to sleep with *him*? When we've both somewhat passive-aggressively made known he's totally not worthy of you? Really?"

But when I get closer, I can see they're merely relaxing with glasses of ice water, and I'm struck for maybe the millionth time at what an odd couple they are. You couldn't tell when they're sitting, but Mom's about two inches taller than Dad. She's pretty bohemian—my grandmother used to say she dresses like a "flower child," even though she was born too late for Woodstock and all that. Today, for example, she's wearing a flowy yellow-and-orange blouse over jeans that are cut off right above the knee, and her long, light-brown hair is tucked back under a red bandana.

My father is more straightedge, though with a slightly European flair. Right now, he's wearing khaki shorts and an A.C. Milan soccer T-shirt he picked up about eight years ago during one of our trips to see his side of the family in Italy. Everyone tells me I look like him, even Mom, who claims I'm "all Agresti." I guess Dad's thick, almost-black hair and brown eyes genes won the DNA battle over Mom's fairer features, though I did inherit a taste for cheesy made-for-TV movies and the dimple in my right cheek from her.

They met when my mom was backpacking through Italy after graduating from college and my dad was a waiter at a café in Milan. He offered to give her a tour of the Duomo cathedral where he was once an altar boy, and the rest is history. When I ask them what attracted them to each other, my mom always says, "He had a great head of hair," which will make my dad respond with, "She tipped well."

I think of what I'd say if someone asked me what attracted me to Hunter: He saved me from being the new-girl social outcast.

I notice then how my parents' clothes are grass-and-dirt-stained. "What were you guys doing?"

"Cleaning out the gutters and patching up holes on the roof," Mom says.

"You went on the roof?" I practically yell. "Are you trying to make me an orphan?" Not that the roof is that high—the old farmhouse is two stories tall—but I was afraid of them falling *through* the roof.

The house was built by my great-great-grandfather in 1910 and not much has been updated since then.

"El, you know we can't afford a roofer," Mom says. Dad just kind of stares off in the distance when she says this, and I instantly feel bad. It's not really his fault we're broke.

For years, my dad had wanted to open his own restaurant, and he finally got enough investors together about five years ago. He opened Agresti's in our old town, Green Ridge, and food critics loved it. It was crowded every night and making decent money, so my parents bought a bigger house. It made enough money that Dad was able to hire a business manager, Dave, so he could go on vacations and not work weekends and stuff like that.

Except Dave basically screwed us out of all our money and we had to shut down the restaurant. My father didn't get out of bed for almost two weeks after this all went down. I'm not sure I can describe what it's like to watch your father give up on his dream *and* be incredibly in debt.

That led to us moving to Ringvale Heights, to the farmhouse, which has seen better days. Its weather-beaten white clapboard siding is in desperate need of a power washing, the slightly crooked black shutters are hanging on by some gravity-defying miracle, and there's only one bathroom, tiled in 1950s Pepto-Bismol pink. But the mortgage is paid off and my parents only have to pay taxes on it, which is much cheaper than having to rent a new place.

In an effort to not bring the family morale down any further, I try to keep my feelings to myself. But honestly? Having to change schools in the middle of your junior year was beyond crappy.

Whenever I think of what was lost, I remind myself that I now have Hunter, so it worked out in that respect, at least.

"How was the lake?" Mom asks, and the whole sex thing comes rushing back.

"Oh, it was fine," I say, pulling my shoulder-length hair into a ponytail, trying to appear casual.

"Anything life-changing happen?"

I know she's joking but it's like she *knows*.

"Ha. Not today."

"But it will tomorrow," my dad says. "Just wait till you start cooking in your class!"

"Marco, don't pressure the poor thing," my mom says with a laugh. "She may have inherited my cooking skills for all you know."

"I seriously doubt home ec will change my life," I say as I head inside. "If I really need to learn to cook, I can always learn from the master."

My father beams.

But seriously. Moving to a new high school in the middle of your junior year changes your life. Getting into your first-choice college changes your life. Actually having sex with your boyfriend changes your life.

Home economics class?

Not so much.

CHAPTER 2

I'm having the dream again. I'm back in seventh grade and standing on the sidelines of a gym class basketball game. My classmates are some variety of laughing, pointing, and staring at me because I'm wearing my old scoliosis brace over my clothes instead of under them. Danny Flatt comes up to me, sneering, and says, "No guy is ever going to want to have sex with you, Robot Girl." This makes everyone in the room start laughing and pointing and staring harder, and then they all start chanting "Robot Girl!"

For some reason, the only thing I can say before I run out of the room is "Spaghetti."

The sad thing is, aside from wearing the brace over my clothes, that probably could've been a typical day in middle school for me, even my lack of a formidable comeback. So it's a relief to wake up twenty minutes before my alarm is set to go off, even though I realize I am crying and my nose is running. The last time I had the dream was right before I started at Ringvale Heights High and I'm guessing it was spurred on this time by the fact that Hunter didn't return my call or texts last night.

I'd tried to go to bed as though I wasn't bothered by the lack of communication, even though Hunter and I either spoke or texted every night before going to sleep. But I pretty much tossed and turned till about four in the morning.

Maybe Hunter had stayed too late at Brynn's and was too tired to talk or send a text saying we'd talk in the morning. I ponder this and other various scenarios as I plod down the hall to the bathroom. I make sure to be quiet, since Dad got home from the Italian restaurant he works at a little after midnight and Mom doesn't have to go to work at the new age store in town until 11:00 a.m.

I endure an intermittently hot and cold shower. I have no idea when the water heater was last replaced—my guess is it was sometime around the Kennedy administration—but at least I feel awake, though with a gnawing feeling in my stomach. I've clearly got a case of first-day-of-school nerves. I had them my first day at RHHS back in January, so it makes sense.

What's sad is that I didn't really ever have a problem with school at all until seventh grade, the hellhole of doom that inspired my dream this morning. Jodie and I were both at Chester Arthur Middle School, and since we hung out with the geeks, we both got picked on a bit, though not more than any other geek.

That's until the scoliosis testing happened.

Yes, thanks to the school nurse being concerned about the curvature of my spine, and my doctor agreeing with her, my parents were told I'd have to wear a brace if I didn't want to be all hunched over and crooked by the time I was forty. The brace was a mix of plastic and elastic and was way uncomfortable, but luckily, under my clothes it totally was not obvious. Except, one day in social studies, Danny, who thought himself quite the class clown, but was really just a dick hiding behind "humor," went to go snap my bra strap and instead hit the brace.

"Oh my god, what *is* that?" he laughed.

When I didn't answer, he yelled, "What, are you a robot?" He found this super hilarious and from that day on would yell "Robot Girl!" and other various insults whenever he saw me.

His friends got in on it and, for the next two years, they all made fun of me whenever I was in earshot. I didn't want to tell any of the teachers because that would probably just make the situation worse.

My friends told me to not give them the satisfaction and just ignore it, but it was incessant, and I had no idea how to stop it. Danny and his friends started throwing food at me in the cafeteria and making fun of the fact that I was interested in meteorology ("Hey, Robot Girl! Is there a ketchup-packet downpour in your forecast?") and picking on me on class trips ("Don't forget to bring Robot Girl's oilcan!"). It got so awful, I broke down and told my parents about it . . . which was a bad move because they told the school, who called Danny and the gang's parents.

They were quieter about their bullying after that, but in a way that was worse, because it felt creepier. I didn't need Danny whispering "Robot Girl" at me when I passed him and his friends in the halls or staring at me for the length of an entire class. It felt vaguely sinister.

Then Jodie decided to go to St. Catherine's for high school, since her mom worked there as a history teacher and could get Jodie in for free. I asked my parents if I could go, because the idea of an all-girls school, free of boys, sounded like heaven. Since the restaurant was doing well and they knew how much trouble I was having, they agreed. And St. Catherine's was amazing. Don't get me wrong, it had its share of bitchy mean girls, but they mellowed out by the time junior year rolled around, and our small class was actually kind of close.

So when I was told I had to go to public school again, I was terrified. I didn't have that much exposure to guys my age, and for me, they were still evil. I was the average-looking new girl who was pretty much poor. I didn't have the scoliosis brace anymore, but I knew if people wanted to find something to tease you about, they would.

I basically flew under the radar the first week, sneak-eating my lunch in the back of the library so I wouldn't have to face the humiliation of eating alone in the cafeteria. But one day, I'd been forced out of my hiding spot because a college fair took over the library, and while I was annoyed at the interruption, it was quickly eased when I remembered Penn State, with its incredible meteorology program, was going to be there.

After losing most of my college tuition money, I was worried I'd have to drop it from my list. Still, I figured maybe I could talk to the admissions counselor about financial aid, because I wasn't quite ready to give up on the idea yet.

When I got to the Penn State table, however, it was empty, with a sign on it that read: "Be right back." I must've sighed really loud because a voice behind me said, "I know, right? I bet they're hanging out with the person from my table."

I turned around and there in front of the vacant Princeton table stood Hunter, all button-down shirt under a brown sweater and jeans. I didn't have much exposure to guys my age, but I was definitely attracted to the preppy type, and his Bambi eyes didn't hurt, either. I tried to hide the fact that I had no real idea how to converse with a boy my age—and apparently I did it well, because by the time the admissions counselor came back, Hunter had asked if I wanted to hang out with him and his friends, and I've managed to avoid being a target of wide-scale teasing since.

I'm putting my contact lenses in when my phone rings, and I sigh with relief. It's probably Hunter telling me when he's coming to pick me up—all summer, he drove my broke, car-less self around, even to my job at the shoe store three towns over. "It's what boyfriends do," he'd say when I'd thank him. "It's what *good* boyfriends do," I'd correct him.

But when I pick up the phone, my heart sinks a little when I see it's Jodie. And then I feel bad about that because she's my best friend and she never calls this early, so it must be something important.

"What's wrong?"

She laughs. "Good morning to you, too!"

"Sorry. You never call this early. I got worried."

"Nothing's wrong. I just realized this is our first first day of school that we're not spending together since we've known each other and I wanted to wish you luck!"

"Aww," I say, and I feel tears prick my eyes. "Like I don't miss you enough already!"

"Sorry! I'm about to microwave those smelly breakfast burritos you hate. Do you miss me now?"

I giggle. "Ugh, maybe not so much."

"Are you working tonight?"

"Yeah, until seven. Can you stop by?" Jodie and I live about forty minutes away from each other now, but my job at Cityscape Shoes is only twenty minutes from each of our houses. It's a good meeting point for a quick say-hello meeting.

"I don't think so. I have Chinese class." I can hear her rolling her eyes. Jodie was adopted from China when she was eight months old and when she turned six her parents decided that it was time for her to start understanding her roots, so they enrolled her in a Chinese language class. Jodie claims she has no desire to go track down her ancestry in China, but I think it's because she's terrified of flying—she's been on exactly one flight in her life, and Jodie's ensuing melt-down annoyed the flight crew so much that they asked her family to get off the plane. But she endures the classes because, as she says, "It'll look good for USC," her dream college . . . which means she has to get over her fear of flying at some point in the next ten months.

"So," Jodie says, and pauses dramatically. "Did you and Hunter talk more about *the big date*?"

"No. He never called me or texted me last night, so now—"

"Hold up. Don't start overthinking this. He's a dude, of course he's not going to be eloquent about it. I bet he's showing his excitement in other ways."

"Like how?" I ask.

"Um, like going out and buying truckloads of condoms and beer? Or maybe engaging in an arm-wrestling match with another guy? You know, to show off his newfound manliness."

I start laughing. I don't know where I'd be without her and her quick wit.

"Besides, it's the first day of school, and you always love that. Don't let the sex thing overshadow it. Seriously, what guy isn't excited about finally having sex?"

"Thanks. You've certainly got a lot of wisdom for this early in the morning."

"I've learned to embrace coffee," Jodie says. "Anyway, good luck today."

"You too. Say hi to St. Cat's for me."

After hanging up, I notice that I start to feel a bit better, maybe because the nerd in me actually *does* love the first day of school.

I check my phone one last time before I leave, and when there's no text from Hunter, I head out on foot.

When I get to school, the senior parking lot is filling up with cars and I fight back the sudden envy creeping into my stomach. I try to remind myself that a car isn't necessary and that it would be a waste of gas for me to drive the six blocks to school every day.

As I walk past the last row of cars, I see Brynn getting out of her Jetta. I remember my pact with myself to be nicer to Hunter's friends, so I call out, "Hey, Brynn!"

She lifts up her sunglasses and spots me, and her color seems to drain.

"Are you all right?" I ask, and she suddenly looks confused.

"Yeah, fine. You just startled me."

"Sorry. How was your sister's dinner?"

It's weird, but she's totally got beads of sweat starting around her forehead, and it's only seventy degrees right now.

"It was great. The whole family was there. By the way, did you remember to make the papier-mâché globe for the Ringtones' 'Mad World' number?"

You mean the song I suggested they do? Of course I remember. I can't say that out loud, though, so I nod. "Yeah, I can bring it in tomorrow."

"Good, because you know Steve is terrible with props and needs all the practice he can get. And he's always forgetting his part in the song. It's like, hi, how hard can it be to remember the bass line? It's not like . . ."

Brynn is positively babbling at this point and I start worrying that she's on caffeine pills. I mean, she's an overachiever and all, but it doesn't seem like her.

"Watch it!" I hear someone yell from behind us and all of a sudden, a figure on one of those BMX bikes flashes past, jumps the curb, and slams into a bench. The bike bounces back and its rider falls off, the bike on top of him. I suddenly feel totally guilty because, in my concern over Brynn's chattiness, I didn't realize we'd been walking in the bike lane.

"I'm so—" I start, but Brynn snaps at the biker, "Why don't you watch where you're going?"

I almost say, "You can't be serious," because it was our fault, but I'm more concerned with the rider. He sits up and pushes the bike off of him and I realize it's Luke Burke, a senior who is a good foot taller than me and who has a tattoo of a lightning bolt on the back of his left calf. In other words, not someone I want to mess with.

"I didn't realize I had to watch where I was going since I had the right of way." Luke smiles, but the passive-aggression is all there.

Then he bends down to pick up his baseball cap, which he puts on backward, and brushes off his elbow, which has a clump of grass stuck to it. "You ladies have a nice day." He smiles again as he locks up his bike and heads inside, and it can only be interpreted as "eat shit."

"He's such a freak," Brynn hisses, and I'm not surprised she'd think us blameless for being in the bike lane. Brynn can *never* admit to being wrong, and doubles down on the self-righteousness when she is.

When we get into the school lobby, I'm relieved when she points to the left and says, "Um, my homeroom is that way."

"Cool, mine's upstairs," I say. "See you at lunch."

"See you," Brynn says before speeding away.

I wonder if I should say something to Hunter about Brynn's odd behavior, but then, I'd actually have to see him for that to happen. As I walk to my homeroom, I pull out my phone and text him.

Are you here yet?

I'm still staring at my phone when someone comes through the door, holding it open for me.

"Oh, by all means, after you," a voice says.

When I look up, Luke is standing there, smiling. I'm afraid if I go through, he'll trip me or something, so I step back. "Oh—I'm—wrong stairway!" I sputter, and head for the stairwell on the other side of the cafeteria.

I feel like Luke is going to say something behind me, but he doesn't. Still, I walk as fast as I can, passing the cafeteria, when I suddenly spot Hunter inside. He's talking to Kim and has this really intense look on his face. Kim suddenly walks off in a huff, and Hunter goes the other way, toward me. I position myself outside the door, and when he bangs through it, he does not look happy to see me. I start to put two and two together. Oh my god. Kim told him I lied about the weather yesterday and now her car is a big mildewy mess.

"How are—" I start.

Hunter just grunts.

"What's wrong?" I ask.

"God, can you leave me alone for just one second?" he practically yells, and it brings tears to my eyes.

Not sure what I'm supposed to say, I step back and let him pass. He does, without so much as a "see you later."

The next time I see him is supposed to be in home ec.

Which means I have an entire torturous day to get through before then.

My heart is pounding when I get to the home ec room, and I've chewed off almost all my fingernails today. When people are upset with me, it always seems to manifest itself physically, and I've barely been able to concentrate all day as a result. It didn't help that Brynn and Kim were mysteriously absent from lunch.

To distract myself, I study the home ec room. There are five tables arranged in the middle, and five "kitchens" around the perimeter. It's obvious much of the room hasn't been updated since the 1970s—each kitchen's cabinets and counters are an alternating shade of reddish orange or avocado. Also obvious is that some funding must have come in recently, because there are newer stainless steel ovens in the walls of each kitchen, and there are two stainless steel refrigerators along the back wall. The cooktop ranges in the counters, however, still look ancient.

Steve is sitting at a table toward the front, so I take a seat with him. He scans the room and smiles. "I don't see any kosher salt, Ellie. You'll have to find another secret ingredient."

"You're so funny, Steve," I say, rolling my eyes.

Steve's still laughing when Hannah Chow, one of the Ringtones' groupies and one of Brynn's friends, takes a seat at our table. "What's up?" she asks, and I'm further relieved.

That's when Luke Burke walks in the room.

This can't end well.

He sees me and smiles. "You again!" he says, and takes a seat at the table next to mine.

"I'm—" But I can't finish what I want to say because Paul Wilder, the school's biggest bully, stalks into the room. He's about six foot five and is built like an eighteen-wheeler, and today he's wearing a thick chain with a Master Lock around his neck. His face is stony and pulls up a chair across from Luke. "Hey, man," Luke offers. Paul tilts his chin at Luke in greeting, but doesn't say anything.

And then Hunter arrives. It's like instinct right then because I'm suddenly delighted to see him . . . until I remember he's angry with me and I have no idea why. He takes the seat next to Steve. Then Brynn walks in and wordlessly sits on the other side of Hunter. She starts digging around her backpack while Hunter looks uncomfortable.

And then it dawns on me: Maybe they've had a fight, too. It would explain why Brynn was so weird around me this morning. But I have no idea what Brynn and I could've both done to make him so upset.

As the bell rings, a short woman with long, curly black hair and glasses strolls in with a mug of tea. "Hello, all. My name is Mrs. Sanchez," she says. "And this is Applicable Life Skills for Young Adults."

She sets her mug down on the counter at the front of the classroom, leaning on the counter as she takes attendance. When that's done, she starts shuffling some papers. "I started this class a few years ago when it became obvious to me that many in your generation are lacking the skills of self-sufficiency."

"Whatever," Paul coughs from the table next to mine.

Mrs. Sanchez fixes him with an amused stare. "I suppose you could run a household effectively, Mr. Wilder?"

Paul leans back in his chair. "Running a household? That's women's work." A.J. Johnson, a senior with close-cropped bleached-blond hair who I've seen working at the local deli, starts to laugh from the seat next to Paul.

I expect Mrs. Sanchez to go on a long feminist tirade like I would, but instead she smiles and says, "Well, what does that say about you, then, being in this class?"

"It says I want an easy A," Paul replies, his face suddenly stony.

Hey! We actually have something in common. Who knew?

"Well, Mr. Wilder," Mrs. Sanchez says. "I regret to inform you that this class is all about responsibility and is not in any way designed to give its students an automatic A. And while it's intended to make all of you eventually thrive in independence, you will be working together as a team, or a family in this case, and that may make it harder. Each table will be considered a family, and you will be competing against the other families in class for points every week. You will only be as strong as your weakest link."

I wonder if I'm considered the weak link at this table, since almost everyone has eaten my failed chocolate chip cookies.

"You earn the points by completing your tasks in a timely fashion, for turning in good work, and for showing teamwork, among other things," Mrs. Sanchez says. "And this is the one time in life where you can choose your family, so if you'd like to be at a different table, you can move now."

I glance around at the other tables in the classroom. The hipster/literary journal kids are sitting together to our left, a group of full-time stoner types behind them. Behind us is a snickering group with two football players I recognize, Bryce Pratt and Anthony Ruggio, because they are ridiculously well-built and have overly gelled hair. They're joined by two girls I've seen around—both with perfectly flat-ironed hair, both always with their heads bent together, gossiping, and hissing harsh "ohmygawwwds."

Then there's the table to our right, which is all guys; Luke, Paul, A.J., and a short, skinny kid with huge brown eyes, Isaiah Greenlow, who I think is a junior, and whose diminutiveness seems completely out of place among these giants.

Everyone seems content with where they are sitting, so no one moves. But I notice Mrs. Sanchez looking at our group. "Hmm, a group of five," she says. I see her scanning the room, and I know she's going to suggest one of us go to another table, but then she says, "Well, everyone else is full, so you'll have to make do."

With that, Mrs. Sanchez passes out a syllabus and starts explaining what we're going to be doing this year: grocery shopping, cooking, laundry, sewing, learning how to make minor household repairs, budgeting, and bill paying.

I try to catch Hunter's eye while this is going on, but his eyes are fixed to the syllabus. This is getting ridiculous. I'm talking to him when we're leaving class, and I don't care if it pisses him off.

The bell rings just as Mrs. Sanchez is explaining that our next class will be learning the basics of budgeting. "Unless dealing with money is also women's work," she says, directly to Paul. He doesn't seem to have any interest in what she's saying, because he takes off pretty much as soon as the bell rings.

I rush to pack up my things because Hunter is moving quickly, and I almost wonder if he's trying to ditch me. An icy feeling creeps into my stomach as I follow him out of the classroom, and practically sprint to keep up with him.

"Hunter," I say, hoping I don't sound desperate, or out of breath for that matter. "What's going on?"

He doesn't answer. This is not fair. It's like this sudden wave of anger comes over me, pushing out the fear for a minute, and as we come into the parking lot, I grab his arm.

"Hunter! What is your *problem*?"

He flings his arm up, knocking my hand off of him, and turns to me. His brown eyes are practically black, and his mouth is set in a thin line. I have no idea who this person is in front of me right now.

"My problem," he says through clenched teeth, "is that I can't deal with you clinging on me. Didn't Kim talk to you?"

For a moment I'm weirdly relieved that he's talking to me and that maybe now that I know what's wrong, we can—wait. Clinging on him? Kim?

"When did I ever cling on you? I just asked what—"

"I can't do this," he says, and opens his car door.

My stomach is churning at this point. "Can't do what?"

"This," he says, gesturing between us. "I can't be with you anymore."

"Where is this coming from?" I ask, feeling faint. It's as if he's pulled a pin from somewhere inside me with those words, and all my energy is draining out.

"It's been coming for a while," he says, and gets into the car. He goes to slam the door, but I grab it.

"Why are you doing this? Is this about yesterday? You said we were okay."

Hunter has one hand on the car door and the other on the steering wheel. He's staring straight ahead, but then he turns his head toward me and his eyes are so cold that I know I don't want to hear what's going to come out of his mouth next. But he says it anyway.

"I don't love you, Ellie."

I feel so weak and dizzy, it's like my soul is being sucked out of me, and I can't even respond. I'm honestly afraid I'm going to throw up. My hands slide off his car door, and Hunter takes that opportunity to slam it shut. He then quickly starts the car, backs out of the space, and drives away, his eyes on the road the whole time.

And I just watch him go.

CHAPTER 3

"I'm going to cut his nuts off!"

This is Jodie's solution to my world falling apart. And it would totally make me laugh if I wasn't completely devastated and sobbing hysterically in my place of employment.

"And then I'm going to hurl him into a fiery pit of lava," Jodie says, stroking my hair as I snuffle. "And then I'll make sure the Ringtones don't do some cheesy memorial concert for him."

The sight of Jodie in our old St. Catherine's uniform, a green-and-blue plaid skirt and white polo shirt, with her signature red USC hoodie should be comforting to me. And it is. But it also makes me feel even more sad that I won't have her with me to face the awfulness tomorrow. I mean, it's a pretty safe bet that all of my RHHS "friends" are going to be taking Hunter's side, sending me back to being alone again.

"I'll pray for a volcano to pop up somewhere in the tristate area just to see that happen," my manager Richard says. For someone who's had to deal with his employee being a bawling mess for the last two hours, he's handling this surprisingly well.

Even though coming to Cityscape Shoes was the last thing I wanted to do after being dumped, I figured it was probably better than going home, where I'd have to admit to my parents that yes, Hunter was indeed aloof and therefore a bad boyfriend. A bad *ex*-boyfriend. But the store's halfway-between-our-houses location meant Jodie, who cut her Chinese class when she got my breakdown via text message, could stop in and see me. The fact that she's so completely angry over this actually makes me feel the tiniest bit better.

"So help me god, I'm about to DM him on Instagram and tear him a new one," she seethes.

"Don't do that!" I say, suddenly alarmed. "He'll think I put you up to it."

"Wow, Jodie, this is a whole other side of you. You're always so sweet and jokey," Richard says. "Who knew?"

Richard is in his forties, but he gets along with Jodie and me really well. He hates television clichés as much as Jodie does, and Richard and his husband, Roy, are big weather nerds, like me. I feel bad that he's being subjected to high school drama right now, but not enough to stop crying.

"Please, he's totally lying to Ellie," Jodie says. "'I don't love you'? What kind of bull is that? He told her he loved her right in front of me two weeks ago when we went to the boardwalk."

Knife. In. The. Heart. I know Jodie didn't say it to hurt me, but a whole new wave of tears starts when I remember the moment she's talking about, when I won him a "Made in New Jersey" water bottle via the get-the-frog-on-the-lily-pad game and he was all, "I love this woman!"

"Maybe there's something going on at home?" Richard wonders. "This did seem sudden, didn't it?"

"It doesn't matter," Jodie says. "He's clearly going through something and making Ellie think she's to blame. That deserves a good telling off, if you ask me."

"But Ellie's too nice for that," Richard says.

"Guys," I hiccup, waving my hand, "I'm right here."

"He has a point," Jodie says. "You are too nice. I know you, Ellie. Don't let this slide."

And suddenly, Jodie's anger has transferred to me. She's right. In twenty-four hours, Hunter has gone from a normal boyfriend to dumping me in the middle of a parking lot, after we said *we were going to have sex*. I don't know how you make a decision like that, then decide you're completely indifferent about your girlfriend, but it's not fair.

After Jodie leaves and I work the rest of my shift without shedding another tear, I plan out what I'm going to write, and when I got home, I let it all out in a text:

> While I guess I have to respect the fact that you want to end our relationship, the way you went about it was completely ass-y. You allegedly don't love me, but having been your girlfriend for the past eight months, I figured I'd deserve something better than getting dumped in a parking lot. I am completely confused, since yesterday we decided to have sex, and today you want nothing to do with me. All I'm asking for is an explanation. You at least owe me that.

I hit SEND before I can change my mind and write something sappy. I sit back in my chair and wait. Then I read over the text again to see if it has the right emotional impact. Then I sit back in my chair again, until checking to see that I texted Hunter's cell number and not his parents' landline. Every time I pick up the phone, I'm forced to see my phone wallpaper, which is a picture of Hunter and me at the top of the Ferris wheel at the local fair. We're smiling with our heads touching, and there's a beautiful sunset behind us. So I quickly delete the pic and replace it with a photo I took of a vicious-looking purple anvil cloud during a hailstorm a few weeks ago.

I try to think if there have been any warning signs of Hunter being a heartless bastard over the last few months. Aside from the last week of him being a little distant, the biggest issue I had with him were his friends, who I knew I didn't really like from the first time we hung out. It was a game night at Hunter's house with Kim, Steve, and Brynn. I was fairly sure the date was going horribly, since Kim kept steering the conversation to classes I wasn't taking and I found something so weird about Brynn's seemingly forced friendliness.

I figured since they'd been longtime friends, they'd have Hunter's ear and tell him to ditch me, and I made myself okay with that idea because I really wasn't jibing well with his group. But something went right, because he asked me out "just us" the next week. We went to the local diner where we talked more about the Ringtones than anything else, but when I gave him some song suggestions, he called me a "genius," and I was delighted to be thought of so highly. Especially since the last time I had really been around guys, they were calling me names and throwing ketchup packets at me.

So when he kissed me, I felt like I had hit the lottery, even if upon our first kiss, my first kiss *ever*, he shoved his tongue in my mouth right away and kind of slobbered on me. But I figured no one was perfect, and maybe he was just inexperienced with the whole kissing thing, like me. Besides, he was cute, and he liked *me*. And it meant I wouldn't have to sneak lunch in the library anymore. What more could I ask for?

I think of that now. *He* asked me to hang out. *He* asked me out on our first date. *He* made the first move. And then he cuts me loose with no real explanation except that he's suddenly lacking feelings for me.

I check my phone again. Nothing.

And then I cry myself to sleep, which is probably much more than a horrible kisser like Hunter deserves.

CHAPTER 4

This is not going to be easy. I know this the second I return to the scene of the crime, the RHHS parking lot, the next morning and an overwhelming sense of nausea comes over me. Luckily, I'm driving my parents' car today, so I can take a moment to gather myself before I get out.

I look at the papier-mâché globe in the passenger's seat. It was the reason why my parents let me borrow the car, since Dad doesn't have to be at work until tonight and Mom is off. I didn't tell them about the breakup, one, because I want to make sure Hunter and I are completely and totally broken up (I mean, what if we get back together?) and two, because I know they aren't fans of Hunter. I feared they'd be relieved or something if I told them and that would just make me feel even worse.

Anyway, Dad saw me getting ready to leave this morning and was all, "It's raining, you don't want to ruin that! You worked so hard on it!" Which almost made me start sobbing, because I'd been putting the globe together for the past few weeks whenever I had a free moment. All I could think about when I was making it was how much Hunter would appreciate it.

I shake my head remembering that now.

I linger in the car, not wanting to go inside just yet. Instead, I stare through the chain-link fence of the house next to the school parking lot. There's a white German shepherd lying peacefully on the grass, sniffing at the damp air and I almost envy him and his lack of angst. I know his name is Montague and that this would be a rare moment for him, as I've heard he's kind of psychotic—like, using-cinder-blocks-as-toys psychotic.

Of course, it was Hunter who told me this, so maybe I shouldn't believe it. I mean, if he'd lie about loving someone, why not lie about something minor like a dog's playtime habits?

That's when I notice Luke roll by on his bike. There's a raincoat-clad figure standing on the back pegs of the bike, hands resting on Luke's shoulders. When she steps off and pushes back her hood, revealing her thick blonde braids, I realize it's his girlfriend, Greta O'Brien. She's a senior and, from what I hear, she's a really good snowboarder, but she kind of scares the hell out of me. She's tall and imposing and loud, one of those girls who gets all "What are you looking at?" if you happen to glance her way. She's always "playfully" pushing her friends or bellowing with laughter. She reminds me a bit of a Viking woman. But from a distance today, she looks kind of innocent in her yellow slicker and braids, like an oversized kindergartener.

Luke and Greta appear to be heavy into a discussion, maybe even fighting. Part of me knows I should look away and not be nosy, but it's somehow comforting to know that even couples who are still together aren't all sunshine and rainbows. I can't hear what they're saying, but Luke is making some really intense gestures with his hands, as if he's trying to explain something to Greta. She shrugs and raises her hands up as if to say "What do you want me to do?" and Luke's shoulders sag.

Greta walks away, and Luke remains behind for a moment, lifting his baseball cap and smoothing his hand over the top of his shaggy light-brown hair. It almost makes me laugh because his T-shirt is beyond wrinkled, but it's his hair he's worried about.

This makes me think of Hunter and how his hair always does what he wants it to do. It's thick and comes down a little past his ears, and he recently got it cut in a way where he has a bit of a coif going on. Like, it appears floppy and wild, but it's actually styled.

I'm glad I don't have to pretend that I find the hair cute anymore, because it seriously kind of makes him look like a douche.

Ugh. I press my forehead on the steering wheel. This is not going to work, this whole tilt-a-whirl-of-feelings thing going on inside me. How can I get through an entire day while at once loving and loathing my all-too-recent ex-boyfriend?

Then I remember I have to see him in home ec, and the anger bubbles up again. There's no way I'm letting him think his cruelty and lack of response to my text has gotten to me. With that, I get out of the car and head inside.

As soon as I step into the main hall, I see Brynn walking toward her homeroom, and my heart speeds up. I know this will be a test, if she acknowledges me. I'm thinking of saying something neutral, like asking if I can give her the globe at the end of the day, but she completely avoids eye contact. Maybe she's afraid I'm going to put her in the middle of this, but I wasn't even going to ask her about Hunter. I was just hoping she'd say hello if I said it first.

I purposely swing by the cafeteria, where I know Kim and Alisha will be sitting. I don't see Kim, but Alisha is at a table talking to a bunch of RHHS TV people. She's laughing, so I head toward her first, since she seems the most approachable. She makes eye contact almost immediately, then drops it, then looks me in the eyes again. "Hi, Ellie," she says, her face pained.

Oh god, please don't let Alisha be weird around me. "Hey," I say, and I realize all her TV station friends are watching me.

"Have you been on The Buzz today?" Alisha asks, lowering her voice.

I shake my head. The Buzz is an RHHS gossip site with a lot of "blind items" about students, paired with complementary photos or GIFs for each. Jared Curtis, one of the guys from my home ec class in the hipster/literary journal group, is rumored to run it, but that's all I really know about it. I don't know anyone well enough to decode all the "this popular basketball player was recently found 'courting' a teammate's mom" type things, so I'm not exactly checking it twenty times a day like other kids.

"Well, it alludes to Hunter dumping you because of—"

That's when Kim brushes by. "Come on, Alisha, we need to get to homeroom."

"In a minute," Alisha says, flustered.

"We need to talk to Mr. Carpenter about the Key Club meeting." Kim won't even glance in my direction.

Without another word, she links arms with Alisha and steers her away from me without so much as a goodbye.

They're siding with Hunter. So that's how it's going to be.

Fresh tears begin to burn my eyes, but I blink them back as I pull out my phone. It's so old that it doesn't hold a charge for very long, but I decide to risk it by loading up The Buzz.

I scroll past items about a beach house that got trashed by some soccer players over the summer and a sophomore who is considering breast implants, and sure enough, the third post has a GIF of a crying Dory from *Finding Nemo*.

CAN'T BAIT THE HOOK

These two geeks are no longer enjoying a harmonious union, as one party was said to be a cold fish . . .

Cold. Fish. The words swim around as the tears start to blind me. The whole school is going to think I'm a prude who won't have sex with her boyfriend of eight months. It's Robot Girl all over again. I'm probably going to get harassed about this until graduation.

And it means Hunter probably told someone he was tired of me not sleeping with him.

But then I notice there's more.

> . . . Sources say, however, that a planned sex outing was on the horizon. Perhaps destiny got in the way?

I squint at that last line, making the tears spill over. What does it even mean? Is Jared saying it's my destiny to be a virgin forever or something since I couldn't close the deal on having sex?

It's only then that I realize my hands are shaking and that several people in the cafeteria are watching me. With my heart hammering, I practically sprint to the bathroom. I make it into a stall before I start full-on sobbing.

I somehow make it to lunch without melting down again, probably because I've reached a phase of "I can't even think about this anymore" numbness. But the humiliation factor is upped when I get to the cafeteria and notice the table I sat at yesterday is empty. Steve is nowhere to be seen. I spot Brynn and Kim, miraculously reappearing at lunch today, at a table with some of their friends from the Politics Club. They don't even glance in my direction.

I scan the rest of the room to see if there's anyone I know, anybody to keep me from being "that cold fish girl who sits alone at lunch." The only person I see is Isaiah from home ec. He's sitting at the end of an empty table, engrossed in some kind of newspaper and seemingly not bothered at all that he's sitting by himself.

That's when the doors to the cafeteria burst open, and Paul comes sprinting through, the head of Harry the Hornet, the school's mascot, under his arm. He's followed by one of the school security guards who pants, "Wilder, you're already going to be expelled for that so you may as well give it up."

Paul ignores him and continues on his mad dash through the cafeteria and out the back door. Everyone else is laughing, or aiming their phones at him to try and record it, or both.

Steve arrives then and drops his backpack on the table. "What the hell was that? Did he have Harry's head?"

"It looks like it," I say, relieved he's talking to me. "You didn't see anything coming in?"

Steve shakes his head. "No, I was just at the guidance counselor. I wanted to drop creative writing and switch into mechanical drawing. Unfortunately, the only time it's available is this period, so I'm switching in tomorrow."

"This period?" I say, feeling my shoulders sag.

"Yeah, sorry about that. I didn't mean to ditch you."

Part of me is relieved that Steve seems concerned about me. But that's completely sucked away when I feel his hand on my knee.

"I'm really sorry about what happened between you and Hunter." He seems sincere, but I don't have time to really analyze it because the hand-on-the-knee thing kind of weirds me out. I quickly jerk my knee away and lock my feet around the chair's legs.

"Have you, uh, been on The Buzz?" I ask.

He looks down at his lunch. I'm not sure if it's because I just yanked my knee away or because of the question. "Yeah. Are you okay?"

"Not really. Have you seen Hunter today? Does he know about it?" I say.

Steve shakes his head. "No. I haven't really talked to him since before he went to Brynn's for dinner the other night. He's been kind of MIA."

To Brynn's for dinner. My stomach starts to knot. I wonder if he told her about the cold fish thing and the "sex outing" and if she advised him to break up with me. Over at their table, she and Kim are laughing hysterically about something. Probably what a joke it was that Hunter would ever date me.

"I hate everyone," I mutter.

Steve gives a light laugh. "Not me, I hope," he says, and his hand finds my knee again.

"Knock it off," I tell him, my voice breaking.

"I'm just trying to be nice," he says, removing his hand.

"Well, you're being a little too nice," I say, standing up.

So this is how it's going to be. Half the school is going to see me as a total prude who won't give it up, and the other half is going to think I was days away from being a raging slut but wasn't good enough for Hunter.

Steve starts to say he's sorry, but I grab my bag and my lunch and leave the room.

I go through the rest of the day practically holding my breath, waiting for someone to whisper "cold fish" at me and for everyone to start laughing, but aside from a few sidelong glances, nothing really happens. Maybe people couldn't decode the blind item about me, since barely anyone knows who I am to begin with.

When I get to the home ec room, Steve and I manage to avoid each other. I'm relieved that he doesn't say anything, because I'm still kind of weirded out by the whole lunch thing.

That's when Hunter walks in. It's the first time I've seen him all day, and he's wearing a dark-green polo shirt that shows off his tan.

He looks incredible in that color, and it hits me, hard, that he isn't mine anymore. And that he told people I'm a "cold fish."

I feel like I'm about to start tearing up, but then Hunter takes the seat diagonally across the table from me, as if going out of his way not to interact with me. The urge to cry screeches to a halt, but my face gets hot and my hands start to shake. I'm suddenly afraid I might blow up right there in the middle of the class, and that's the last thing I want. No way am I giving Hunter the satisfaction of dumping me, then being all, "Don't you see she's crazy? Can you blame me?" So I make myself hyper-into what Mrs. Sanchez is saying.

"Budgeting is the cornerstone to any home, be it a single person, a couple, or a family. Without knowing how to spend your money, you risk not having enough to cover your expenses."

Mrs. Sanchez spends the rest of the class explaining what should be in every budget: utilities, credit card bills, cell phones, food, hobbies, college loan payments, savings, mortgages, and rent. I think of how little money my parents make and how it barely covers anything on the list (I know for a fact they don't have much in savings right now). I doubt anyone at this table has a clue about what it really takes to get by and survive.

Thinking about it makes my insides twist, so I inhale deeply and close my eyes. When I open them, I notice Paul is absent from the table next to ours, and I wonder if he's truly going to be expelled. Luke is following along with the budget lecture and writing in his notebook and A.J. is trying to carve something into his chair with his pen. Isaiah, however, has that same newspaper from lunch on his lap, and he's staring at it intently.

"Mr. Greenlow," I hear Mrs. Sanchez say, and Isaiah looks up. "Could you kindly show me what you're reading?"

Isaiah guiltily pulls his newspaper off of his lap and holds it up. Mrs. Sanchez leans over her counter to get a better look. "*The*

Daily Racing Form?" she says and, with that, the whole class starts laughing.

"Yes, ma'am," Isaiah says, sinking in his seat.

"I'm not sure that's appropriate for class," Mrs. Sanchez says.

"I don't know about that," A.J. jumps in. "I mean, betting on the ponies could be listed under hobbies when you're budgeting, right?"

The class laughs again, and Isaiah sinks farther down in his seat.

Mrs. Sanchez ponders this. "Yes, Mr. Johnson, I suppose it could. That said, reading about Belmont Park isn't going to help when there's a test on this material. So, Mr. Greenlow, kindly pay attention."

"Yes, ma'am," Isaiah says again, folding the newspaper and placing it on his backpack just as the bell rings.

Mrs. Sanchez claps her hands as everyone gathers their things. "Read the packets I gave you yesterday so we can discuss how income affects budgeting tomorrow."

I turn my head, looking for Brynn. I want to ask her to come to my car to get the globe, but I don't see her or Hunter anywhere. Then I remember that there's a Ringtones rehearsal this afternoon in the school theater and they're probably heading there. I can leave it with one of the guys and run out, and Hunter will be none the wiser.

I get to the classroom door at the same time as Luke and have to skid to a stop before I bash into him.

"We have to stop meeting like this," he says.

"Sorry," I say, sidestepping around him.

"She speaks!" he says behind me, but I don't stick around to hear what else he has to say. I check over my shoulder to see if he's talking about me with A.J. or someone, but he's met up with Greta and they're smiling at each other. I guess whatever disagreement they had this morning is over.

It's nice that *some* couples can work out their issues.

I head to the parking lot and grab the globe from the car, then head toward the back door of the theater. If I leave it in the prop room, it'll get found, especially since it's where half the Ringtones go to make out with their groupies during rehearsals.

As I'm about to round the bend that leads to the theater's back door, I pass two girls, freshmen, judging by their general youngness, giggling.

"Who does that, outside and in the open?" one says.

"I know, right?" her friend replies. "It's like they don't care who sees them."

I'm intrigued as I come around the corner, half expecting to see a couple like Luke and Greta going at it. Sure enough, there's a girl leaning against the brick wall by the theater door practically being mauled by a guy . . . in a dark-green polo shirt.

I think I literally stop breathing when the realization dawns on me. It's like my feet refuse to move. I'm just standing there, watching him swallow this girl's head, his hands running all over her body.

"Wait, I need to catch my breath," the girl says, giggling.

I know that voice. Oh my god, this isn't happening.

Hunter backs off from his conquest and suddenly I'm staring straight at Brynn.

"Are you kidding me?" It just comes out, and they both jump. I'm on autopilot and I don't care who sees or hears it. "You get me out of the way so you can be with each other? You *assholes!*"

Hunter digs his hands into his pockets guiltily, but Brynn is totally affronted by this, and there's no way I'm letting her say anything back to me. I spin around and start storming toward my car. I get to the parking lot before I hear Brynn yelling after Hunter and Hunter yelling after me. I realize I'm still carrying the globe and have this urge to hurl it at the both of them.

"Ellie," Hunter yells. For some reason I stop, maybe thinking he'll apologize or something. "You don't have to be like this. I didn't want to lead you on anymore."

It's like this sudden, eerie calm takes over me. I'm done with this. I'm done with *them*. I turn to face Brynn and Hunter and set the globe down, then spin around and start walking to my car before I can burst into tears in public. Especially since there are a good number of people watching this all go down and I know the humiliation is going to sink in in a few seconds.

"You're seriously going to let her call us assholes?" I hear Brynn bark at Hunter, and the eerie calm is gone just as quick as it came. I turn back around, stomp toward them, pull my leg back, and let my foot fly at the globe. In a rare moment of pure athletic skill, it launches in the air and hurls toward a wide-eyed Brynn and Hunter, making them both duck. The globe ends up careening toward the side of the building and slamming into the brick wall with a pathetic thud before it falls into the bushes below.

Hunter and Brynn both stare at me openmouthed, maybe a little frightened. "Oh my god," I hear some girl whisper in awe. Suddenly I'm shaking—there were so many witnesses. What if any teachers saw what just happened? I turn and practically sprint to my car.

"I think her name's Ellie," I hear someone say behind me.

"I didn't know she had it in her," someone else replies.

That makes two of us.

CHAPTER 5

Almost seventeen hours have passed since the globe-kicking incident and it is more than safe to say I am still angry. I know this because my mom volunteered to drive me to school this morning, and instead of being grateful I don't have to walk through another pouring rainstorm, I'm annoyed that she had to interrupt my stewing time. I have yet to tell my parents about the breakup or the resulting papier-mâché carnage.

So of course my mom's all, "Are you okay, love?" as we get in the car.

"I'm fine," I say, studying the chipping "Pink Pearl" nail polish on my left hand. When I made the globe, I'd pretty much destroyed the manicure I had given myself at Jodie's house. At the time, I thought it was for a noble cause. Now the globe is a pile of paste and painted newspaper strips wadded under a bush somewhere, and my nails look pathetic for no reason at all.

"Don't lie, El," my mom says as she starts the car. When I don't say anything she adds, "You've come home the past two days and locked yourself in your room. And then I heard you raising your voice on the phone last night at Jodie. That's not like you."

I knew I wouldn't be able to avoid my parents forever. The night of the breakup, I'd come home from work and declared I was too tired for dinner and went straight to my room. Last night, I scarfed down my dad's famous macaroni and cheese, and then ran to my room to call Jodie, where I filled her in on the day's events, my voice getting higher and higher with every detail.

"I wasn't raising my voice *at* Jodie." I pray the tears don't come. I'd been so outraged the past half day that crying was the last thing on my mind. It was nice to not have puffy, bloodshot eyes for a bit. "Hunter and I broke up."

There, it's out. And she can't question me too much because we're literally a three-minute ride to school and she knows I can't be late for homeroom. Hopefully, she'll forget all about this by the time I get—

"Oh, honey," Mom says, turning the car off. She turns in her seat and places her hand on my shoulder. "Are you okay?"

I shrug. I need to play this well. I can't have her know she was right about Hunter, and I also don't want her and Dad worried about me. They have enough on their plate right now. "I'm doing all right. It's an adjustment."

"Would it be prying to ask what happened?"

"We were just growing apart," I say flatly, silently willing her to start the car again.

"I'm sorry to hear that," she says and, to her credit, she *does* sound sorry. "I want us to talk about this later, if you're up for it. We can have ice cream for dinner and watch that show you love about weather disasters?"

Oh god, Mom, I think, as I stare out the window fighting back tears for real now. *Stop being so nice to me. It'll just make me cry more.*

"That sounds good," I say, glad my voice doesn't break.

Mom squeezes my shoulder before she finally starts the car. It's the longest three minutes of my life before I can say goodbye to her and hurry into school, where I can hopefully break down behind the closed door of a bathroom stall.

A group of students is gathered by the main door when I come in. They suddenly fall quiet and stare at me as I pass, then start whispering when I'm a few feet away.

"That's her!" I hear one girl hiss. "She's the one who freaked out yesterday."

"That explains it," a guy says. "She's like the one girl in the senior class I don't know."

Of course you don't know me, I think. *It's not like anyone was particularly friendly toward me when I first started here.*

Except Hunter. And Alisha.

I think of Alisha then and wonder if she truly is on Hunter and Brynn's side, since she tried to warn me about the Cold Fish thing before Kim whisked her off. But then again, she hasn't tried to contact me or seek me out, so maybe she heard about the globe-kicking and thinks I'm a raging psycho or something.

I remember The Buzz, then, and wonder if my globe-kicking is a featured item. I head to the library, where I plug in my phone and load it up. A GIF of a glittery marijuana leaf is at the top of the feed.

HIGH TIMES

This smarty-pants wants everyone to think she's Miss Innocent, but our sources report seeing her smoking weed at the beach this summer. Multiple times.

I wince. I think this might be Anna Feldman, who's in competition with Kim for number one in our class, and who I've been secretly rooting for to keep Kim from being valedictorian in June.

This is followed by a GIF of an old TV show, where two girls and a guy are embracing, all smiling.

TEAM TRYST

This athletic trio is quite the threesome. They were spotted at a team party disappearing into a bedroom together with multiple reports of endless groans and moans coming from behind closed doors. Now we're wondering who finished first, second, and third?

Yikes. Maybe there's so much gossip grist from the RHHS rumor mill that my outburst yesterday was . . .

THE KICK HEARD ROUND THE WORLD (OR AT LEAST THE SENIOR PARKING LOT)

This new couple had their smooch sesh quashed when a certain cold fish-turned-woman-scorned let her rage be known with a swift kick. Maybe someone should've told her this union was in the works for quite some time?

Wait, what? I feel the blood pounding in my temples as I read it over again. Their relationship has been in the works for *quite some time*?

I can only squint at the screen, dazed with confusion. Was Hunter cheating on me with Brynn? I wrack my brain and deep down, I don't think he was. I mean, I'd be willing to bet they definitely hooked up the night before he dumped me, and the seeds of lust were being planted a little before, if Hunter's distant behavior meant anything. But how was their relationship in the works otherwise?

Quickly, I click on Instagram and load up Hunter's profile. I'm actually kind of shocked to see he hasn't unfollowed me, even though I kicked a globe at his head. Then I realize he's probably just waiting to see if I have some kind of psychotic episode via a sad selfie or something, so he can be all, "Phew, I'm so glad I'm not with her anymore. What a psycho!"

I scroll through the past few weeks of Hunter's photos, but don't see anything out of the ordinary.

Then I move over to Brynn's profile and I see it right away: a selfie with Hunter from last night. She's resting her head on his chest with her arms wrapped around him, and they're both smiling coyly at the camera. Below it is a caption: "Nine years in the making."

And it's invited one hundred and eight likes and nearly thirty comments. I fight the bile rising up in my throat as I read them.

Carrie Torres, a cheerleader and one of the more popular girls in our class, writes: "OMG, you and Hunter are together?!?! I've only been waiting for that since seventh grade!"

Jeez, even Ben Granderson, the hermit of the senior class, is in on it: "It's about time, Panz. We all knew she was crazy about you."

I sit back in my seat, my breakfast threatening to eject itself from my stomach. This is probably the "destiny" that was "in the works": Hunter and Brynn were somehow destined for each other for years. But how obvious was it that everyone was rooting for her?

Because Hunter asked *me* out and was with *me* for the last eight months.

I scroll down past a few more nauseating "Yay! You're dating" responses on Brynn's pic, until I stumble upon one from Hunter's older sister, Lisa: "So psyched for you, little bro. Brynn's so awesome."

There's an empty feeling in my stomach as I let this sink in. *Brynn's so awesome.* Does that mean I'm not?

It hits me then that there's no way I'd ever stack up to Brynn, even if she is a know-it-all with bratty tendencies. She's known these people forever, and familiarity probably outweighs her flaws. She isn't the villain in this scenario. It's me. I had thrown a wrench in the epic love story of Hunter and Brynn, which was apparently obvious to everyone but me.

Like, if this were a bad TV show, Brynn would be the one the audience is rooting for because she and Hunter have been friends forever, and she's been choking back her feelings for him. She's about to tell him when some new character—me—is foisted onto the show with the express purpose of keeping the main characters apart. Naturally, Hunter and I don't belong together simply because Brynn and her feelings exist.

I'm about to sign off when I get some sudden inspiration. I uncheck the box near Brynn's name and unfollow her and then do the same on Hunter, Kim, and Steve's profiles. I debate unfollowing Alisha, since I haven't seen or heard from her, but something deep down tells me not to.

I make my way out of the library. Right away I notice Hunter coming toward me, and the rage comes flooding back. If he makes eye contact with me, I plan on glaring at him as hard as I can.

But his eyes are on his phone as he texts, and he's smiling. Suddenly his phone rings and he answers, not even seeing me. "Hey, you," he purrs. "I dreamed about you last night."

I swear to god.

He's so absorbed in his conversation that he doesn't notice me pass him. *Obviously* he gets to be happy while I'm the one with enough emotions to fill an entire telenovela.

And then I remember I have to see him and Brynn again in class. Together.

I spin around and turn back to the main hall. Then I march into the guidance office and make an appointment with the office assistant.

I'm getting the hell out of home ec, and nobody can stop me.

Despite not having any more run-ins with Hunter and Brynn, I'm still feeling rage-y by the time I return to the guidance office for my appointment around midday. I only have one thing on my agenda this afternoon, and it's to not be spending last period with the lying, exhibitionist lovebirds every day. I have no idea what other elective I could possibly take, but even an extra gym class is more appealing than being in close proximity to Hunter and Brynn as they undress each other with their eyes or whatever heartless cheaters do when they're together.

I hear my phone buzzing from my backpack and find a text from Jodie.

> How's it going, Lionel Messi?

Only Jodie can make me laugh at myself right now. It's the first time I've smiled in days.

> **Trying to switch out of home ec.**

> Don't give them the satisfaction of running away from them!

I'm about to respond, "Do you really want me in the general vicinity of knives and meat cleavers with those two around?" when the door opens to my counselor Mrs. Gillroy's office. She's wearing a dark conservative suit, which contrasts with her bright, flaming-orange blouse. If my emotions could be a color right now, they'd be that.

"Mary Ellen, good to see you again," Mrs. Gillroy says. "What brings you here today? Did you want to start thinking about your admissions essay for Penn State?"

"No, but I can't believe you remembered I want to go there." We had a brief college discussion when I first transferred back in January. There are roughly twelve hundred kids at RHHS, which is like three hundred in the senior class alone—and yet she can recall a minor conversation she had with me.

Mrs. Gillroy smiles. "It's my job. Also, I loved how passionate you were about meteorology. Have you thought about joining the school TV station to get some experience being in front of the camera?"

"I have a part-time job," I remind her. "You know, to help pay for college."

She nods. "I'm aware of that, but the TV station films in the morning and they wouldn't need you every day after school. Surely you could fit it into your schedule?"

"Possibly. But they already have a weatherperson," I say. "Also, I want to do the more scientific side of meteorology over broad-casting."

"Still, you may end up wanting to be in front of the camera later, and you can pick up some helpful skills there," Mrs. Gillroy says. "Even if you end up in the research aspect, you never know if you'll be called upon to be an expert on TV someday."

I know she's right about this. But the thing is, I'm kind of terrified of being on camera. The idea of kids being like, "Oh my god, it's the globe-kicking cold fish!" makes me want to puke.

Mrs. Gillroy is staring at me, so I say, "I'll think about it," to get her off my back a bit.

"Good," she says, then consults a folder on her desk. "Ah, so you're here to switch a class."

"I want to switch out of Life Skills," I say, and she immediately raises her eyebrows in surprise.

"That's intriguing. It's one of our most popular electives. Is it not demanding enough for you?'

Don't try reverse psychology on me, lady. Not today.

"I'm just not sure I need to understand budgeting and cooking and sewing and all that at seventeen," I say, knowing it probably sounds completely lame.

Mrs. Gillroy smiles. "If you're not going to learn it now, when are you? Being on your own in college will probably come as less of a shock if you have some idea of what it's like to be self-reliant."

"I *am* self-reliant," I say, and I know it comes out super defensive.

She stares at me hard, as if she's trying to figure out if she should say what's on her mind. Finally, it comes out. "I feel like this may be coming from somewhere else. Honestly, in all my years of doing this job no one has ever wanted to drop that class from their schedule."

Oh, crap. What if my blowup yesterday got all the way to *school administration*? I feel heat creeping up my neck into my face. "I—"

"Is there something you're trying to avoid? Or someone, maybe?"

I can't help it when it comes flying out of my mouth. "*You* try being in close proximity to the guy who broke your heart and his new girlfriend for the next nine months."

She eases back in her seat and tents her fingers. "So you want to drop this informative, helpful class—that will help you for the rest of your life—because you can't move on from an old relationship?"

"Old? He just dumped me two days ago. And he moved on really quickly. He may have even been cheating on me." I add that last part because, really, is the gravity of adultery lost on anyone?

But Mrs. Gillroy is unmoved. She just stares at me, like I'm somehow trying *her* patience. "Mary Ellen, do you really want to be the type of person who runs away from difficult situations? Who can't take a challenge?"

Spending an entire school year with Hunter and Brynn isn't my idea of a challenge, it's out-and-out torture. Still, knowing that Mrs. Gillroy obviously doesn't see my unending heartbreak as a good enough reason to drop a class, I can't think of anything to say.

"Exactly," she says, taking my steamed silence as confirmation. "Which is why I'm denying your request to switch out. What doesn't kill us makes us stronger, you know?"

It *is* going to kill me to see Hunter and Brynn be all lovey-dovey with each other, but I know I can't win this fight.

"You don't look so thrilled with this," Mrs. Gillroy says.

I clench my teeth, kind of fed up with her unsympathetic platitudes. Everything I say to her gets countered back to me, so I just shrug as angrily as possible.

"Well, if there's anything else I can help you with, let me know."

"Yup," I grumble, grabbing my backpack.

"Make an appointment with me when you start filling out your college applications!"

Maybe I should forget about meteorology and change my career choice to guidance counselor, since all you apparently have to do is dole out clichés and make people feel bad about feeling bad. That sounds easy enough to me.

But then I guess that would be *unchallenging*, wouldn't it?

Sigh.

CHAPTER 6

I've got a huge case of "don't mess with me" by the time I get to the home ec room. If I have to spend the rest of the year watching this train wreck, then I intend to let everyone know how unhappy I am to be here. It's better than being the sad and hurt victim, which is probably what Hunter is expecting me to be.

Hunter and Brynn arrive at the same time. Their heads are bent together, and they're smiling as if sharing some sweet, cute little secret.

Vomit.

When they see me glaring at them, both of their faces stiffen and they swallow hard as they sit down at our table. I'd like to think they're feeling guilty, but I'm not sure either is capable of it. More than likely they're afraid of me, because Brynn makes a point to leave an empty seat between us. Like that space will stop me from kicking another globe at her or something.

After the bell rings, Mrs. Sanchez leans on her counter and peers at our table over her glasses. "It appears as if Paul Wilder has been expelled for his little stunt the other day."

It's only then that I notice Paul's chair at the table next to ours is still empty. I'm relieved that I won't have to be dealing with him, but what does that have to do with us?

"And since your group has five people, and our assignments will call for groups of four, I was hoping one of you would volunteer to join Paul's family to replace him."

I feel my face grow hot as I scan my table. There's Steve and Hannah, both Hunter and Brynn's friends. And then there's Brynn, Hunter's new lady love. And the man of the hour himself. All of them are staring at me.

They expect *me* to volunteer to go.

You have got to be kidding me.

I mean, these people may be my new sworn enemies, but I'm not trading them for a group of delinquents and the opportunity to relive my middle school angst for the next nine months. No way, no how.

When none of us says anything, Mrs. Sanchez laughs. "I guess you're all really tight. But you'll still be in the same class. Surely one of you can join another group."

Nope. Not me. Luke is staring at me, probably relishing the idea of teasing and laughing at me on a daily basis.

"I'm afraid if one of you doesn't volunteer, I'll have to pick someone," Mrs. Sanchez says, annoyance rising in her voice. Good, let her pick. I'm not being pushed out of this group as if *I've* done something wrong.

"We don't bite, yo," A.J. says, tipping his chair back and lacing his hands behind his head.

Brynn leans toward Hunter and whispers, "I can't believe her."

"Can't believe what, Brynn?" It comes out of my mouth before I can stop myself.

Brynn's mouth hangs agape as she struggles for something to say. I feel kind of vindicated.

Until Luke speaks up. "Hey, Mrs. Sanchez. What if we pick someone? Will that make it easier?"

Mrs. Sanchez sighs. "Seeing as how this group is too stubborn to do anything, I think that's a wonderful idea, Mr. Burke."

Luke smiles and I just know what's coming next. "I think there's a little too much testosterone in our family, right, guys?" he says, nodding at his group-mates. I close my eyes, preparing for my utter humiliation.

"Okay," I hear Luke say, and I suck in my breath. "We'd like Brynn."

Huh? I open my eyes and exhale. Brynn is completely slack-jawed. "Me?" she squeaks.

"Ms. Potts, gather your things and join their group," Mrs. Sanchez says. "I think this is a more than sensible solution since none of you are volunteering."

"B-but," she sputters, looking helplessly at Hunter, who is shaking his head in dismay.

"*Now*, Ms. Potts!" Mrs. Sanchez snaps, clearly at the end of her patience.

And that's when Brynn starts to cry. Like, her nose gets red and tears spill over. Her hands are shaking and she lets out a little sob as she pushes in her chair. Hunter makes a grab for her free hand. Hannah tries to pat her on the back. It's like Brynn's being shipped off to a war zone or something. And it makes me realize I'm now going to be viewed as the monster of the group for daring to stick to my guns.

"Oh, for the love of god," I grouch, standing up and grabbing my backpack. "*I'll* go."

Brynn is totally stunned into silence as I huff over to the next table and sit down in Paul's vacant seat with a heavy plunk. I don't look at any of the guys and will my hands to stop shaking. I stare straight ahead at Mrs. Sanchez, who shakes her head, perplexed. I'm kind of confused myself, though I'm not really thinking rationally right now. All I know is there's no way I'd let Brynn play the martyr, as if her anguish was somehow worse than the pain she and Hunter inflicted on me.

It's only then I notice the guys in the group are all gaping at me.

"Hey," A.J. mouths, wiggling his eyebrows at me. I quickly turn my attention back to Mrs. Sanchez.

What have I done? Oh god, *what have I done*?

Mrs. Sanchez is oblivious to my horror as she walks around the room, placing unmarked manila envelopes on each table. "Inside these are different income brackets for your family. We have everything from 'Grad Students on a Budget' to 'Dual Income Investment Bankers.' You will also find your monthly expenses and you'll have to figure out a realistic budget for your family based on this."

The classroom is suddenly buzzing as everyone opens their envelopes to find out their status. A.J. is momentarily distracted from harassing me and grabs the envelope off our table.

"May I do the honors?" he asks.

The guys nod, and A.J. unhooks the gold clasp on the envelope. He reaches in and pulls out a stack of papers bound together with a binder clip, and reads something on top of the pile. His smirk fades away.

"You've got to be kidding," he says. He sits back in his seat, disgusted, as he tosses the papers on the table. Clipped to the top of the stack is an index card, with "Single Mother, Two Kids" written on it in thick black marker.

"Maybe it won't be that bad. Maybe the mom's some big-shot executive," Luke says, picking up the stack. He peeks under the index card at the first sheet of paper and his face falls. "Oh. She's a bus driver."

A.J. and Isaiah are shaking their heads at the stack of papers, as if it somehow has the capability to know it's disappointed them. Luke, however, is studying me. I decide now is as good a time as any to let him know he can't intimidate me, so I shoot what I hope is a defiant look back at him. But instead of mocking me or making some creepy gesture, his eyes quickly shift away, the tips of his ears turning slightly pink.

I'm momentarily confused, but then I notice Steve and Hannah high-fiving, Hunter pumping his fist, and Brynn, having done a complete emotional 180, dancing in her seat. Hannah is holding their papers, and I squint to read their index card: "Husband and Wife Investment Bankers, Two Kids."

Of course.

"Now," Mrs. Sanchez is saying, "every month you will be responsible for paying the bills in your pile. You'll find a current budget for the family attached, but you will be making changes to it based on your income. The goal is to have some money left over each week to go into savings."

Isaiah is skimming through the pile. "Well, it looks as if we're making thirty-eight thousand dollars a year."

"In this area? With two kids?" A.J. says. "There's no way this is going to work."

I'm kind of surprised he's even aware of how far thirty-eight thousand dollars goes. A year ago, I had no idea how much money a family would need to get by. Now I'm all too familiar with it. I didn't suspect other kids in an area as middle-class as Ringvale Heights would have to worry about such a thing.

I've noticed Luke has stayed pretty silent on the subject, but he's reading one of the pages.

"The mom is in the process of paying off hospital bills for her recently deceased husband," he says quietly, and I'm surprised at his sober tone.

Everyone at the table is silent as this registers. Well, everyone but A.J.

"Hey! How are we going to be able to make this budget work?" he says accusingly at Mrs. Sanchez. "We've got bills coming out of our ass and barely any money coming in."

"Please refrain from swearing, Mr. Johnson," Mrs. Sanchez says, but she smiles. "I know your income is pretty low, but with a little smarts and teamwork, you'll make it. I promise. Now, let's move on to picking out names for your families. Maybe think of something that invokes the lessons of this class or teamwork!"

Teamwork. I survey the group at my table: A gambling addict in training, a loudmouth, and a tattooed goliath who may or may not be crushing on Brynn. "Making it" is somehow going to be impossible.

Out of the corner of my eye, I see Hunter tickle Brynn, which makes her squeal. It doesn't help that Hannah is giggling at their tickly shenanigans because they're just *so* adorable together.

"What about Breasts, Legs, and Thighs for a group name?" A.J. says. "It falls under the food thing because it refers to a chicken!"

"I don't think Mrs. Sanchez will dig that too much," Luke says with a laugh. He cocks his head at me, as if he's waiting for me to weigh in on the situation. Probably so he can make fun of me. I just keep my mouth shut.

"Okay, how about the Home Economics Homeboys?" A.J. suggests.

"I'm not exactly a boy now, am I?" I say, annoyed.

"No, we were all under the impression that the long hair and pierced ears were a big attempt at a disguise," Luke says, rolling his eyes, and I feel my face grow hot with annoyance.

A.J. snickers, but Isaiah doesn't say anything.

"Well, what if we take the letters from each of our first names and make it an antonym," A.J. says.

I'm about to sigh over his word misuse when Luke surprises me and says, "I think you mean acronym, bro, but that sounds like it could work."

"Cool, so we get an A and J for me since my real first name is Andrew-James," A.J. says.

"It's just an L for me," Luke says.

Isaiah pulls out a piece of paper and writes out an A, J, L, and I. Then he points his pen at me. "Do you go by Mary Ellen or Mary?"

"Now, now," Luke says. "Don't assume. Maybe people call her 'Agresti.'"

"Uh, no one calls me that," I say, staring straight ahead, waiting for him to drop another insult on me.

"Well, then, that's a shame. It rolls right off the tongue," Luke says. I can't tell if he's being serious or sarcastic.

Then I turn back to Isaiah. "You can call me Ellie."

He adds an E to his list and we study the letters.

"What about IJEAL," I say. "It sounds like 'ideal.'"

"It sounds like something nasty," A.J. says with a wrinkled nose. "Like it's what happens when a guy—"

"Uh, hold it right there," Luke says with a laugh. He lifts up his hand, revealing a tattoo of a bike tire mark on the underside of his arm. "Let's remember there's a lady present."

"Wait!" A.J. says, his pale skin suddenly flushing with excitement. "What about this?" In big block letters he spells out: JAILE.

"Jaile?" Isaiah's face is incredulous.

"As in 'this class is a prison I can't escape'?" I say. I can't help myself.

"As in the most badass name this class will have," A.J. says, tapping the paper with his pen. "Think about it. We're competing against the other groups for points, right? So we can intimidate them right off the bat with our name."

Before anyone else can say anything, a brown-nosey voice I know all too well calls out, "Mrs. Sanchez! We have a name!"

"Well, tell us then, Ms. Potts," Mrs. Sanchez says, smiling at Brynn's National Honor Society level of enthusiasm.

"We're calling ourselves Synergy!" Brynn says, as Hunter beams at her. Of course he would. She comes up with SAT words—even though I don't think it makes that much sense for a home economics class—for their group name, and I come up with "ijeal."

"What exactly does synergy have to do with a home economics class?" Jared Curtis wonders from the literary/hipster kid table.

"We're going to be working as a group toward our cause," Brynn sniffs haughtily. "And what's your name going to be? The Hipster Posers?"

Jared informs her that his family is going to be called the Bukowskis, after Charles Bukowski, whom the whole group apparently admires. The table of football players and ohmygawd girls will be Jersey Strong, and the stoners go completely unironic and call themselves the Bakers.

Mrs. Sanchez peers at them over her glasses, as if to say, "Seriously?" but she doesn't fight them on it. Then she turns to my table. "And what about this group over here?" she says. "Have you picked a name?"

I clear my throat. "Not ye—"

"We're the JAILE family, bitches," A.J. says, pumping his fist at the rest of the class.

I close my eyes and inhale deeply as the whole class howls with laughter, and to make matters a billion times worse, I can hear Brynn snorting among them. When I open my eyes, I see that Mrs. Sanchez's head is tilted with curiosity. "And how did you arrive at that name?"

"Because they're bound for juvie," I hear Anthony snicker from the Jersey Strong table.

"Why don't you shoot some more steroids into your brain, douchebag," A.J. snaps, and Anthony sneers at him.

"Mr. Johnson, that's enough of that," Mrs. Sanchez says. Then she looks at us expectantly. She still wants an answer to her question.

"We just mixed up all the letters of our first names and came up with it," Luke says.

Mrs. Sanchez smiles. "That's very creative and a very good representation of what your families are supposed to be about . . ."

Convicts? Felons? Chain gangs? That's what you're supposed to think of in a home economics class?

". . . Individuals coming together as a unit to learn and get tasks done. And believe me, you will need every member of your family to get points in your weekly rankings. Nice job, JAILE family."

I peek out of the corner of my eye to see the Synergy family shaking their heads, annoyed. That's when Hunter rests both his hands on Brynn's shoulders and gives her a massage, as if to ease her disappointment at not being the "smartest" in the class.

Fighting the urge to simultaneously burst into tears and puke, I force myself to turn my attention back to my table.

Luke grins at me wickedly. "Excited to spend the next nine months in 'a prison you can't escape,' Agresti?"

Seriously. What have I done?

CHAPTER 7

Apparently, there is a right and a wrong way to do dishes, and Mrs. Sanchez is going to make absolutely sure that we don't ever wash the plates before the forks, so help her god.

"You waste room in your drying rack that way," she says, scrubbing some spoons from her kitchen at the front of the room, the next day.

Every family is standing by the sinks in their assigned kitchen; one side of our double sink is filled with sudsy warm water, and there's a drying rack on our counter. We're supposed to follow along with Mrs. Sanchez as she pulls out utensil after utensil, identifying them, then washing them. It's about as thrilling as you'd expect.

"In our class, this will be known as a pancake turner, *not* a spatula," Mrs. Sanchez says holding up an instrument I've called a spatula most of my life. After she washes it, she holds up the thing I use to scrape cake batter off the sides of the bowl. "*This* is a spatula."

I look at my family members. Luke seems to be trying to see how long he can balance on one leg, A.J. is making bubbles with our bottle of dish detergent, and Isaiah? Well, he's at least drying the dishes that I dunked into the soapy water and rinsed with the tap.

But he doesn't say anything the whole time he's drying, as if he's completely riveted by Mrs. Sanchez's lecture.

Though I guess my group seems a little more focused than the guys of Jersey Strong, who appear to be using their Dutch oven and cast-iron frying pan as makeshift weights.

"Okay, kids," Mrs. Sanchez says, and the tone of her voice gives me hope that something exciting is about to happen. "On to pots and pans."

I'm about to sigh heavily, when I hear Hannah giggle from Hunter and Brynn's group.

"We have a lot of pots and pans we'll be using in this class," Mrs. Sanchez is saying, but now Hunter and Brynn are suppressing smiles as they glance at each other. Why on earth is this so—

Oh my god.

Pots and pans. Brynn Potts and Hunter "Panz" Panzic. *Potts and Panz.* They've been going out for less than a week and they already have a supercouple name. Maybe this is why they got together, because when your names are just so sickeningly cute when paired, how can you *not* be dating? I look at Hunter and Brynn and their shmoopy-woopy expressions and I have a sudden urge to yank the hose from my sink and take aim at them with the water on full blast.

It doesn't help that Mrs. Sanchez keeps uttering the offending term, without seeming to notice the giggles it elicits.

"Now, when you're putting away your pots and pans, make sure . . ."

Synergy is now all giggly, even Steve. Hannah adds an "Aww," when she sees one of the adoring gazes Brynn and Hunter keep sharing.

"Jesus, shut *up*," A.J. hisses, momentarily distracted from his bubble making. The group gives him a collective scowl, like, "Who is he to tell us what to do?", but they do indeed shut up. If Mrs. Sanchez has noticed this quiet outburst, she doesn't make it known, because she goes on explaining how you store lasagna pans and loaf pans.

Part of me wants to thank A.J. for stopping the madness, but then, he didn't do it for me. I mean, it's not like he's got ESP or something. Plus, he's back to making bubbles with the soap, and completely ignoring Mrs. Sanchez as she identifies a ginormous roasting pan. I start getting annoyed when I realize that Isaiah and I are probably going to be the only ones to pass the upcoming cookware quiz, which means we'll be the only ones to get points for the family this week.

Mrs. Sanchez finally wipes her hands on a paper towel, a gleaming mountain of dishes next to her on the drying rack. "Okay, now I want you to put the dishes away, and identify them among yourselves as you go."

Oh, this should be fun. I take the stopper out of the sink's drain and glance at the clock. There's still twenty minutes left of class.

"Maybe it would be faster if we pair off and put certain things away," Isaiah says.

"Works for me," A.J. says, grabbing a dish. "This is a cake pan," he says.

"No, it's a pie tin," Isaiah says slowly.

"I can tell I'm going to learn a lot from you, dude," A.J. says. "Pie tin," he repeats to himself as he puts it in a cabinet next to the sink.

Luke comes up next to me. "So, I guess it's you and me and the utensils," he says.

"Uh, sure," I say as I grab a handful of silverware and baking tools from the drying rack. Luke opens the utensil drawer and holds a hand out. "Scalpel," he demands in a monotone voice.

"We don't have a scalpel," I inform him, unable to hide the annoyance in my voice.

Luke slaps his hand to his forehead dramatically. "Man, I knew I should've been paying attention." Then he shakes his head exasperatedly. "I was making a joke. You know, ha-ha?"

"Oh," I say, feeling my ears get hot. "I didn't get it."

"Of course you didn't," Luke says with a sigh.

"What's that supposed to mean?" I snap.

"You don't seem like the chill type. Can you hand me the measuring spoons?"

I thrust them at him. "You don't even know me," I say, hoping my voice sounds measured and not as angry as I'm feeling.

"Fair enough," Luke says. "But you seem kind of wound up is all."

Maybe the news of the breakup hasn't reached everyone after all. Or maybe Luke is just tremendously out of the loop. "In case you haven't noticed, I'm not exactly thrilled to be in this class. I have my reasons for being 'wound up,' as you put it."

"Psh," Luke says, nodding in the direction of Synergy. "Like those losers are worth your anger? I tried to get Brynn away from that table, but you were having none of that, were you?"

I chew my inner cheek, not really knowing what to say. Though deep down, I think I'm relieved he has enough taste to not have a crush on Brynn.

"Anyway, it's no excuse to be rude to everyone else."

So he does know. He just doesn't care. I place the utensils on the counter, afraid I might be forced to commit murder with a butter knife or a grapefruit spoon.

"Don't tell me how to feel," I say, irked when tears start forming in my eyes. "And if I'm being rude, maybe it's because you seem like you're out to get me or something."

I'm surprised when Luke's face falls. "I wasn't trying to—"

"Whatever," I say, wiping my eyes. "Let's just get this done."

"Okay," Luke says quietly, turning back to the drawer. "Can I have the spatula?"

I pick it out from the pile and hand it to him wordlessly.

"No, the, uh, spatula."

I realize I've handed him the pancake turner. "Sorry," I say, my face flaming. Here I'd thought this whole time that he wasn't paying attention, and now it seems like I wasn't.

The last of the soapy dishwater is disappearing down the drain, making this nasty, gaspy-sucking noise as it goes.

If I didn't know any better, I'd think the sink was making a declarative statement about my life at the moment.

CHAPTER 8

Mrs. Sanchez says the average American spends forty-one minutes a week grocery shopping. It's probably an ordinary experience for everyone else, because they either share that time with people who are halfway normal, or, even better, get to shop alone. But if the average American had to endure those forty-one minutes with the JAILE family, there's no way they'd make it out of the produce section without wanting to bludgeon themselves to death with a butternut squash.

This is the only acceptable course of action when one of your "family" members uses fruit to portray the anatomy of a woman.

"Look," A.J. says in a high-pitched voice, holding two grapefruits up to his chest, then dancing with them in place. "I'm just like Carlina Crawford."

Of course he'd name-check a former porn star turned YouTube influencer and infomercial queen.

"You're Canadian?" Luke says innocently. He's looking at me, as if he knows something like this is *just* a bit inappropriate with a girl present and also like he's worried I may go off on them as a result.

"Among other things," A.J. says, hefting the grapefruit up higher on his chest.

I just close my eyes and shake my head. After Luke's comment about me being rude, I'm pretty much going out of my way not to say anything. So if the guys are going to behave badly, let someone else call them on it.

I suppose spending last period at the Shop & Save is better than being stuck in a classroom washing and identifying kitchenware. And Mrs. Sanchez certainly seems excited at the prospect of us learning to food shop according to our budget. She's given us color-coded maps and fake money and even managed to get a cashier to total us all up at the end, even though we're not really paying for the food and taking it home. She's been doing this for so many years, the employees know her by name and they tell us to seek them out for any help.

If we come in under budget, we get points added to our group total. We've allotted ourselves $100 to buy food for the week. To put that in perspective, Hunter and Brynn's group has a $300 budget for food, so no, we're not expecting to get very far, food-wise, or in our little in-class competition.

"My boobs are the biggest in all the land," A.J. says in his high-pitched voice.

I throw a desperate look at Luke, who's still in the produce section, but he's no longer paying attention to A.J.'s antics because he appears to be FaceTiming Greta on his phone. And he also appears to have no sense of an indoor voice.

"Yeah, I'm at Shop & Save!" he practically yells.

I squeeze my eyes shut. *I will not say anything. I will not say anything. I will not say anything.*

Isaiah, at least, has his head in the game. He carries over a bag of potatoes and sets it down in our shopping cart. "They can get several nights of side dishes out of those."

"Good call. They're on sale, too," I say, noting their price.

"My bra will be a forty-six triple deeeeee," A.J. sings from behind us, still cradling his fruit breasts, as Luke yells to Greta, "Yeah, it's crazy, we're grocery shopping for class. Wait, holy crap, look at this lemon. Doesn't this look like Mr. Roydon's head?"

Isaiah and I watch Luke turn his phone toward the lemon in his left hand, and we both sigh audibly. We make eye contact then and I don't want to say we both burst out laughing, but we kind of chuckle.

"Jinx," I say.

A.J.'s arms must grow tired because he puts the grapefruits back. "So, like, what are we starting with?"

"We need breakfast and we're close to the cereal aisle," I say, studying our list. "Then we can move on to lunch, dinner, and snacks."

Luke mercifully has ended his call and returns to our cart, lifting a bag of oranges so we can see them. "I already got some of the snacks. Seventy-nine cents a pound, and three pounds here. That should get them through a few snack times."

Color me impressed—he can apparently FaceTime and food shop simultaneously. But I'm still playing it cool, so I say, "That'll work," as neutrally as possible. Luke swings the bag of oranges around like he's a ninja.

A.J. wrinkles his nose as we make our way into the cereal aisle. "It sucks that this family doesn't have any room for some kind of junk food. Like where's the ice cream? The cookies?"

"Yeah," Luke says, "but can you do this with ice cream?" He pulls some of the oranges out of the bag and starts tossing them in the air. I'm about to blurt out, "What are you doing?" when he starts to juggle them. I'm momentarily mesmerized as the oranges move expertly through the air and back to his hands again. It's not like when you see people *trying* to juggle—this seems as natural to him as blinking. "See?" he says calmly, not taking his eyes off of the flying fruit. "Not only are oranges food, they can be used as toys."

"Damn, Burke, where'd you learn to juggle?" A.J. says.

"Circus school," Luke says nonchalantly, as he catches the oranges, one behind his back, no less, and returns them to the bag.

"No, for real," A.J. says.

"I'm serious," Luke laughs. "I did a summer camp for circus training once."

"So you can, like, fly on a trapeze and tame lions and shit?" A.J. says, staring at Luke in awe.

Luke shakes his head. "No lions. And I tried the trapeze, but it wasn't me. I got pretty good at tumbling and balancing, though." He leans over my shoulder and looks at our shopping list. "So, can we afford two boxes of cereal this week? With three people eating it every morning, it'll probably go quick."

I'm still wrapping my mind around the idea that Luke is a closet acrobat, but I manage to say, "If we get the generic, store-brand cereal."

That's when the Bukowski family strolls into our aisle with a cart full of things like steaks, strawberries, and Italian cookies. Their group has the income of a single, fifty-year-old accountant with no kids and apparently money to spare.

Jared, the alleged great mind behind The Buzz, who likes to laugh at his own jokes and wear berets "ironically" (today it's a red-and-blue striped one), gazes into our cart. "Well, if it isn't one of our rival *familias*," he says. I can see the wheels turning in his head as he surveys our nearly empty cart and then the bag of oranges in Luke's hand. He turns back to his group and stage-whispers, "Orange you guys glad we're not part of the JAILE family?"

Of course they all laugh, much louder than necessary, if you ask me.

"Yeah, well, your accountant guy's only got his steak and old-lady cookies to keep him warm at night," A.J. says, folding his arms and smiling. "At least we have proof our bus driver lady has gotten laid."

Jared shrugs. "Well, good for her. Maybe she can turn to stripping to make some extra cash." His group snickers as he leads them past us. "And look on the bright side, guys—you'll be eligible for food stamps. Ta-ta." He gives an obnoxious wave as he goes.

A.J.'s face is a flaming shade of red and his nostrils are flaring as the giggly Bukowskis exit the aisle. Like, I know A.J. has a low boiling point, but I feel like there's something deeper at work here.

Isaiah starts to push the cart forward quickly and Luke follows his lead. It's like we all know we need to get A.J. past this before he murders Jared in the cereal aisle.

"Uh, I think we can get two bags of the generic Cheerios, right?" I ask.

Luke shakes his head vigorously. "No, no. Give them some variety. Store-brand Cheerios and Rice Krispies." He gives A.J. a sympathetic clap on the shoulder, then jogs to catch up to the cart.

We manage to get through the processed foods aisles pretty quickly, mostly since everything outside of pasta, soup, and canned vegetables is pretty pricey.

Mrs. Sanchez had been eager to point out that supermarkets are laid out with the perishable foods outlining the perimeter of the store. I didn't need her to tell me this because, outside of the produce section, the perimeter of the store is usually lined with refrigerator/freezer equipment, which almost always makes me shiver for the duration of any food-shopping trip.

I groan inwardly. I mean, I may be dressed appropriately for the seventy-eight-degree temperatures outside, but I should've been prepared for this, since I get chilly on most supermarket trips. The second we enter the meat department, the first wave of coldness hits me.

"What kind of meat do we want this week?" I ask, trying to ignore the goosebumps erupting on my arms.

Luke makes a face. "I don't know. Can we afford any of it?"

"It's not like they can't eat meat," I say, trying to rub some feeling back into my arms. "They can still afford ground beef and minute steaks and stuff."

"Sounds like you're pretty versed in this," Luke says, studying a package of minute steaks.

"Yeah," I say, and my teeth chatter a bit. "My dad's, uh, into food."

"Here," Luke says, untying his navy-blue hoodie from around his waist, and extending it toward me. "We can't have you dying from hypothermia before we hit the dairy and frozen food sections."

I just kind of stare at him. I can't explain why, but it feels a little weird to put on Luke's sweatshirt. The last time I wore something of a guy's, it was Hunter's. Offering you an extra layer—it's the type of thing a boyfriend does for you, not a fake family member.

"It's okay," I say, waving my hand. "I'll live."

Luke shakes his head. "I'll leave it on the cart if you should decide you don't want to freeze to death."

I clench my jaw to keep my teeth from chattering as the guys examine all the meats. They end up debating whether to buy a whole chicken or a pack of chicken cutlets.

I push the cart and follow as they decide, my ice-cold hands resting on Luke's sweatshirt. It's soft under my fingers and I can imagine it keeps warmth in nicely.

"On to the dairy aisle!" A.J. declares, and I realize we have to get through that and the freezer section. So I pull the sweatshirt off the cart and shrug it on. It's huge, but despite its size, I like that it covers every one of my cold, exposed body parts like a tent. It must be new, because the inside still has that fleecy, soft feeling and isn't yet pilly and rough.

If Luke notices this, he doesn't say anything. In fact, he's more fascinated by the types of frozen breakfast foods, which we can't afford, of course. "For the cost of four breakfast biscuits we could buy three cartons of eggs," he says, shaking his head.

The sweatshirt, surprisingly, isn't completely wrinkled, unlike the blue-striped T-shirt Luke's wearing right now. It smells of some woodsy-fresh fabric softener, overtaking the scent of lilac body splash I'd used this morning. My hands are completely covered, so I push the sleeves up as best I can, knowing I probably look ridiculous. But I no longer feel like I've been stranded on Antarctica in a bikini, so the sweatshirt is staying on. For now.

By the time we have to meet back up with Mrs. Sanchez at the checkout line, we've filled our cart with what we calculate is about ninety-eight dollars' worth of food. Three meals a day and snacks for seven days, plus a roll of toilet paper, some paper towels and store-brand glass cleaner.

"No one's going hungry on our watch, bitches," A.J. says.

"Too bad you guys can't eat real food," a voice says from behind us.

We all turn around to see Jared and the rest of his group in line with their cart. I'm kind of dumbfounded. Their cart had been so much fuller than ours earlier and they just finished?

A.J. is downright glowering at Jared, but the line is moving forward, so he doesn't say anything.

I notice Hunter and Brynn's group is standing near the exit, apparently done for the day. Hunter fans Brynn with one of those free local real estate magazines, and Brynn giggles and playfully slaps his hand.

I almost lose my lunch.

"Okay, JAILE family, let's see how you did," Mrs. Sanchez says. The four of us gather near the front of the register, and our food follows us on the conveyor belt, a store employee unloading the cart and the cashier scanning all of it.

"Did you find this task challenging?" Mrs. Sanchez wants to know.

"It was kind of hard, considering we're dirt-poor," A.J. says. "But we'll definitely be under budget."

Mrs. Sanchez smiles. "See, I told you money isn't everything in this class, you have to be—"

"Okay," the cashier says cheerfully. "Their total is one hundred three dollars and fourteen cents."

"What?" I say, my family members making similar statements of disbelief. The cashier's face falls and she checks the receipt.

"There's no way," Isaiah says. "We calculated twice. It was ninety-seven dollars and seventy three cents"

"Did you include sales tax in that?" Mrs. Sanchez asks, disappointment in her voice.

Luke nods. "We even took something out of our cart to make up for that."

I notice Isaiah is staring at our "purchases" that are being stacked in crates to return to the store shelves. Then he points at something. "Those weren't ours."

We move as one to the end of the register, and the guy putting the food in the crates backs away. A.J. rifles through the crate Isaiah pointed at and this look of total realization and rage crosses his face as he pulls out . . . a bag of Italian cookies.

"Those weren't in our cart, Mrs. Sanchez," Luke says.

"You!" A.J. booms suddenly, and we turn around to see him pointing at Jared, whose purchases are now being loaded onto the conveyor. "You put those on the belt when we weren't looking!"

"Prove it," Jared says, folding his arms.

"Prove this," A.J. spits back, and knocks the beret off Jared's head.

"Hey!" Jared says, uncrossing his arms and pushing A.J. with a surprising amount of strength for an underground gossip blogger.

"Boys!" Mrs. Sanchez barks. "This needs to stop right now!"

A.J. leans forward to push Jared back or worse, but Luke is suddenly behind him, pulling him back toward the windows, away from the register.

"Let me go," A.J. says.

"It's not worth it," Luke mutters.

Of course, Hunter and Brynn and their group have to come running over, and their shoulders sag in disappointment that the fray has been broken up before they got to see anything. I don't realize I'm staring at them until Hunter's eyes lock on mine. For a minute I have this reflexive urge to smile at him, but I fight it and probably end up looking like a psychotic clown. Hunter doesn't react, but I notice he's staring at my torso with something resembling curiosity.

I glance down and realize I'm still wearing Luke's sweatshirt, which explains why Hunter's eyes go from me to Luke and back at me again. Luke, who is blocking A.J. from even seeing Jared, is totally oblivious. Hunter turns around too quickly for me to identify what he's thinking.

"JAILE family and Bukowski family," Mrs. Sanchez says sternly. "I'm deducting thirty points from each of you for your lack of conduct today."

A.J. gestures at us. "But Mrs. S, they didn't do anything. I'm the one who—"

"That doesn't matter, Mr. Johnson," Mrs. Sanchez says, her face totally unamused. "One family member's actions reflect on the rest of the family. Hopefully you learn that by the end of the year."

A.J.'s nostrils flare, like he wants to shove Jared's beret down his throat, and Luke positions himself in front of him again.

"This totally blows," Luke says when Mrs. Sanchez is out of earshot.

Isaiah shakes his head. "Yeah, you pulled A.J. back way too fast. You could've at least let him get a punch in."

I almost laugh.

"I'm sorry, guys," A.J. says, shoulders slumping.

"It's not *your* fault," I say. "We did the lesson right." Luke blinks several times, like he's surprised I'm being cool with this.

On the way back to school, Luke manages to keep A.J. away from Jared. The whole class is buzzing as we move, the near-fight being the closest thing to action they've seen since I kicked a papier-mâché globe at Hunter and Brynn's heads. Maybe I should be grateful to A.J. for putting my public meltdowns on the back burner.

We get back to RHHS about twenty minutes after the end of last period. Most of the cars have cleared from the senior parking lot, and only a few kids are hanging around the halls when I grab my things from my locker.

When I go back outside, I notice Luke unlocking his bike from the bike rack, and I peel off his sweatshirt. "Hey," I say, jogging over and handing it to him. "Thank you. I think I would've lost a few limbs to frostbite if not for this."

"You're welcome," Luke says, putting his arms through it and shrugging it on. He sniffs the shoulder of the shirt and wrinkles his nose. "Looks like I'm going to smell like flowers now."

"I'm sorry," I say, my face growing hot.

He laughs and climbs on his bike. "Don't sweat it, Agresti. See you on Monday."

"See you," I say.

I watch him ride away and sigh, trying to ignore the scent of woodsy freshness lingering on my shirt.

CHAPTER 9

I don't know that I have many talents, but over the last few weeks, I've gotten pretty good at pretending I'm not eating when, really, I'm scarfing down an entire sandwich . . . in tiny pieces. My secret lunchtime routine has escaped the notice of the school librarians, and I'm hoping I can keep it that way till June.

But it's going to be a challenge today because I've packed a Thermos with my dad's famous chicken and gnocchi soup. Its deliciousness has been calling to me like a siren song from my backpack all day. Eating something so conspicuous in total secrecy is going to be a little tough, however.

I plunk down by the computers, and check over my shoulder to see if any of the librarians have somehow wandered back here. They seem busy helping a freshman history class find information on the Revolutionary War, so my hope is that they'll be distracted just long enough for me to eat the whole thing.

I manage to unscrew the top and pause for a moment to savor the scent of the soup. When Dad made it last night, he'd said, "You've seemed a little stressed lately. I thought this might help." The weird thing is, I haven't thought that much about Hunter the last few days,

and this is extremely exciting because it means I'm totally getting over him and I may be able to—

"No eating in the library!" a voice booms.

My stomach drops as I look up to my left. Sure enough, there's a librarian standing by the railing of the second-level annex, frowning down at me with disdain. I'm one of those kids who kind of fears any type of authority—a grown-up yelling is all it takes to make me feel bad. Being called out like this makes me feel four years old again.

"I'm sorry," I croak as I screw my Thermos lid back on. My face is on fire as I walk past the gawking freshmen. For the rest of the school year they're going to remember me as the girl who almost took out the entire library computer system with a Thermos full of soup.

Reluctantly, I trudge to the cafeteria, where the low hum of lunchtime hits me when I step through the open doors. Two teachers are standing by the entrance chatting. I scan the room for an empty table, but it appears as if I'm the only one who hides during lunch, because the cafeteria is pretty crowded.

"Excuse me, is this your lunch period?" one of the teachers asks.

"Uh, yeah, I'm just looking for a place to sit," I say.

"There are plenty of seats," the teacher says, gesturing at the tables ahead of us.

Yes, there *are* plenty of seats . . . at tables already occupied by groups I'm not a part of. Like, I'm sure the cheerleaders would just love it if I wandered over and pulled up a chair and was like "Hey, gals! Nice day, isn't it?"

That's when I notice Brynn and Kim are staring at me from their table. I don't want to give them the satisfaction of being smug about my friendlessness, so I take off to the left and walk as if I know where I'm going. Worst-case scenario, I can exit through the cafeteria's back doors and hide in the bathroom for the remainder of the period.

And then I spot Isaiah. Like the last time I saw him in the cafeteria, he's sitting by himself at the far end of a table, the other end occupied by teachers discussing some papers. Isaiah's back is turned, so he doesn't see me until I'm pulling out the chair across from him.

"Hi," I say. "Mind if I sit here?"

A look of confusion, followed by recognition, followed by just a hint of annoyance crosses his face and I instantly feel bad. I should've known. Isaiah is a classic introvert and just because we're "family" doesn't mean I can crash his solitary time.

"Hey," he says back, finally. I take this as my okay—or, okay enough, anyway—and sit down. That's when I notice he's got the racing section of the *Ringvale Heights Gazette* folded in half on the table next to his lunch, and he appears to be marking it up with notes. I must have interrupted his horse-studying time. I want to ask him about it to be friendly, but I feel like I've already imposed enough.

"Don't let me interrupt your reading," I say. I pull out my Thermos and physics textbook to let him know that I'm going to be concentrating on studying and have no desire to be a Chatty Cathy.

He eyes me warily, but doesn't say anything else.

I absorb myself in elementary particles. It goes down a lot easier while getting to enjoy the creamy soup, which I relish eating publicly and not having to hide.

"What is that?" I'm so startled, I literally jump a little in my seat. I look up and see that Isaiah is staring at my Thermos cup.

"It's chicken and gnocchi soup. My dad made it. He's a chef," I tell him.

"Is that why you're taking home ec, to follow in his footsteps or something?" he asks.

"No. But my dad was happy when I told him I'd signed up for it. I

guess he likes that I'm taking an interest in cooking, but he knows I don't want to be a chef."

He nods. "My mom's a dermatologist and my dad's a pharmacist. I don't want to do their jobs, either."

"Do you want to do something with horse racing?" I ask.

His eyes start to sparkle as he nods enthusiastically. "I'd like to be a trainer. You know, the person who gets the horses in shape for races and stuff. The problem is, I only get to see them when we're driving through the farm areas. My mom doesn't like horse racing."

"So you've never been to a racetrack?" I don't know much about horse racing, but I assume this would be like if I'd never watched The Weather Channel or something.

Isaiah frowns and shakes his head sadly. "My grandfather was a jockey after he emigrated here from Jamaica. He got thrown from a horse, hit his head, and went blind. I guess my mom doesn't want that happening to me. But it sucks."

"Well, maybe someday she'll change her mind," I say hopefully.

Isaiah shrugs, unconvinced. Then, he goes back to his reading and I go back to mine, and it might be the best lunch I've had since coming to Ringvale Heights High.

For some reason, lunch with Isaiah has made me a lot more optimistic about things. Like, I don't know what tomorrow will bring, but if he's open to me sitting there again, I'll have found an actual lunch buddy.

A lunch buddy I didn't meet through Hunter. This is huge.

I'm even psyched when Mrs. Sanchez tells us that today's cooking lesson is going to be difficult. "You'll be making sautéed vegetables, rice, and Texas toast, so you're going to need every person in your group to pull his or her weight today in order for this to work."

I'm closest to our apron drawer, so I pull out all four of them and place them on our kitchen counter. They're all a little worn and none of them match. I take a faded red-and-white-striped one so that one of the guys is forced to wear the green-and-yellow flowered apron with yellow ruffles, or the one that says "I Heart Chocolate." It's given me my own private chuckle the past few weeks.

Brynn is also reaching down into her family's apron drawer, which is in my direct line of sight. Like a distress signal, I kind of can't avoid seeing the bit of red sticking up past the waistline of her jeans.

A thong. And not just any thong. A *red lace thong*. And Brynn once said in her most judgmental voice, and I quote, "Why would any woman subject herself to wearing butt floss?" Which means there's only one reason for this turnaround: She's wearing it for her boyfriend.

My insides twist on cue.

She hands Hunter an apron, and they simper at each other.

I feel my stomach churn and I steady myself on the counter with both hands. So much for being over it.

"You all right?" Luke asks as he ties on the flowery apron.

I nod but can't say anything. Hunter and Brynn have been dating for a few weeks and are probably already boinking like crazy. I had him for eight months and could barely even bring it up in conversation.

I tie on my apron and think of my own underwear collection, which is mostly cotton with flower prints or polka dots and then Christmas trees and Santas for December. They're cute, but definitely not *sexy*. Maybe Hunter dumped me because my underwear wasn't hot enough for him?

Isaiah is looking at our recipes for the day. "I can do the rice. Who wants the Texas toast?" A.J. raises his hand, and Luke volunteers to sauté the vegetables. That puts me on "prep," which means I get to chop the vegetables and think about Brynn and Hunter having sex while I have a knife in my hand.

Mrs. Sanchez claps her hands together. "I'll be checking over your written materials for your budgets next week. We won't have much time to work on them in class, as we'll be cooking this week, so you will probably have to work on it on your own time."

"What do you mean, 'on our own time'?" A.J. asks.

"Exactly that, Mr. Johnson. You won't have enough time to complete your task in class, so you're going to have to get together as a group during your free time to work on it."

A.J. crosses his arms. "That's BS."

Mrs. Sanchez's eyes narrow and she puts her hands on her hips. Even in her Snoopy apron, she suddenly looks intimidating. "Excuse me, Mr. Johnson?"

The whole class has stopped mid-preparation to watch this exchange. Even Jared's bright-green beret, tilted forward on his head, looks interested.

"This class isn't supposed to be this hard. I didn't take it to do stuff *outside of class*. It's total bullshit."

"In the hallway, *now*, Mr. Johnson," Mrs. Sanchez says, pointing toward the door.

A.J. sets his jaw and stalks out of the room. He doesn't even look back at Mrs. Sanchez, whose shoulders sag as she follows behind him. "Get started on the lesson, guys," she says. "I'll be back in a second."

We set to work right away without a word. Isaiah starts boiling water for the rice while simultaneously buttering some bread and sprinkling garlic powder on it, while Luke digs out our giant frying pan. Our sautéed vegetables are carrots, snow peas, and green onions, so I just have to cut up the carrots and green onions.

I'm about to start chopping the onions when I realize I need some paper towels to pat them dry. There's a whole stash of them in the classroom pantry, so I quickly make my way over there. I have to squeeze by Synergy's kitchen to do so, and just as I pass, Brynn's demanding voice assaults my ear. "Would you guys mind if we finished our budget before the weekend? Hunter and I are going camping and we won't be here."

I freeze in place. They're going camping? Like Hunter and I were supposed to go camping? So they can have hot sex and Hunter can tell Brynn about my lame underwear choices?

I don't realize that I'm staring at them until Hunter looks directly at me and his face falls.

"Camping?" I say, not taking my eyes off of him. "*Our* camping trip?"

Brynn drops her eyes in fake dramatic fashion. "Oh, sorry, Ellie. I didn't mean for you to hear that."

"Oh, please," I snap, my voice getting higher. "You waited till I was in earshot to say it. You're not sorry about anything."

Brynn's face contorts into an indignant glare. "Not everything is about you, Ellie."

I'm breathing heavy, like I've just run a mile and not merely walked about five feet. "Yeah, you made that pretty obvious since you moved in on my boyfriend while he was still with me. God, you're a real piece of work, you know that?"

Brynn can't seem to formulate a response outside of a couple sputters and sighs.

"Let it go, Brynn," Hunter says, touching her arm.

"*She* needs to let it go," she says, shrugging his hand off of her. "You wanted to be with me just as much as I wanted to be with you." Then she fixes me with a hard stare. "And it's not my fault she doesn't know what a girlfriend is supposed to do."

The words sting like a slap across the face and tears start

burning in my eyes, and to make matters worse, I hear one of the Jersey Strong girls whisper, "Oh shiiiit!" and some people giggle in response. Which means what I feared is true: The whole school knows I'm a virgin of my own cold-fish doing.

A.J. and Mrs. Sanchez re-enter the room then, and Mrs. Sanchez totally notices that something is going on. "Everything all right?" Actually, it's more of a statement, as if there's no other acceptable answer except "yes."

"It's fine," Hunter says, but his eyes are on me, pleading to not make any more of a scene.

"Yes, fine," I say, though my voice cracks and betrays me. "I need some more paper towels, though, so . . ." I stride into the pantry as the tears spill over. I can't do this. No matter how much I think I'm over this, I'm always going to be the one who got dumped while Brynn gets to shop at Victoria's Secret and do the nasty with my ex in the woods, and everyone will be on her side.

While I'm the girl who yells at them in front of everyone like a lovelorn psycho.

I sink to the floor, wracked with silent sobs, and I'm glad the classroom activity has resumed because I'm never going to be over this. Ever. And I'm never going back out into that classroom. Or at least not until class is over.

That's when Isaiah sort of tiptoes into the pantry and, in a low voice, says, "Hey. Are you all right?"

"Fine," I chirp. "I just need some—" but before I can finish, an involuntary wave of tears comes over me, and I'm totally sobbing again.

"I'm sorry," I gasp.

"Oh no," Isaiah says, frowning. "I didn't mean to make you cry!"

"It's not you," I say, tearing off a paper towel from one of the rolls next to me, wiping my eyes. "It's them. You saw. The *whole effing class* saw."

"But you didn't do anything wrong, and I think the, uh, *whole eff-ing class* knows that."

"But they think Hunter dumped me because," I pause, and it literally makes my heart hurt to say it: "I'm uptight."

Isaiah scowls. "You give him too much credit. That guy's completely ridiculous."

In spite of everything, that makes me giggle. "Gee, Isaiah, tell me how you really feel."

"No, seriously. He cheated on you with her, right? That's just . . . wrong. Like, really wrong. He doesn't deserve to have someone crying over him in a pantry. Or anywhere else for that matter. He's pathetic."

I study Isaiah for a moment. He's keeping his distance like most guys do when they see a girl crying. But what he just said is the emotional equivalent of a pat on the back. I mean, Jodie can tell me that, but since she's my friend, she's automatically on my side. I think back to Luke telling me they're not worth it last week, and now Isaiah. They don't owe me anything and yet they're seeing this from my point of view.

I give him a wobbly smile. "Thank you."

Luke pokes his head into the pantry then. "Everything okay in here?"

I take a deep breath, thinking of Hunter and Brynn's self-righteous faces. "I will be. But we need to beat Hunter's team."

Luke raises an eyebrow, his eyes twinkling with amusement. "In today's task or all year?"

I blink hard, and feel my pulse start to quicken at the thought of being better at something than the both of them, the hyper-competitive overachievers. At the thought of taking them down and putting their smug asses in place. To show them that they're not better than me.

"All. Freaking. Year," I say.

A.J. wanders into the pantry then. "Is this a team meeting?"

"Yes," Luke says. "Agresti wants to annihilate Synergy."

"I'm down with that, yo," A.J. says, rubbing his hands together. "As long as we beat jackass Jared's team, too. That guy's such a dick."

Luke, Isaiah, and I all mutter our own distaste for Jared while nodding vigorously.

I pull myself up from the floor, an exhilarating feeling of determination surging through me. "Okay, well, we need to get back out there and get a jump on our meal."

We head back into the classroom and set to work, washing, chopping, and frying. Luke tosses the snow peas and carrots in the frying pan. He caught on to the technique of sautéing before the rest of the class (for example, Jared is sautéing across the room and doesn't seem to notice that a snow pea has landed on his beret) and I wonder if his circus training has helped him with hand-eye coordination or something.

Brynn and Hunter start giggling over something then, and I reflexively inhale deeply and clutch my knife's handle super hard.

Luke leans over toward me. "We've got this, Agresti."

I gaze up at him and nod. "We sure as hell better, Burke."

This makes him burst out laughing, loudly, and the entire Synergy team turns to shoot us a disapproving look.

I chop my onions as methodically as possible and ignore them.

They don't know they're going down and it's going to be so, so epic.

CHAPTER 10

Deciding to obliterate Hunter and Brynn's group has become my new fuel, to the point that I wonder what other aspects of my life I can apply this to. It's invigorating.

The problem is, I don't have enough of a social life to be out there one-upping them in much of anything else. It's completely evident all weekend, when, after Jodie catches a cold and can't hang out, I'm stuck in the house with my parents, who are all hover-y and "how are you doing, honey?" I appreciate the support, but this only drives the point home that I've wasted the last eight months of my life not making any friends outside of Hunter's group.

So I spend most of Sunday reading The Buzz archives in the hopes of spotting some old gossip about Hunter and Brynn, but instead learn maybe too much about my other classmates: The high-achieving junior who, as of last March, was probably getting shipped off to rehab for an Adderall addiction (I know that this actually happened a few weeks later to Madison Sawyer, a quiet girl in my gym class. She has yet to come back to RHHS); the lovers' spat that broke out in the cafeteria and revealed one party cheating with at least two other people; a sophomore boy who feared coming out to his family so he was "man-whoring it up with as many girls in his class as possible."

And then I feel gross for reading every word.

So a few days later, when I see a poster declaring that the RHHS TV station is looking for camera people and editors, I figure this is a sign, both literally and figuratively. Hunter hates the TV station—what better way to be like, "I don't care what you think," than by doing something he despises?

And it's two birds with one stone, because the next time I meet with Mrs. Gillroy, I can be truthful when I tell her I took her advice and joined the TV station—and editing keeps me from being on camera, which is key.

After school, I poke my head into the newsroom, where there's one of those news-anchor desks with a green wall behind it. Chris Phan, one of the anchorpeople who was also in my French class last year, is sitting behind the desk with a pen tucked behind his ear, reading a bunch of papers and shaking his head.

Hunter used to make fun of him for being so intense about the TV station—"He acts like it's freaking CNN and not some stupid home-room time-killer," he said. Meanwhile, Hunter once flipped out because all the guys in the Ringtones didn't have their hair parted on the same side. For a performance at a peewee hockey game.

"Hey, Chris," I say, and he jumps, knocking his knee on the anchor desk.

"Oh, hey," he says, rubbing his knee. "What's up?"

"Mrs. Gillroy told me to come down here because I'm interested in being a meteorologist and—"

"Do you know football?" His eyes are full of hope, like my answer is the key to our existence or something.

"Uh, yeah, kind of," I say. I learned about it from Mariana, the bartender at my dad's old restaurant. She was from western Pennsylvania and obsessed with the Pittsburgh Steelers. I don't understand football completely, but thanks to her, I do have a basic grasp.

"Thank you, god!" he says, clasping his hands together. "Have you ever been on camera before? Wait, never mind, we're stuck so we need you no matter what."

"Stuck?" is all I say because a sudden sense of doom has come over me. I don't want to be on camera.

"Yeah, our sports reporter is out with a broken ankle and her backup has the flu."

It hits me then. "Wait, Alisha is the sports reporter. She broke her ankle?"

"Yeah, it was a bad break," he says, flipping through some of his papers. "She tripped in gym class. Had to have surgery and everything."

I think back to the last time I saw Alisha. It was that day in the cafeteria, when she got pulled away by Kim. This whole time I thought she'd been avoiding me because of the breakup. I almost *unfollowed her* on Instagram. I'm pissed at myself for being so thoughtless and—

"So we're short-staffed and we need someone to interview Rashad Bryant, the football team captain, about his sacks record. Do you know anything about that?"

I'm relieved to say "No." If I don't know what's going on, how could I possibly interview him about it?

And if I can't conduct the interview, I can't possibly be on camera, and then become some serious fodder for The Buzz, or worse, give Hunter and Brynn something to laugh hysterically about, can I?

Chris waves his hand. "No worries. He's about to break the record for most sacks in school history. You just have to ask him how he feels about that."

I'm struck dumb momentarily. I don't know enough about

sports—jeez, I don't know enough about *this school*—to be asking questions in a journalistic capacity. Particularly while on camera.

This on-camera thing is going to be a real problem.

But Chris must take my petrified silence for an affirmative answer, because he continues with, "We need to get this in before tomorrow morning's broadcast since he could break the record during Saturday's game." He consults his Apple watch, oblivious to my openmouthed panic. "You've got about an hour before football practice ends. You can catch him after and just ask him a few questions."

Um, no.

The only thing I know about TV journalism, outside of my beloved Weather Channel, is what I see during the ten o'clock newscast that my mom watches. And then there are those prime-time shows with those reporters who jump out of bushes to accost someone about their defective products or ask how it feels to be let off for the murder of their mistress. In all those cases, the reporters, even the jump-out-of-bushes sort, are ballsy. And bubbly. At the same time. That is *so* not me.

And god only knows what Jared could cook up about me stammering my way through an interview, looking like a total idiot.

I still haven't said anything when Chris hands me one of his papers. "Here are some questions you can ask him."

I've seen Rashad in the halls and in the cafeteria. He's about six foot three and all muscle. He's crazy popular and he's in honors classes with Hunter, so I know he's smart enough to figure out I don't have much of a clue about football.

"I'm going to get in touch with Willow Goldstein, our camera-person, and you can meet her back here in a half hour or so," Chris says. "Okay?"

I desperately want to say, *No, it's not okay. I just wanted to own my ex, but this is something else entirely,* but I still haven't regained the power of speech. Besides, I'm afraid I'll look like a coward. So I just nod.

Chris smiles and shuffles his papers. "You're awesome, Ellie. Thanks."

But when I pass out from fright?

On camera?

He's not going to think I'm so awesome anymore.

A half hour later, after studying the mini-script and questions I'm supposed to ask, I'm standing in front of the mirror in the bathroom, trying to cover the zit that's formed right next to my nose. I take a deep breath and will the lines to ease out of my furrowed forehead. I am going to do this. I am fully capable of asking questions. It's just talking to another human being.

On camera. And shown to twelve hundred of my peers.

Oh, who am I kidding? I exhale loudly as I turn away from the mirror. I don't want all of RHHS snickering over my zit or taking note that I'm bloated or that my voice is really, really high when it's recorded. I don't want to give them anything to pick on. I was Robot Girl once, and that's more than enough for me.

Maybe I can fake being sick. Yes, that's it. I've got a sudden stomach bug or something. Chris doesn't have to know it's the "I just want to fly under the radar, thanks" flu.

I march back to the studio, working on my best "sick face" and practicing what I'm going to say in my head. I'm so caught up trying to look deathly ill that I almost crash into a tiny blonde girl carrying a camera and a footstool. She smiles when she sees me. "Oh, hey, you're Mary Ellen, right? I'm Willow, your cameraperson."

I blink down at this sprite of a girl: I'm only five foot five, but

Willow is barely cracking five feet. I'm surprised she doesn't collapse under the weight of the camera.

"It's so great that you're doing the sports report," she goes on. "Like, girl power, you know?"

"Yeah, girl power," I say weakly. There's no way I can get out of this now. Not with Willow playing the feminism card.

"Chris says I'm supposed to help you out," Willow says. "Have you ever been on camera before?"

"Not unless you count home movies," I say, forcing a laugh.

"Well, then, we can practice a bit," Willow says. "That'll help you get a feel for it."

Willow leads me to the hill above the football field, also known as The Nest, home to the RHHS Hornets. "We can interview him here. It'll set the tone for the story," she says.

Down below, football and cheerleading practices are going on simultaneously. I can hear whistles and the crashing of helmets and shoulder pads mingling with a cheer that includes a lot of clapping and chanting, "Sting you, fling you, the Hornets are gonna bring you pain."

Willow hands me a microphone, then climbs up on her stepstool and aims the camera at me. "Remember to talk into the mic. And smile, too."

When Willow nods, I project my voice as loudly as I can. "When the Hornets face the Ford Hill Tigers—"

Willow moves the camera down for a minute. "Talk loud, but don't scream," she says. She then gives me the thumbs-up. "You're doing great!"

We work at this for about five minutes when music starts blasting from the field.

"Is that going to interfere with the sound?" I ask.

"It might," Willow says. "Let's wait for Rashad in the senior parking lot. There won't be anything going on there to distract us."

"Sounds good," I say, giving silent thanks that one of us knows what she's doing.

While we're waiting, we manage to record the intro for the story. And I only need six takes to finally get it right.

Since Rashad is for all intents and purposes a giant, it's not hard to spot him when he makes his way into the parking lot a half hour later. When he sees us waiting on the curb, he stops short.

"Hey, R-R-ashad," I say. "CouldIaskyouafewquestions?"

He stares at me blankly and I'm terrified that this is someone else I've mistakenly thought was Rashad Bryant for the last nine months.

"It's for RHHS TV," Willow pipes up, plopping down her footstool and climbing up on it.

I nod. "We want to ask about you breaking the school record for sacks."

Rashad checks his phone. "Okay, but I've only got five minutes. I have to pick up my sister at karate practice."

Five minutes? I feel my hairline break out in sweat. There's no room for mistakes with only five minutes.

Rashad motions for us to follow him to his car, where he drops his backpack on the trunk, rubs his hands together, then looks at us expectantly.

Willow lifts up her camera and she nods at me with a big smile. "We're rolling!"

"Uh, okay. So, Rashad, when—"

Willow lowers the camera. "Your microphone!" she reminds me.

"Oh," I say, suddenly remembering that I'm holding it. Rashad gives me a wary glance and I pray he can't see my hands shaking. "Okay, so, Rashad, when did it first occur to you that you'd break the school record for tackles?"

"You mean sacks?" he asks, his face totally neutral.

I feel my face turning bright red. "Oh, god. Yeah, sorry." *Ugh.*

Rashad doesn't even have to think. "I'd say last October. I had a good first few games and Coach Abbott was like, 'Hey, you know you can break Joe Howard's record, right? And I was like, 'Okay, that's something to strive for.'"

I smile and nod, which seems to encourage Rashad to open up about how he met Joe Howard last year at a banquet. Thank goodness, I think I'm actually going to get through this. But as he goes into how Joe was chock-full of advice, there's a strange snarling "*arrr*" noise—it almost sounds like a vicious cross between gasping and gargling—from somewhere to the left.

"You started as a quarterback. How did you make your way into defense?" I ask, just as there's a more audible "*arrr, arrr.*" I begin to fret that some kind of hellmouth has opened behind me and that a bloodthirsty demon is about to unleash its fiery wrath on us. I mean, that would be my luck. I can't turn around because the camera is straight on me, probably capturing the look of paralyzed fear on my face.

Rashad doesn't seem fazed at all, and answers above the murderous sounds behind us, which are growing louder.

And then I remember: Montague. As if on cue, I spot the white German shepherd behind the chain-link fence beyond Rashad's shoulder. And he's dragging one of his infamous cinder blocks around while making those heinous noises. When he makes eye contact with me, his tail wags excitedly. And then, I swear to god, he nudges the gate open with his nose and practically prances toward us, tail whipping back and forth, tongue lolling out of his mouth.

I see Willow's face go slack from behind the camera. I feel my own face stiffen as Montague's thick tail whacks me in the leg and he starts barking excitedly. Why? Why is this happening right now? When I'm already making a fool of myself for the dumbest of reasons? It takes everything in me to keep my hand from shaking and my eyes on Rashad and keep my face looking neutral instead of the all-out panic that's suddenly coursing through me.

Rashad, though, doesn't miss a beat, as he launches into a story about how he once played quarterback and defensive tackle in one game. And he does all this while petting Montague, who keeps jumping up, trying to lick Rashad's face.

Just one last question, thank god.

"Any thoughts on playing Ford Hill?"

"Yeah," Rashad says, rubbing his hands together. "We're going to tear them apart."

"*Arrr! Arrr!*" Montague dances around between us.

I smile at Rashad and turn back to the camera, knowing I look like a crazy woman, and say the first thing that pops into my head. "And it seems Montague would agree!"

Willow waves her hand, reminding me I have to add, "The Hornets play here at The Nest on Saturday afternoon at one p.m. Back to you in the studio," and with that, we're done.

When I turn back around, Rashad is actually smiling and cooing, "Who's a good boy?" as he leans over and pets Montague, who has now rolled over on his back for a belly rub.

"I have no idea how you stayed so calm," I say with a laugh, as I lean over and scratch Montague's ears. "I thought I was going to lose it."

Rashad shrugs. "Aw, he just wanted to make friends. And I know we were short on time, so I tried to be professional about it."

I smile at him gratefully. "Thanks."

The three of us quickly make our way over to the fence, calling Montague so he follows us. I hold the gate open for him as he trots back inside, and shove the latch down so he can't get back out. He lays down next to his cinder block and sighs, seemingly content with the amount of havoc he's wreaked for the day.

"I'm going to run this back to the studio so they can edit this by tonight," Willow says as she folds up her footstool. "See you later!"

"Thanks for everything, Willow," I say as she scampers off. "And thank you for your time, Rashad. Good luck on Saturday."

"Thank you. Mary Ellen, right?" he says.

"Oh my god, I never introduced myself," I say, slapping my hand to my forehead. "Yes, I'm Ellie Agresti."

Rashad opens his car door. "I've seen you around. You were going out with Hunter Panzic, right?"

"Yeah," I say flatly. "Why?"

"Oh, nothing. I just know he's not too big on school sports and stuff is all. I thought you might be the same."

"No," I say. "I like sports. I'm not that good at playing them. I mean, I totally suck in gym class. But I like watching them."

Jesus, Ellie, he didn't ask for your life story.

"Well, you should try to get out to at least one game, they're a lot of fun. We've got a good team this year." With that, he climbs in his car and backs out of the parking lot. He waves at me before he leaves, and I wave back, looking like an idiot with the microphone still in my hand.

I'm fidgeting in my seat in homeroom the next morning. The news portion of RHHS TV is airing on the classroom flat-screen, and half of my classmates are sleeping through it. The others aren't paying much attention. Apparently, there's a quiz in one of the history classes and a lot of kids are cramming for it now.

All of this bodes well for me. If no one is watching, then they won't notice my zit or that I totally suck at interviewing people.

A story about the school nurse's twenty-five years at RHHS

is wrapping up, and Mia Mullholland, one of the anchorpeople, smiles at the camera. "And in other milestone news, the Hornets' Rashad Bryant is about to set the school record for sacks. Mary Ellen Agresti has that story in sports."

This weird feeling of pride suddenly swells through me at hearing my name. It ebbs away just as quickly when my smiling face takes up the whole screen and my voice is way, way higher than I *ever* thought it would be when I asked the first question.

"Hey," Tom Arriston says, tapping me on the shoulder from behind. "That's you!"

All I can do is nod. My eyes are glued to what surely is going to be a train wreck, what with my voice sounding like I'd been main-lining helium before the interview started, and Montague's antics about to come.

Willow, thankfully, had zoomed in on Rashad for most of the inter-view, so I'm only shown when I ask a question. Montague bursting into the scene is totally obvious, however. I can hear some of my homeroom mates giggling and ohmygod-ing over it and I'm afraid to turn around to count just how many are joining in. Of course they'd wake up and stop studying now. *Of course.*

I squirm through all two minutes and twenty-eight seconds, even if my screen time is minimal. Rashad, for his part, is great. He could totally be interviewing on ESPN in a few years, he's that at ease in front of the camera.

"We're going to tear them apart," he says finally, and that's when the camera zooms back and I'm suddenly smiling at the camera, all, "And it seems Montague would agree!"

And that's when my class, seemingly holding in their laughter till now, all start roaring. And not in a "Ha-ha, Robot Girl's got a scoliosis brace" sort of way, but in a "That was actually funny" sort of way.

"That was awesome," Tom says, tapping me on the shoulder again with his pen.

"Seriously, Montague was so loud!" Julia Ashito says next to me. "How did you keep your composure through that?"

"I honestly have no clue," I admit, and both Tom and Julia laugh.

Later in the morning, I get a text from Alisha, responding to a "get well soon" basket of cookies I'd sent her:

> Thank you for the sweet eats! I'm feeling a lot better now, especially with the aid of cookies. Heard you kicked ass in your interview with Rashad. When I'm back, we're going to the diner to celebrate! Welcome to RHHS TV, Ellie!

The relief I feel over Alisha still wanting to be my friend is enough to power me through the day, but then there's the added bonus of kids in my classes coming up to me and saying how much they loved the interview. And here I'd thought that no one even knew who I was for the last nine months.

I mean, even in home ec, Rebecca Rizzo, who's part of Jared's family, is like, "Montague's so freaking crazy. It's a major feat holding it together like you did."

I'm about to say "Thanks!" when Jared gives her a dirty look, probably for fraternizing with the enemy. His group is only ten points ahead of ours, so that could be why.

"What's a major feat?" A.J. asks, returning from the pantry with a box of tinfoil. We're making cinnamon toast, and he's in charge of lining our cookie sheets.

"Ellie's interview," Isaiah says. "Did you see it this morning?"

"I did," A.J. says. "I thought Montague was going to eat you guys."

That he doesn't make a snarky comment about the interview is a compliment in and of itself, so I take it.

I feel someone staring at me, and when I glance up, I notice Hunter look away. I wonder how much of that conversation he'd heard. I also suddenly ache inside, wondering what he thought of the interview. And then I kind of hate myself, because of course, like anything TV-station-related, he'd probably think it was dumb.

This seesaw of emotions I have for him is never-ending.

"Maybe you could interview Montague next," Luke says. He's standing across from me, digging out oven mitts from our drawer. "You seem pretty good at charming people, so a psychotic dog should be nothing."

I narrow my eyes at him, thinking he's being sarcastic, but he smiles. "Nice work, Agresti," he says, and pats me on the shoulder with an oven mitt as he makes his way over to the oven.

I accidentally make eye contact with Hunter then. He quickly turns his attention back to washing dishes, but not before I can note the slightly wounded expression on his face and his slouching shoulders. I think he, dare I say it, might be a bit regretful.

I suddenly want to give Montague a big pat on the head.

CHAPTER 11

Over the next few days, the sight of Hunter and Brynn doesn't send me into a tailspin. In fact, aside from one teary moment at Cityscape Shoes when a friend of my mom's came in and asked if I was still seeing "that boy with the hair who sings," I've been holding it together. Funneling all my feelings of sadness and anger into beating them in class—we're currently trailing his group by five points, and it's super irritating—seems to have been the cure-all.

I still go out of my way to avoid their haunts, though. And that's how I run into Chris, when I'm taking the long "actively avoiding the cafeteria" route to my homeroom.

"Ellie!" I hear him call. I peer over my shoulder and see Chris waving at me from the open doorway of the TV studio. "Hey! How would you like to do another story for us? Alisha's got a doctor's appointment this week and we need help."

"What kind of story?" I'm worried he'll make me investigate the teachers' union or something that would require me to be sneaky.

He takes a long sip from his iced coffee before finally saying, "We'd like to do a piece on Luke Burke."

Of all twelve hundred Ringvale Heights students he could've

named, that is the last person I expected to hear him say. He takes my furrowed brow for confusion, because he goes on to explain, "He's, like, this huge competitive stunt biker. He just won a local competition last weekend. And there's talk he could make it into the X Games in a few years."

I must be wearing an expression of complete shock, but Chris is all, "So do you know him?"

"I do. I had no idea."

Chris' brow furrows. "You guys aren't close, are you?"

Weirdly, I feel my face flush. "No! He's just in my home ec group."

"Okay, I just don't want this to be a conflict of interest or anything. Anyway, you and Willow could go down to where he trains and interview him, ask him a few questions about his training, you know, stuff like that."

I mean, it's too weird for me to be interviewing Luke, right? What if I screw up and make him look bad in front of the whole school? And then we have to spend the rest of the year together in the same "family"? But I can't tell Chris about my paranoia.

"Um, okay," I say.

"Good," Chris says, walking away. "We'll need it for Tuesday's broadcast, so if you can get it in by Friday, that would be awesome."

"I'll ask him today," I say, and he gives me a peace sign over his shoulder as he heads for the cafeteria.

This should be easier considering I already know Luke.

So why is there a giant knot forming in my stomach right now?

The prospect of asking Luke for an interview looms over the rest of my day and the knot in my stomach just gets bigger and tighter. I mean, we've talked in class, but I realize we've never had an actual conversation, hence why I didn't know about his successful biking career. It's going to be completely strange for me to be all in reporter mode and to talk to him as if I *know* anything about him or something.

My hands literally sweat as I wait for the last bell to ring—I figure I can ask him after class, aka when there's less of a chance of anyone seeing him laugh in my face and turn me down.

You're not asking him out, I think as I watch the classroom clock. *This is to publicize himself.*

When the final bell rings and Luke exits the room, my heart starts to hammer.

Calm down, I yell at myself. *You wore his sweatshirt for crying out loud.*

I jog to catch up to him as he hits the main hallway.

"Hey, Luke," I say, taking a deep breath to try and slow my pulse. "Can I talk to you about something?"

Luke stops and narrows his eyes, almost like he's afraid of what I'm about to say. "Uh, sure."

I just blurt it out. "RHHS TV wants me to profile you."

Relief floods his face and he stands up a little straighter. "Me? Really?"

"Chris Phan told me you won some kind of biking competition last weekend?"

Luke shrugs. "It was just a local thing."

"Still. How come you didn't say anything?"

"I don't know," he says, shoving his hands in the pockets of his jeans. "It's not like we share everything with the group, you know."

He has a point. "Well, maybe now more people will be aware of it."

Luke rubs his chin and seems to think it over for a long time. Finally, he says, "If you promise not to make me look like a douche, I'll do it."

"Huh? You're like an anti-douche."

Luke laughs. "That's probably the best compliment I've ever got."

I feel the tips of my ears burning, making it obvious I'm delighted this exchange has turned out better than I thought.

"Do you train somewhere near here? Maybe I can interview you there?"

"Sure," he says. "How about tomorrow? The skate park is over on Hampton Avenue, about five minutes from here."

"It's a date," I say, instantly feeling ridiculous. I feel the red creep from my ears to my entire face.

If Luke notices, he doesn't say anything. Instead he's all, "Cool, see you tomorrow."

I'm about to head to my locker, when I hear, "Hey, Agresti!"

I turn back around and Luke is smiling. "If you win a Pulitzer someday, I hope you remember this interview as the start of your success."

"You better be *on* in that interview, then," I say.

"Oh, I'll be so on, you won't know what hit you," he says, pointing at me, then winking.

I roll my eyes, but when I walk away, I feel myself smiling.

"So what's Luke's deal?" Willow asks as she drives us toward the skate park the next afternoon.

"He's apparently really good at bike tricks and stunts," I say. "He won a local competition last weekend."

"Well, that explains him being with Greta. She's really good at snowboarding, so I guess the extreme sports connection makes sense."

"A real power couple," I say, forcing a laugh. Even the thought of Greta makes me nervous. Her larger-than-life personality must extend past the school's walls.

"Yeah," Willow says. "But my ex-girlfriend was in her math class, and she said Greta's supposed to go up to Canada for Olympic trials training sooner or later. I can't imagine Luke's going that way for college."

I don't have a response for that. Despite our friendly exchanges of late, I'm not exactly one to be weighing in on Luke's relationship. Still, I'm not sure how long-distance relationships work, especially when someone's in another country.

"This must be it," Willow says, turning the car into the parking lot of the Ringvale Heights Indoor Skate Park and Biking Facility.

Willow lugs her camera toward the building and I carry her footstool for her. There are two scrawny-looking kids, wearing pants and shirts that are way too big for them, standing on the ramp leading up to the building. They're both holding skateboards, and when they see us coming, they eye us up and down.

"Hey," the kid wearing an orange hat drawls.

"Hello, ladies, you coming to film me?" his green-hatted counterpart asks, cocking his head at us. "I'm the best thing you've ever seen."

"What are you, twelve?" Willow asks, looking more amused than annoyed.

"Age ain't anything but a number," he says, winking.

Willow rolls her eyes. "Glad to see they've added charm classes to the middle school schedule."

"I'll be your Prince Charming if you'd like," orange-hat guy says, wiggling his eyebrows.

"Agresti! Willow! You beat me here!"

The four of us turn around, and I see Luke riding toward us on his bike. The boys' faces both fall.

"Hey, Luke," I say, waving and trying not to laugh.

Both boys stand up straight. "Hi, Luke."

Luke looks from the boys, back to Willow and me.

"These guys giving you a hard time?" he asks. "They're in my beginner BMX class and I'm not above making anyone run suicides as a warm-up."

"No, Luke," the green-hatted kid says. "We were just—"

"—hitting on us," Willow says matter-of-factly.

Luke's eyes widen. "Wow, you guys are a lot ballsier these days, huh? When I was your age, I wouldn't even dream of looking at such enchanting women, let alone hitting on them."

Enchanting? I have to choke back a laugh.

"We're sorry," the orange-hatted kid says. "We saw the camera and got excited."

"That's understandable," Willow says. "Everyone likes the idea of being on camera. Except for Ellie, of course, even though she's pretty good at it." She gives me a hip bump.

The boys skate off and we make our way up the ramp leading into the building. Luke holds the door open for us. "Shall we?"

I'm so close when I scoot past him that I can smell the woodsy fabric softener again, coming off his fitted, bright-blue T-shirt, which he wasn't wearing in class before. "Enchanting?" I say, choking back a giggle.

"What? You're light years out of a seventh grader's league," Luke says with a smile. "Plus, they could use a good vocabulary lesson. The only word they know to describe girls is 'hot.'"

I start to laugh when a voice booms out, "Hey, man! Junior Vert Champion Luke Burke is in the house!"

We both turn to see a grinning, skinny guy with a crew cut walking toward us.

"Hey," Luke says. "This is Willow and Ellie. They're filming me for my school TV station."

"Sweet," the guy says, then bows. "I'm Vince, if you should ever want to cover BMXers who aren't half as good as this guy right here."

Luke shakes his head. "Too bad you go to St. Mark's."

I take a minute to scan the giant room. It's like a gym, except there's a variety of ramps set up at different angles all over the place. There are even stairs and handrails in the middle of the room, where this gangly blond kid is practicing jumps on his skateboard. At the far end of the ramp-riddled expanse is what looks like two giant ramps facing each other.

Luke must be following my gaze because he's like, "That's a half-pipe. I'll show you my moves on that today. Have you ever watched a BMX vert contest before?"

Willow and I shake our heads.

Luke smiles. "That's okay, most people outside the extreme sports world don't know it exists."

"Well, all of RHHS is going to know it after this!" Willow says.

"He's gonna blow your mind," Vince says.

Luke frowns. "Don't set them up for disappointment, man."

Vince chuckles. "Are you kidding me, dude?" He shakes his head at Willow and me. "This guy right here is a machine."

Luke looks at the ground, but he's fighting a smile, and I can tell he's enjoying the praise. "So, how should we do this?" he asks, rubbing his hands together.

Willow lifts her camera up. "Why don't you show us some of your moves, then Ellie can interview you after."

"Sounds like a plan," Luke says, shoving a helmet on and squeezing some elbow guards over his arms. "See you on the other side."

"We can sit down there," Vince says, pointing to the edge of the half-pipe. "He'll only need the middle section."

"Great," I say. "Maybe you could explain some stuff to me as he's doing it."

"My pleasure," he says, smiling. We climb to the top of the ramp and sit on the edge, our legs dangling. Willow positions herself across from us, with her camera trained on Luke, who's at the far end of the half-pipe. He starts riding up one side of the ramp and the bike jumps in the air, turning slightly.

"That's a 180," Vince says. "It's a pretty basic move. He had that thing nailed like the first week."

"Have you known him long?" I ask, as Luke does another 180 on the other side, a little faster this time.

"Since he started here when we were thirteen," he says. "He's a natural. I've been doing this since I was nine and I can't do half the stuff he does."

Vince cups his hands around his mouth. "Stop being modest. Do your thing, dude!"

Luke gives a thumbs-up and rides to the other end of the pipe, climbing up one side. He sets himself there, then rides down, up the other side of the ramp, going much faster and higher than he did with the 180.

"Here we go," Vince says, clapping.

I'm holding my breath as he moves up and down the sides of the pipe, the bike climbing higher into the air every time he leaves a ramp. On each jump, he executes a trick, like a 180 or taking his hands off the handlebars as the bike flies upward. Half of me is terrified he's going to come crashing down at any moment and the other half is in total awe. His movements are so controlled and fluid. Graceful, even. It's like the juggling, only way more . . . masculine.

When Luke finishes his last move, which involves his legs splaying out and the bike twirling underneath him before he catches it between his feet, I start clapping. I mean, there's no other reaction one could have after seeing something like that.

Vince just laughs and shakes his head. "I told you. He's the real deal."

Luke guides his bike to the bottom of the pipe, where he removes his helmet and runs a hand through his hair. He's breathing heavily when he looks up at us. "What did you think?" he calls.

I struggle to find the right words to describe it, and end up blurting out, "That was totally hot!"

Vince literally falls over laughing when I say this and I feel my face start flaming.

"No, not in that way. You know, like the moves were awesome, you know 'hot.'" I say quickly, with air quotes and everything, but Vince laughs even harder. Luke's face is red, but it's probably because he was just defying gravity a moment ago and the blood had no other place to go. I'm relieved that he's smiling.

"I'll take hot," he says, riding over to us. "Hot is good."

Willow, mercifully, doesn't say anything about it. Instead, she runs over and high-fives Luke. "That was awesome. Maybe the coolest thing I've ever shot!"

"Just wait till I do this interview," Luke says, puffing out his chest. "You ain't seen nothing yet."

Is it weird that I never noticed how broad-shouldered Luke is until now? I mean, I have class with him every day so this is something that probably should've—

"Earth to Ellie," Willow says with a giggle.

"Sorry. I'm trying to get my questions in line in my head, so I don't have to look at my cards," I lie.

"I was just asking if you wanted some water before we started."

"No, it's okay. Let's do this."

Willow climbs up on her footstool and I run a hand through my hair and adjust my glasses as she sets up the camera on her shoulder. The camera light turns on and she points at us to start.

"So, how did you get into BMX biking?" I ask, remembering to aim the microphone at Luke when I'm done.

"Well, I was kind of a hyperactive kid and I was always moving around. Like, I couldn't sit still, and I was always on my bike," Luke says. "I started doing stunts when I was about thirteen, and after my dad died, I just really wanted to focus on something, to take my mind off of it, so I threw myself into the whole BMX thing."

I'm so taken aback by this response—I had no idea his father died—that it takes me an extra second or two to remember my next question.

"When did you start entering competitions?"

"About a year after that. It took me about another year to start winning stuff, but with the right coaching and a lot of practice, I started to do pretty well."

Luke goes on to talk about his coach, whom he trains with on weekends, and how he works at the facility as a teacher four days a week to help pay for everything.

"How do you balance all that with school and friends?" I ask. It wasn't even a planned question. I'm genuinely curious.

Luke smiles sheepishly. "Most of my friends are here, so it's easy. But I admit, some of my grades take a hit because of this. But this is my dream, you know? If taking my time to perfect a move here means I don't get to study as much and I get a B+ instead of an A, I can deal with that."

Finally, I ask my last question. "So, what's your ultimate goal?"

"To get to the X Games, maybe make it on a pro tour when I'm older. I'd like to go to college part-time, too, so we'll see how that pans out. I just want to be the best I can at this. Whatever it takes, you know?" Luke smiles and I notice how well the blue of his shirt brings out the color in his eyes. I wonder if he did that on purpose.

I turn back to the camera. "If you want to see Luke ride, come down to the Ringvale Heights indoor skate park and see for yourself. You won't be disappointed!"

When Willow lowers the camera, I turn back around to Luke. "I hope it's okay I said that."

"Sure, why not?" Luke says. "I always perform better with an audience. Especially when they think I'm 'hot.'"

I shake my head. "I'm never going to live that down, am I?"

He grins widely. "Nope."

"Well," Vince sighs dramatically. "I hope people come to watch, even when this guy's a star and has flown the coop. I'll be all lonely here by myself."

"Get on your St. Mark's TV station," Luke says, clapping him on the shoulder. "Publicity is key, man."

"Then I'd better go practice my pitch," Vince says, batting his eyelashes. "I don't have your baby blues to help in the convincing."

Luke playfully whacks him on the shoulder with his elbow pads as Vince grabs his own bike and moves toward the half-pipe.

"Do you want to ride with me, Ellie?" Willow asks. "I'm headed back to school to drop the camera off."

"It's okay, I'll walk. I live less than a mile from here in Ingleside."

"No way. I'm in Ingleside, too," Luke says. "You can walk me home, then."

"How chivalrous of me," I laugh, slinging my backpack over my shoulders. I hope he doesn't notice how surprised I am that he'd want to hang out with me.

When we get outside, the sun is starting to sink low in the sky. It's still warm, and the air smells like fresh-cut grass that's been drying in the sun all day. It's probably my favorite time of year, those few weeks after summer before fall really takes over.

Luke walks beside me, pushing his bike. "Why didn't I know you lived in Ingleside?" he says.

"Well, we only moved here in January," I tell him. "Have you lived there long?"

"My mom and little brother and I moved here about five years ago, after my dad died," he says. "My mom couldn't afford our old neighborhood, so we moved to a smaller house. My mom remarried last year, but she loves the house, so we're staying put for a while."

"I'm sorry to hear about your dad," I say. "I had no idea."

Luke shrugs. "It was a while ago. He had cancer and it totally sucked. He's the one who told me to take my riding more seriously, and since it was kind of his last wish, I did it. Luckily, I love it." He smiles at me and I think he's only doing it for my benefit, as if to say, "It's sad, but don't worry about me."

He hops on his bike and stands on the pedals, moving the bike in a slow, snake-like pattern as we walk. "So, what about you? Why did you move here?" he asks as he rides in figure eights around me.

"Bankruptcy, pretty much." I'm surprised how easily that came out. It's not like I go around telling everyone this story, but I feel like Luke's not going to judge me. "My dad used to own a restaurant in Green Ridge, but we had this shady business manager, Dave. One day my mom was cleaning the office, she came across some opened bills that were marked "past due." It turns out that Dave was stealing money to help pay off his gambling debts and was paying child support to a former mistress who'd had his kid."

"Jesus," Luke says. "What kind of asshole was this guy?"

"Oh, it gets better. To try and make up for all that, he invested the money that was left into some pyramid scheme and got screwed. And then he lied about filing our taxes, too. The restaurant was in so much debt, my dad closed it down, and used what we had in savings to pay off the taxes we owed and all the investors and creditors."

Luke's eyes are practically bugging out of his head.

"And that led to us not being able to afford our house anymore and it was really awkward living in Green Ridge, where everyone either felt sorry for us or thought we had something to do with the money disappearing, so we decided to move here to take over my grandmother's old house. It's paid off, so the only thing my parents have to worry about is the taxes," I say.

Luke stops in his tracks, his brow furrowed. "God, that totally sucks. I'm sorry you had to deal with that."

"Yeah," I say. "If you go to college part-time, maybe you could major in business or something, so you can manage your money yourself."

"My stepdad told me the same thing," he says, nodding. "What's your dad doing now?"

I tell him about the restaurant where he works and how he still seems regretful whenever anything money-related comes up. "I mean, I tried not to complain too much when we moved, but I think he knew how much it blew to have to switch schools in my junior year."

"But then you must've met Hunter pretty quickly," he says, studying his handlebars as he hops off the bike and walks next to me again.

"I did. But those were eight months of my life I wasted. I mean, I barely made friends with anyone else because of him."

"Well, you're making up for lost time now," he says, and smiles again. "I mean, you were kind of quiet when I first met you, but you're pretty all right, Agresti."

I stare at Luke for a moment. The sun is setting behind him, making his flip-y hair glow with reddish highlights. I want to thank him—for saying I'm all right, for the interview, for bucking my preconceived notions of him and not ever making fun of me, but I'm—

Honk!

Luke and I both jump and look over our shoulders. A red pickup truck is coming toward us from behind, music blasting from its stereo. I step to one side of the street to let it pass, but Luke stays where he is. He waves at the truck, and suddenly, a blonde, pig-tailed head leans out of the passenger side window. "Luke Burke! You're a hard man to find."

My heart suddenly starts to pound and I'm not even sure why.

Luke smiles, but it doesn't quite meet his eyes. He ends up waving at the driver of the truck, a guy from my gym class, Evan Fishman.

"I finished my training sesh and swung by the park, but you weren't there," Greta says, climbing out of the truck. Her face is flushed, and I assume she's invigorated with athletic energy, because Greta doesn't seem the type to blush at the sight of her beloved. She turns around and smiles dazzlingly at Evan, who winks and waves before driving off. Greta gets close to Luke, and he leans down to give her a quick peck on the lips. I'm silently grateful that no full-on PDA takes place.

"Ellie just profiled me for the school TV station," he says.

Greta eyes me up and down. "Oh, right. You're the girl who did that interview where Montague went crazy. That was awesome."

I don't know if she means the interview itself or Montague's antics, but I say "Thanks," anyway.

"Are we still doing dinner at your house tonight?" Greta asks, turning back to Luke.

"Yeah. My mom told me to ask you because it's chicken casserole night."

"Great," Greta says, linking arms with him. "She makes the best chicken casserole and I'm *starving*."

It's sort of awkward walking with them, and they thankfully veer toward a cute tan bungalow with dark-green shutters. Two rows of gorgeous yellow and purple chrysanthemums line the walkway leading up to the house and its inviting-looking porch swing. It's like something out of a lemonade commercial. "This is me," Luke says, jerking his thumb in the direction of the house. His voice almost sounds apologetic.

"Oh, okay. Thanks again for the interview."

"When do I get to see it?" Greta asks.

"Tuesday morning," I say.

"Awesome," she says, then narrows her eyes. "Like, I want to make sure this thing really happened and you weren't, like, hooking up or something."

Horrified, I glance at Luke, whose eyes are huge, his mouth hanging open.

Greta laughs loudly. "Oh, man. The looks on your guys' faces! Like you two would ever be together." She's a mess of giggles as she climbs the stairs to the house.

Luke lingers behind, his smile betrayed by his furrowed brow. "You're good to get home from here?"

"Of course. It's only a few blocks away," I say, plastering on my own smile. "See you in class."

I move forward, hoping that I'm not sweating as badly as I feel like I am. I peek over my shoulder and see that Luke is on his porch steps, watching me. He raises his arm and waves.

I wave back and start walking again, forcing myself to think about my history homework, what I'm getting Jodie for her birthday in January, my college applications . . .

Basically anything besides what Greta has just said.

CHAPTER 12

If someone told me a few weeks ago that Luke and I would be friends, I'd sincerely ask if they'd been smoking crack. But we kind of *are* friends now. Like, since the interview, we say "hi" in the halls (Luke seems to like excitedly cheering "Agrestiiiii!" whenever he spots me), and we've walked home from school together three times. We've even started texting every now and then—mostly discussing assignments in classes where we have the same teacher, but sometimes Luke sends a funny GIF or YouTube video.

And in home ec a week after the interview, I'm folding aprons and humming Beyoncé's latest hit when Luke starts dancing along.

I stop mid-hum and peer up at him.

"Don't stop the music, I've got a good groove going," Luke says, spinning around and dropping a bowl full of baking utensils into the sink. "But hold it just a second because I have to run this bag of flour back to the pantry."

"Yeah, Ellie, thanks for getting that stuck in my head," A.J. says as Luke scurries off.

Mrs. Sanchez reminds us then to have our monthly budget ready by this coming Friday. "And this week I want you to find a family activity that fits in your budget and factor that into your planning."

There's a knock on the classroom door then, and Mrs. Sanchez goes to answer it.

"Great, our family can, like, take a walk up the block," A.J. mutters.

"There has to be something cheap they could do," Isaiah says as he shakes excess flour off his T-shirt.

It's only then that I notice Bryce Pratt and Anthony Ruggio are eyeing Isaiah from Jersey Strong's kitchen on the other side of ours. Or should I say, they're eyeing Isaiah's shirt, which has a running racehorse printed on it. Bryce covers his mouth as he laughs, then says something to Anthony, who peeks around Isaiah to get a look.

I can see what's going to happen here, and I'm already not amused. Mrs. Sanchez is totally distracted, talking to Mr. Lee, the woodshop teacher.

"Why are you so into horse racing? Are you like a bookie or something?" Bryce says.

"Or are you, like, into horses in a sexual way?" Anthony says, which makes Bryce crack up.

Isaiah, to his credit, doesn't bludgeon them with our rolling pin, like I would. "I'm very interested in thoroughbred racing," he says, as if that's going to be enough for them.

Bryce clutches his hand to his chest. "Well, if it's *thoroughbreds*, then it must be a worthwhile pursuit."

I narrow my eyes. "Leave him alone."

Over Bryce's shoulder, I see Luke come out of the pantry, taking in the situation.

Anthony finds this completely hilarious. "Aww, what, are you two in Gamblers Anonymous together or something?"

"Gamblers Anonymous, yes!" Bryce cackles, offering a high five.

There's such a surge of anger in me in that moment that I almost feel as possessed as I did when I kicked the globe at Brynn and Hunter.

"That's not even remotely funny. And, for your information, we're going to Glenwood Park for our family activity," I say hotly, even though it's a total lie. "Because I like horse racing, too."

Isaiah and A.J. are gaping at me like I've lost my mind, but Luke pulls his phone from his pocket and steps over to all of us. "Yeah, they have a family day there every Saturday in October." He scrolls through his phone, then pulls up an ad proclaiming "Family Fun Day at Glenwood Park Racetrack" for this coming Saturday. I don't know how the stars aligned for that, but I'm glad.

I don't realize we've attracted Synergy's attention until Hannah jumps in with a "Um, that's for *real* families."

"And Mrs. Sanchez just wants us to find an activity, not actually do it," Brynn says.

"Well, we're clearly just more motivated than you, yo," A.J. says, catching on.

I nod, even though I'm thinking, *Wait, do we really want to all hang out on the weekend?*

"Uh, you have to be eighteen to bet on horses in New Jersey," Hunter says as if we're all idiots that this hadn't occurred to us.

"You don't have to be eighteen to go to the track," Isaiah says. "Just to bet."

Luke shrugs. "But if we wanted to, I could bet. I'm eighteen now, so—"

"You're eighteen?" I cut him off. "Since when?"

"Since last week," he says.

I don't know why, but I suddenly feel bad. "Your birthday was last week and you didn't say anything?"

Luke shrugs. "It's not a big deal. I mean, it's not like Christmas." His eyes light up when he says this.

"Christmas?" I say with a raised eyebrow.

"Yeah, Christmas," he says, rubbing his hands together. "It's my favorite time of year."

The idea of six-foot-five, tattooed Luke being overtaken by the Christmas spirit is almost too much for me to handle, and I burst into giggles.

"What?" he asks.

"I'm just picturing you with tinsel in your hair and stars in your eyes as you wait for Santa."

"No, no, I'm not like that," he says, his eyes twinkling. "I only wear the stringed popcorn."

"Ahem," A.J. says, and I realize everyone is staring at Luke and me. Especially Hunter, and even Mrs. Sanchez, who has returned. I quickly turn back to the sink.

Synergy, Bryce, and Anthony retreat back to their kitchens then, muttering about what a bunch of weirdos we are.

"So, we're really going to do this?" A.J. says. "The racetrack? Like with shady dudes smoking cigars and people blowing their life savings away?"

"And also the place where families go to watch horse races," Luke says.

"Awesome, I'm in," A.J. says.

"You guys really want to go to the racetrack?" Isaiah says, his eyes wide in disbelief.

"Yeah, why not?" I say. "I like horses. They're cute."

"And Glenwood Park looks beautiful," Luke says. "It's a nice way to spend time outside, you know?"

I'm suddenly struck with an idea and turn around. "Mrs. Sanchez? If we actually do our family activity, can we do a report on it in our monthly budget and submit it for extra points?"

Mrs. Sanchez straightens up and smiles. "I think that's a wonderful idea, Ms. Agresti."

I can feel Brynn scowling at me without even having to look, it's amazing. I even hear Hunter mutter something under his breath.

"Okay," Isaiah finally says, still looking unsure. "But I don't know if my mom's going to let me go. She hates the racetrack."

"Even for a class project?" A.J. says. "It's an, uh, educational outing."

Isaiah bites his lip and shrugs.

"Maybe we can have Agresti drive, since moms trust girls more," Luke says, and I nod, knowing my parents are going to be home on Saturday and won't need the car. He smiles broadly. "And Agresti's every mom's dream. She'll give us mom cred."

Mom cred?

I shake my head at Luke. "Whatever it takes, especially with points on the line, I guess."

He winks at me in response.

"I'm leaving," I call into the basement Saturday morning. My parents are down there organizing stuff to sell at flea markets for some extra money. "Thanks for letting me take the car."

Mom comes up the stairs carrying an armful of old board games. "Have fun. It's you and your home ec group, right?"

"Yep," I say, grabbing my jacket. "A.J., Isaiah the horse racing fan, and Luke."

Mom's eyes suddenly light up. "Luke's the one I've seen you walking home with, right? The hunky one?"

I freeze as I'm shrugging the jacket on. "I guess?"

"You guess you walk home with him or you guess he's good-looking? What's going on there, anyway?"

"There's nothing happening there," I snap, my heart suddenly hammering, and Mom flinches. *She's only teasing you. Calm the hell down, Mary Ellen.*

"Sorry," I say. "What I mean is . . . he has a girlfriend. We're just friends."

Mom nods like she gets it, but I'm alarmed at how my initial instinct was PMS-levels of defensiveness.

I'm saved when my dad emerges from the basement with a box of books. "Have a good time with the horses. But if any mafia goons approach you, tell them you're Italian, but not *that* Italian."

"It's not going to be shady. It's Family Day."

"Doesn't the mafia call themselves a family? Then this might be the ideal setting for them."

That actually gets me to laugh, and I'm glad. Clearly, I'm feeling jittery about this whole experience and I chalk it up to being nervous about spending an entire day with all the guys. What if we have nothing to say to each other beyond our class assignments? It's going to make for an awkward afternoon.

I walk outside and I'm greeted by a beautiful fall day. It's sunny and warm, the sky is bright blue, and there's a light breeze blowing through the red and yellow leaves. I have no idea if this is good horse-racing weather, but it seems like it should be.

I'm unlocking the driver's side door when I see Luke coming up the street. I freeze, wondering if my mom is watching from behind the curtains.

He waves. "You ready for Family Day at the Races, Agresti?"

"As ready as I'll ever be," I say.

"We are fam-il-y," he sings in a high-pitched voice as he opens up the front passenger's side door. "I got all my, uh, classmates and me."

"You may want to stick to biking," I say, giggling as I start the car.

We pick up A.J. first. He insisted that I could get him at his dentist's office, which is a few blocks from here. "I have an appointment in the morning for a cleaning. It'll just be easier for you to get me there," he'd said. We find him waiting by the curb.

"Yo," he says, opening the passenger side back door.

"Any cavities?" Luke asks.

"Huh?" A.J. says, sounding confused. "Oh, no. Not this time."

"On to Isaiah's we go, then," Luke says.

"I'm glad his mom is letting him come," I say.

A.J. leans forward. "Do you have a strategy for meeting her?"

Since Mrs. Greenlow wants to meet the person doing the driving, Isaiah says I'm the only one she wants to meet.

I shrug. "Apparently I have mom cred, so that's what's going to win her over."

"You do!" Luke says, "You're . . . what's the word? Wholesome!"

Wholesome? Seriously? The PMS-ish feeling comes rushing back and I'm suddenly cranky. "What is *that* supposed to mean?"

"It's not a bad thing," A.J. says. "You're just not, you know . . ."

"The type of girl no guy wants to date?" I spit.

"Take it easy," Luke says, patting my shoulder. "Why would you think that?"

I know exactly why. Because apparently I was so *wholesome*, my boyfriend dumped me for a girl who wasn't. But I don't say that. "I don't know," I sigh, feeling bad that I'm getting so angry over the Hunter thing for the bazillionth time.

"Believe me," Luke goes on. "I didn't mean it like a bad thing. You just know who you are and you're okay with it."

"And moms love that sort of thing," A.J. says. "Like, you're not going to lead anyone down the wrong path or some shit."

I shrug. "Well, then both your moms are going to be disappointed because I'm really going to take you to an underground fight club and not the racetrack."

A.J. thumps back in his seat. "Man, that would be epic."

Wholesome. God, let's see how long it takes me to move past that one.

We pull up in front of Isaiah's house, a sprawling pale-yellow ranch with immaculate landscaping and a weeping willow tree in the front yard.

I take a deep breath and unbuckle my seat belt. "Well, here goes nothing."

When I knock on the front door, Isaiah steps out, followed by a thin woman in a cardigan, her big brown eyes solemn. They look so much alike my mom would say, "She could've spit Isaiah out."

"You must be Mary Ellen. I'm Elena," she says with a slight Caribbean accent. She sticks out her hand and when I shake it, I make sure to have a firm grip. My father says he doesn't trust anyone with a weak handshake.

"So, we're going to go now," Isaiah says, gesturing over his shoulder toward the car.

"Just a minute, honey," Mrs. Greenlow says. "I want to make sure you know the rules here."

"I know, no gambling. And no talking to anyone but my friends."

I suddenly feel all melty inside at being referred to as Isaiah's friend. But then I realize it's probably just less formal than saying classmates.

"Isaiah tells me you're a good student and are respectful and that the other boys are, too, it's why I'm allowing this," she says. "I don't mean to seem so overprotective, but I know how racetracks can be and I just want to make sure you'll look out for each other."

"Well, it's Family Day," I say, wracking my brain for anything optimistic to say. "I bet there will be lots of parents and kids. Maybe even grandparents!" *Maybe even grandparents?* How is that reassuring? Good god.

"Thanks again for letting me go, Mom," Isaiah says, probably wanting to get out of here before I say something else stupid.

Mrs. Greenlow smooths her hand over his hair with a small smile. "Have a good time. And text if you're going to be late."

When we get into the car, she waves to us from the porch. I can't help but notice her forehead creases and I feel bad.

"I'm sorry about that," Isaiah says from the back seat. "If we were going to the outlets or something she wouldn't have been all crazy like that. I just didn't want to lie to her."

"No worries, she wasn't crazy at all," I say, smiling at him in the rearview mirror. "We're just glad she let you go."

It's a chatty ride to the racetrack—apparently Mrs. Sanchez is married to a bodybuilder and A.J. found his profile on Instagram last night—and there are no awkward silences or anything, which deep down I had feared. Like, it's close to impossible to be quiet when pondering how much protein Mrs. Sanchez and her husband have to cook to keep him in that kind of shape.

We pull into the crowded parking lot of the racetrack, which we can't see since it's obscured by a large building. There are a lot of little kids running around, and the smell of barbecue is coming from somewhere beyond the main gate.

"A guy in a pink suit and gold chains just walked in there," A.J. marvels, pointing inside the gate.

"Hey, guys who like pink suits and gold chains have families, too, you know," Luke says, and I can't help but giggle.

"We're going to need a program," Isaiah says after we pay our entrance fee. He points to an old man in a green visor, who's holding up what looks like magazines, then digs into his pocket and pulls out a dollar, which he hands to the man.

"Good luck today, sir," the man says, smiling at Isaiah.

"Oh, we're not betting," Isaiah says. "We're here for Family Day. I just want to see who's racing."

The confused expression on the man's face is priceless as he eyes all of us, trying to place how we are all "family." But he smiles again brightly. "Well, have a good time, regardless!"

We pass an area that looks like stables, right in front of the main building. There's an odor of hay and manure, which makes A.J. pinch his nose. "Why they gotta smell like that, man?"

"They're very large creatures," Isaiah says seriously. "Their waste is going to be bigger and smellier than most animals."

"And that's where they bring the horses before the race?" Luke says pointing to the stable-y looking area. "Where you can see them before you bet on them?"

Isaiah nods, his eyebrows raised as if he's impressed. "How did you know?"

Luke shrugs. "I did some research."

I try not to smile when I picture Luke sitting up all night looking up horse racing online. It's kind of sweet that he'd read up on it.

We enter the main building and it's bustling with people. There's a soft hum of voices echoing off the high ceilings, which have banners hanging from the rafters. There are pictures of jockeys' outfits stitched on them, with a name of a horse underneath it and a year. Isaiah points to the more famous horses and explains what they meant to the racing industry. On the side, there are ticket booths with the words "Betting/Claiming" on signs above them, and there are lines of people gathered at each one.

And right in front of us, up a walkway, and beyond an expanse of green benches and small fence is the racetrack itself. It's bigger than any type of sporting venue I've ever seen. I mean, I guess it would have to be since the track is over a mile long. The rich red-brown dirt of the track encircles a park-like area, with trees and a pond and a scoreboard-looking thing in the middle.

Isaiah's eyes are huge as he takes in the whole scene, and a smile is spreading on his face. "This place is more beautiful than I thought."

This time when I feel the smile coming, I don't even try to fight it.

CHAPTER 13

"Go! Go! Gooooooooooo!"

This has become the word of the day. Also in our vocabulary: "Come on, [fill-in-the-blank horse name], come on!" As in, we all pick horses we want to win and bet against each other. Not with money, but with "Whoever wins this race gets off dish duty on Tuesday" or "The person whose horse comes in last has to say something nice to Jared this week."

Of course, Isaiah has picked the winner for three straight races, so he's not going to have dishpan hands nor have to man up and tell Jared his beret choice is awesome. Even though his knowledge is giving him a distinct advantage, he tries to explain odds to us, why certain jockeys are better than others, and breeding, but it's kind of a lot to take in. Especially when horses with names like "Snack Attack" and "Barbie's Dream Horse" are running. Like, how could I *not* pick one of them when they are so awesomely named?

But Isaiah is completely in his element, as my mom would say. It's a total 180 from his in-school personality. He's chatty and giggly and even talks smack to us before the races. Like, I never thought

I'd see the day when Isaiah would point at us and be all, "You guys are so going down, it's not even funny." It's delightful.

"This place is pretty happening," Luke observes by the time the fourth race rolls around. And by "happening," I think he means, "holy cow, there's a lot to look at." Like, there are actual families here today, moms and dads and grandparents with kids. Upon seeing the aged, I felt vindicated for my stupid comment to Mrs. Greenlow earlier.

There's a picnic area that has a karaoke stage and clowns giving away balloons to kids. At one point, a clown starts waving us over, and Luke freezes in place and is like, "Guys, clowns scare the crap out of me. I can't go over there." And this leads to the awesome moment where the entire JAILE family admits to also being terrified of clowns ("That clown probably wants to kill us in our sleep" is how a saucer-eyed Isaiah puts it) and we all literally run in the other direction.

There's also a DJ from one of the local radio stations handing out bumper stickers and T-shirts to passersby as songs blast from the booth. A.J., after rocking out on air guitar to "Bohemian Rhapsody" in front of the booth, was declared "pretty righteous" by the DJ, so now he's walking around with a "Rock On with Classic Rock 102.7" bumper sticker stuck to his chest.

But then there are the die-hard gamblers. Like, you can spot them right away. They're generally men, but there's a few older ladies studying the forms, too. There are people in tracksuits and others in khakis and polo shirts, the stressed-out looks on their faces betraying their Preppy for the Poolside garb. Their intensity is at once amusing and frightening and somewhat sad.

It's funny, but A.J. is probably the anti-die-hard-gambler, insisting on going to see the horses before the race, pantomiming the trumpeter's song when the horses are called to post, and then jumping up and down when they sprint toward the finish line.

Everyone seems to be enjoying the day and I'd say it would have been completely perfect, except that Luke keeps getting texts every now and then that make him frown or shake his head, momentarily distracting him from the festivities.

"Everything okay?" A.J. finally asks before the fourth race, when Luke shoves his phone in his pocket and sighs.

"Yeah," he says tightly. "Greta and I just can't figure out what we're doing tonight."

Oh. For some reason I feel the need to divert my attention elsewhere.

"Okay," Isaiah says, opening up the form, either oblivious to Luke's angst or just trying to change the subject. "We've got eight horses in the fourth race." The names of the horses running are:

1. PICKADILLY
2. THAT'S SOME ISH
3. WEATHER OR NOT
4. RED SHIRTED
5. CLARENCE LEMONS
6. MYT QUINN
7. BOSSMAN BRYAN
8. LORD BERGAMOT

"Oh my god!" I say, tapping Weather Or Not's name. "I'm totally picking number three!"

"Why?" Isaiah asks, looking genuinely interested at my enthusiasm.

"Come on, that name is awesome, I just have to!"

"Well, his odds are seventy-five to one. And it's Red Shirted's race to lose. He's the favorite."

"I know, but he's my pick."

"So when the horse finishes dead last, you'll be the one"—he pauses for a second—"going up to Anthony on Monday, asking him what kind of protein shake he uses."

"Fine. I'm willing to take that bet," I say defiantly.

"If you guys don't mind," Luke pipes up, "I may go put two dollars down on Red Shirted. I mean, what's the point of being eighteen if you can't do things like a legal adult?" It's weird, because he's staring right at me when he says this, like he's trying to tell me something.

Then it dawns on me: He probably wants a girl's advice on dealing with Greta. "Um, I'll come with you," I say, and his face relaxes, so I'm glad I read that right. Though I'm not exactly sure I'm the relationship authority over here.

We work our way through the crowds to the main hall where the betting booths are. I wait for Luke to say something, because I don't want to be like, "So, you're in the doghouse over date night, huh?"

Finally, he stops short and runs a hand through his hair. "Are we cool?"

"Cool?" I repeat, wondering if I've somehow missed something.

"Yeah. I didn't mean to insult you by calling you wholesome."

I laugh. "Luke, that was hours ago."

"I know. But you seemed really upset by it. I just wanted to apologize if it's—"

I hold up my hand. "It's okay. It was a knee-jerk reaction, I guess. And there are definitely worse things to call someone."

"Good. I really didn't mean it as something bad, you know," he says. "Anyway, why do you like that horse so much?"

"Uh, the name is kind of meaningful to me. I want to be a meteorologist."

Luke's face lights up. "That's so cool. Do you want to be one of those people who sends up weather balloons? I've always wanted to know what they figure out from those things."

I try not to gawk at him in wonder, remembering how Hunter's crew used to be so dismissive of all that. "I think I want to do research, so it would involve weather balloons. Study weather patterns and storm systems and stuff. I'd love to do something weather-related for NASA," I tell him. "People usually get disappointed that I don't want to go the glamorous route of TV."

Luke nods. "So, what brought on this love of weather? Was it so you could predict snow days? Because that's totally what I'd be in it for."

I can't help but laugh. "No. It's more to do with tornadoes, actually."

Luke stops in his tracks, beneath one of the large windows of the main hall. A beam of sunlight is touching his head, making his hair glow all holy-like, as a look of complete fascination crosses his face. "Tornadoes? How? You're from New Jersey!"

"I know! But we were doing this cross-country drive when I was eight and when we were going through Nebraska, we almost ran into one. The sky got all green and it got really still, and then, way down the highway, we saw the funnel cloud. I'll never forget it—it was really thin and spindly, not like the one in *The Wizard of Oz*. And then the tornado sirens started to go off."

"Jesus," Luke says, his eyes wide. "What did you do?"

"Well, my mom just kept driving, all calm as a cucumber, but my dad started freaking out, and he was all, 'We need to get off the road!'" I pause. "He's from Italy. He's not really used to that sort of thing."

Luke shakes his head. "I'm not so sure I'd be so good around one, either, but go on."

"Anyway, we were passing this barbecue joint and the owner and his daughter saw us as they were making their way down to the storm cellar. They waved at us to come in and said tornadoes were in the forecast all morning. I was so fascinated about the idea of knowing a storm like that was going to come—and that you'd have a special room to hide in when one hit. Anyway, it didn't end up hitting where we were, but I didn't shut up about it for the rest of the day. When we finally got to our hotel, my mom turned on the Weather Channel for me and that was that."

Luke smiles, looking like he's going to laugh.

"Oh, god," I say. "I really sound like a nerd."

"No, that's the thing. You're, like, glowing over this. It's clear that it's what you're supposed to do."

He's looking at me with what might be admiration and I'm weirded out that his approval pleases me. I don't know what to make of it, so I clear my throat and point to the betting/claiming windows.

"I think you need to go to the booth that guy is using." At the window, there's an older guy in a white blazer, his black shirt opened up to reveal a lot of chest hair and some giant gold medallions. He's totally balding, except for two small tufts of hair over his ears, and he's carrying a fancy-schmancy cane. He folds a huge wad of cash into a gold money clip.

"Dude, that's totally how I want to look when I grow up," Luke says with a laugh. "Maybe he knows that booth is good luck or something."

When we get to the booth, a middle-aged lady with big, feathered blonde hair looks at us expectantly from the other side of the window. "How can I help you today?"

"I'd like to put two dollars on the next race, the number three horse, Weather Or Not."

I stare at him in disbelief. "Luke, if it's not going to—"

"Win, place, or show, sweetie?" the lady asks.

"To win," Luke says, slipping two dollars through the slot in the window. He turns to me with a cocked eyebrow.

I laugh. "You're crazy. His odds are terrible, you heard Isaiah."

"You won't think it's so crazy when this horse brings in like a hundred and fifty bucks," he says. "I'll need a money clip like our friend just had."

I shake my head, still laughing. I guess it's only two dollars, but deep down, I'm touched he'd go with my horse.

"Don't laugh, honey," the betting lady says. "You can make him buy you something pretty if he wins!"

She thinks we're together. *In that way.* This should make me embarrassed, but I'm having too good a day to let any inferences, right or wrong, get me down.

"Hmm," I say, squinting at Luke, whose face is slightly red. "I think I'd like a new spatula! A bejeweled one!"

Luke grins. "Done," he says, as the lady in the booth hands him a slip of paper with his bet printed on it. "You're definitely worth a bejeweled spatula. Maybe a gold-plated pancake turner to go with it."

We head back to our group cracking up and Luke doesn't say anything about his pick. When Weather Or Not is loaded into the starting gate, he nudges me with his elbow and it's hard to suppress a grin.

"Agresti's feeling good about this race, I can tell," Luke says, and I bite my lip to keep from laughing.

When the race starts, the horses are all clustered together and it's hard to see who's where, except Red Shirted, who's leading them all by a few yards. But then, about halfway through, one horse starts challenging Red Shirted, and when the speed-talking announcer says it's Weather Or Not, I suck in my breath. By the time they hit the homestretch, I can feel the vibration under my feet from the horses' hooves as they thunder toward the finish line. It's Red Shirted and Weather Or Not totally neck and neck with the rest of the pack falling farther behind with each stride.

The crowd is going nuts, and you hear all the people who bet on Red Shirted yelling, "Come on, four!" I'm literally clutching both sides of my head as the two horses draw near the finish line, their heads bobbing rhythmically and so, so close together.

And that's when Red Shirted makes one last sprint and pushes past Weather Or Not, and crosses the finish line first. I exhale and it feels as if I'm deflating on the inside, which is so weird considering I'm not the one who had money on the horse.

"Wow, Weather Or Not came out of nowhere!" Isaiah says.

That's when I finally look at Luke. His face is registering disappointment, but then his eyes meet mine and something strange happens—we almost immediately both start laughing. Hysterically.

"What's so funny?" A.J. wants to know as we both double over.

"Oh, Agresti's just not going to get a bejeweled spatula is all," Luke gasps, which makes me laugh so hard I start crying.

Isaiah looks confused, but then A.J. announces he's hungry and suddenly we're moving as a group to the concession stands, Luke and I working through our residual giggles as we go.

"Ellie, is that you?" a woman's voice calls.

We turn around as a group, where a tall dark-haired woman in a Glenwood Park polo shirt is standing behind us smiling.

I feel my eyes light up. "Mariana!" I turn to the guys. "She used to bartend at my dad's old restaurant. She taught me all about football."

"I wish she'd teach *me* about football," A.J. says dreamily.

She runs over and gives me a hug. "I thought it might be you. How are your parents? Are they here today?"

"They're good but they're home. I'm here for a class project." I glance at her shirt. "And you're working here now?"

"I graduated two years ago and I've been doing some work with the horses here since then. And you're here for a class project? Have high school classes really changed that much since I left?" She laughs.

I explain to her about the family activity and point to Isaiah. "He's the reason we're here today."

Mariana gives Isaiah a big grin. "Are you interested in horses?"

"Interested? He's like a horse genius," A.J. says. "I'd trust him to bet my life savings for me. All fifty-three dollars of it!"

Isaiah looks at his feet, though I can see he's pleased by the praise. "I do a lot of reading. I want to be a trainer someday."

Mariana seems to be thinking something over. "Do you work with horses at all now?"

"No," Isaiah says, shaking his head. "I'm only sixteen, plus my mom isn't a big fan of horse racing, so I'm probably going to have to wait till I go to college."

Mariana nods. "You know, I do some work over at the equine therapy center and they could use some help with feeding and grooming the horses. I know it's not racehorses, but you can get some basic experience. They're all very patient and sweet. I could even give you my card to give to your mom, if she wants to talk to me."

"Oh my god, that would be amazing," Isaiah says, and his huge smile makes my heart grow ten sizes. Luke catches my eye and grins.

Mariana fishes out a card from the backpack she's carrying, then shakes Isaiah's hand and grins. "I'll see what I can do. We could use a smart kid like you around there."

Isaiah just beams at her. I think, along with being super psyched to work with horses, he may be just a bit in love as well.

"I have to get down to the stable." Mariana squeezes my arm. "It was so great to see you again, Ellie. Tell your parents I say hi."

"Will do," I say. "And go Steelers!"

A guy in New York Jets sweatpants turns around and scowls then, and Mariana laughs as she walks away.

A.J. punches the air victoriously. "Take that, Bryce and Anthony, Isaiah gets to work with a total babe *and* horses.

"She seems really nice," Isaiah says, hearts practically taking the place of pupils in his eyes.

"So, Family Day turned out to be everything we dreamed it would be and more," I say drily.

"Mrs. Sanchez is going to be so psyched," Luke says. I notice his nose is a little pink from having been in the sun most of the day. I wonder if Greta will notice it too and if their plans for tonight were ever solidified or if they're still fighting. I wonder if she'll be pissed that he was out with us having a good time and getting a slight sunburn while they were arguing.

And then I force myself to stop wondering. Because it really isn't any of my business, after all.

CHAPTER 14

It's kind of crazy how much I, with my lack of athleticism and only mild interest in sports, enjoyed our day at the races—and it has little to do with the fact that we ended up getting twenty extra credit points for our outing. Okay, that's made me pretty psyched, too. I mean, Brynn's face totally fell when she saw Mrs. Sanchez scrawl the new standings with Synergy in third place. Behind us.

But, two weeks later, I decide to take up Rashad on seeing a football game, and Jodie agrees to go with me. I find myself kind of hoping that the guys are going to go, too. I mean, we had fun at one kind of sporting event, why not another?

"So," I say as we clean up after making cupcakes. "How do you go about buying tickets for football games here?"

"You just show up. You buy a ticket at the gate when you walk in," A.J. says as he swirls frosting on a cupcake with such care and ease that I'm momentarily mesmerized. He has such a knack for it that even Mrs. Sanchez was admiring his handiwork earlier, telling him he should consider pastry school. A.J. shrugged it off.

"Oh," I say. "I thought maybe you bought them in advance."

"Are you covering it for the TV station?" Isaiah asks. "You'd probably get to sit in the press box."

"No, I'm going with my best friend, Jodie. We both kind of wanted to see a real-deal high school football game. Are you guys going?"

I notice Hunter's head whip up when I say this, but I ignore him.

"I'm covering for my boy Patrick at the deli," A.J. says.

"My grandma's visiting," Isaiah says. "But it sounds like fun."

We all turn to Luke, who blushes and glances down.

"I'm hanging out with Greta after my training session," he says.

A.J. and Isaiah make "ooh!" noises but Luke ignores them.

"But you'll have a great time," he says to me. "Lawndale's tough. Man, I wish I could go. I forgot they were playing this week."

"Why not bring your lady?" A.J. says, batting his eyelashes.

"She's not exactly into football," Luke says, shrugging.

Maybe it's for the best, then. I'm not sure I'd want to spend an entire game with Greta joking about Luke and me having an affair. I literally shudder at the thought.

"Cold, Agresti?" Luke asks. "Don't have my sweatshirt today, I'm sorry to say."

I can only laugh nervously in response.

"I don't know why anyone would go to a football game," I hear Hunter say, and it makes me freeze.

"Yeah, all you're doing is telling the mouth breathers they rule the school," Steve agrees.

Mrs. Sanchez wanders over to inspect their cupcakes then, meaning I can't turn around and say something sassy to them like I want to. Especially when I hear her award them fifteen points for making the most difficult frosting, which no one else in the class tried, which means they're only five points behind us now. The deep, irritated sigh I let out doesn't go unnoticed by Luke, who smiles.

"Easy, there," he says, patting my shoulder. "We'll hold 'em off, don't you fret."

"Who's fretting?" I say, forcing a grin in the hopes of making myself actually believe that.

In the eight years I've known her, I've never seen Jodie so excited for a sporting event.

"How do I look?" she asks when she arrives at my house that night. "I mean, I know I'm dressed for a day in the rain forest, but aside from that?"

I laugh because Jodie's giant USC rain poncho obscures everything but her head and her rain-boot-clad feet.

"You're more than set for tonight's conditions," I say.

"When's this rain supposed to start, anyway?" Jodie asks as she stands in front of my bedroom mirror, gathering her long dark hair into a ponytail. "I suppose you've consulted your BFF the Doppler radar?"

"It's not supposed to start till after nine, so we'll be dry for most of it." I decide to leave out the part about the wind that will be picking up from a coastal low that's making its way north. Once it starts to rain, it's going to be a mess.

As Jodie and I walk over to the school, the wind starts to whip up. Luckily, it's unseasonably mild for October, so we don't need anything heavier than our sweaters and ponchos to keep us warm.

When we get to RHHS, the parking lot is bustling with cars and people. Most of the crowd is dressed in the Ringvale Heights colors, navy and gold, but there are a few people wearing Lawndale's red and white. The RHHS marching band is off to the side, tuning up, so there's a weird mix of various instruments, accompanied by the thumping of car stereos. There's a buzz of excitement and Jodie grabs my elbow.

"This is so freaking cool!" she says.

"Ellie! Hey!"

We turn around and see Alisha in her band uniform coming toward us. Her foot is in a walking boot now, so she doesn't need crutches, but it still looks uncomfortable.

"I didn't know you were coming tonight! And, oh my god, it's Jodie! So good to see you!" Alisha envelops Jodie in a big hug and Jodie laughs.

"I must've made a big impression at the boardwalk," she says, and I realize that's the last time we all hung out. It was only August, but it seems like years ago.

"We've never been to a high school football game," I tell Alisha.

"I need to check it off on my 'teenage rites of passage' bingo card," Jodie adds.

Alisha's eyes light up. "Oh, speaking of teenage rites of passage, I'm having a party—well, my brother is having a party—next Friday, if you guys are around. Our parents are going to Vermont for a wedding and he wants to invite the whole senior class. I have no idea where we're going to put everyone, but he insists it will work."

Alisha's twin brother, Darpan, is incredibly popular. He's just like Alisha, in that he's super friendly, but he's on the soccer and baseball teams, which means he's friends with mostly jocks who are into the whole party scene. Which means it could get out of control pretty quick.

"I need to see," I say, hoping I don't sound ungrateful for the invite. I mean, I'd love to hang out with Alisha, but at a loud, raging party?

"Come on, El," Jodie says, tugging my sleeve. "I've never been to a co-ed kegger. I need to see if every TV show and movie has been lying to me all these years."

Alisha leans forward and lowers her voice. "And if you're worried about Brynn and Hunter being there, don't. Kim is apparently having some kind of wine and cheese party that night."

The conspiratorial glint in her eyes makes me laugh out loud. "Okay, then that's working in its favor."

"And, seriously," she says, "I won't be going crazy partying or anything. You guys could keep me company."

"Alisha!" Across the parking lot, I can see a girl in a band uniform waving at her. "We're heading down soon!"

Alisha nods and gives a thumbs-up to the girl. Then she turns back to us. "I hope you'll both come! Good to see you again, Jodie! And I'll see you Monday, Ellie!" she says, limping over to her fellow bandmates.

"That party is going to be so epic," Jodie says, linking arms with me. "And no, you're not getting out of it, Mary Ellen."

"I wouldn't dream of not having a front-row seat to my classmates puking up copious amounts of beer."

Me. At a huge party. I don't know if I should laugh or be completely terrified.

We head down to the field, which is so brightly lit, the grass practically glows. We take a seat in the bleachers, off to the side of an area that's roped off for the RHHS band. I see Mrs. Gillroy, wearing an RHHS shirt, sitting arm-in-arm with a guy, who I assume is her husband, wearing a navy-and-yellow baseball cap. I also see several of my teachers spread out among the vast seating area, and recognize a bunch of my classmates.

The RHHS band starts to march onto the field and the PA system crackles to life and a voice announces, "Ladies and gentlemen, please welcome the Ringvale Heights High Fightin' Hornets marching band. Under the direction of Maria Francis, they will be entertaining us this pre-game with a medley of hits from the 1980s."

There's a burst of cheering from our side of the field, and most of the people near us are watching attentively as the band forms a giant Pac-Man, but Jodie sits up straighter and scans the bleachers.

"I didn't realize we get musical entertainment and—" She suddenly clutches my arm, scaring the crap out of me. "Oh my god, that guy is so freaking hot!"

"Who?" I ask, looking around.

"That guy!" She points to a guy walking up the aisle on the other side of our section. I suck in my breath.

"That's Luke, from my home ec class."

"Wait, this guy is in the JAILE family and I'm only now hearing about him? Good god, woman, how do you not see this? He's a total fox."

"He's supposed to be with his girlfriend tonight," I say, ignoring the heat creeping into my face. "I wonder if she's here?"

"Well, ask, genius," Jodie says.

"You mean call him over here?"

"Yes. I'd like to meet him."

I'm worried that if I call him over, Greta will find us, and we'll have to sit with them for the rest of the game. I worry she'll make another weird comment about Luke and me. I worry what Luke thinks of her saying stuff like that. And I worry that I'm worried about it.

Jodie nudges me with her foot.

Fine. "Luke!" I call, and I see his head turn in our direction. His eyes light up and he waves. He searches for an empty row of seats and makes his way across toward us.

"Ellllll," Jodie whispers. "You need to at least make out with this guy."

"Jodie!" I bark, then lower my voice. "He has a girlfriend! And he's not even my type."

Jodie rolls her eyes. "Except he is. He's hot. Every girl likes a hot guy."

"Then maybe *you* should like him," I say.

"No, I'm fully devoted to pining over Joaquin, the new guy at work. Besides, you're bright red right now, so I think you know exactly what I'm talking about."

I don't get to argue with her because Luke has reached us. I notice he's carrying a golf umbrella. "Fancy seeing you here," he says.

"I thought you were going out with Greta tonight?" I say. I can feel my face get even hotter when I say Greta's name.

"She ended up going into the city to meet up with some of her snowboarding friends from Canada. She told me it'd be a lot of shoptalk, so I stayed home," Luke says, his face totally neutral. "But at least I get to see the game now."

"You should totally sit with us," Jodie says smiling at him.

"Unless you're meeting friends," I say. "No pressure."

"No," Luke says, "I was actually hoping to run into you!"

Jodie kicks me, but she distracts Luke from seeing it by scooting down our bleacher, dragging me with her and opening up a seat for him on the end. Next to me.

"Oh," I say, "Luke, this is Jodie."

Luke sits down and his smile broadens. "Nice to meet you. Are you a big football fan?"

"Ha, I'm not the biggest sports gal, but I do anything for a friend," she says, elbowing me.

"She also can't turn down seeing guys in tight pants," I say, starting to giggle, and Jodie shakes her head.

"Just because Joaquin was wearing those tight jeans that day doesn't mean I was checking out his butt. I am many things, but a silent sexual harasser is not one of them."

I'm kind of relieved I have Jodie on the defensive, thus momentarily preventing her from going on the offensive with me. I turn to Luke. "She has a crush on a new guy she works with at Retro Mania in the mall, but she can barely talk to him," I say.

"Why not?" Luke says.

"I just never know what to say. I don't have a lot of experience with guys," Jodie says with a shrug.

"I wouldn't worry about that," Luke says. "Like, you're doing a great job of talking to me. Don't sell yourself short."

Jodie's brow furrows. "Really?"

"Really," Luke says.

Jodie sits up straighter. "Okay, maybe I'll try tomorrow."

This crazy warm feeling grips my heart then and I smile gratefully at Luke. He winks back in return.

The game is pretty close. The score seesaws back and forth between us and Lawndale, and by halftime, Lawndale's up 17–14. The wind has really kicked up and the smell of rain is in the air. I wonder if they'll get the whole thing in before the monsoon hits.

I'm impressed at how well Jodie and Luke are getting along. Within ten minutes, they realize they both love *Saturn Quest*, this Netflix comedy/sci-fi show. Jodie tells Luke it's her dream to write for a show like that, and Luke tells her all about BMXing and how I've seen him train.

"Why didn't you tell me you interviewed him?" she says, elbowing me, then jerking her thumb in my direction. "She's so mysterious, this one."

I'm about as mysterious as a toothbrush, but I'm kind of amused that Jodie is painting me as a lady of intrigue. Maybe let Luke think I've got some deep secrets or something.

"And she's one of the funniest people you'll ever meet," I say, jerking my thumb in Jodie's direction. "That she thinks Joaquin wouldn't be into her is crazy."

"So, when did this Joaquin dude first catch your eye?" Luke asks, and Jodie launches into detail about how Joaquin started at Retro Mania three weeks ago and how he seems almost impossibly shy. Luke ends up giving Jodie tips on how to talk to him, and even this old guy sitting behind us, a football player's grandfather, weighs in with, "Sometimes, all it takes is a smile."

After that, Jodie high-fives the old man whenever something good happens during the game.

When the RHHS band takes the field for the halftime show, Jodie stands up. "Anyone want a soda?"

"I'm good," I say, also standing up, "but I'll come with you."

"No, I can handle this," Jodie says cheerfully. "I saw where the snack bar was when we came in."

She is so doing this to give Luke and me alone time. I know her too well.

"*Okay,*" I say, blinking hard at her.

"Luke, you want anything?" she asks innocently.

"Well, if you insist," Luke says, fishing some cash out of his pocket and handing it to her. "Can you get me a Coke?"

She waves the money off. "It's the least I can do for all the boy advice you've given me," she says, making her way up the bleachers.

"She's awesome," Luke says. "You guys are a lot alike."

"In some ways, we're like twins," I say. In other ways, I want to kill her.

"You guys been friends long?"

"Since the fourth grade," I say. "It's going to be weird next year, when we're at different colleges. I mean, being at two different high schools is hard enough. But I guess if we could survive middle school together, we can survive anything."

"That sounds heavy," Luke says, his eyes full of concern.

"Oh, it was nothing life-threatening. I just got picked on a lot in middle school, and Jodie got picked on for sticking up for me."

"Really? You?" he says, his eyebrows raised in surprise. "You're so . . . What did they pick on you for?"

I'm so what? I want to ask, but I jump right in with the scoliosis saga.

Luke narrows his eyes. "Why would anyone bully somebody for something like that? God, if I had been at your school . . ." But he doesn't finish his thought.

"So were you always defending your classmates like some kind of superhero?" I ask teasingly.

"Uh, not really. It was weird. My dad died when I was in the sixth grade, so after that, it was like I didn't care about anything. I think I was popular before that, but after, I didn't give a crap anymore. Thankfully, my real friends stuck by me, because I was a bit of an ass to people for a while. Not in a teasing way, though. I just couldn't deal with anything and I got pissy easily."

"But that's totally understandable. You were coping with a loss."

Luke manages a small smile. "I think a lot of people thought I hated them when I didn't. Man, I was a charmer back then."

"I have to admit," I say, laughing. "I thought you hated me when we first met . . ."

"Oh, god!" Luke says, looking alarmed. "I didn't mean—"

". . . but I realize now that you were just joking around. I was being too much of a bundle of nerves to figure that out back then."

Luke sighs. "Well, *I'm* going to admit that I thought you were a bit like Brynn at first, because you were always hanging out with her. But I saw that look on your face when she bitched me out the first day of school. You looked like you wanted to punch her."

"I did! God, she was so rude to you. I'm sorry I didn't say anything to defend you."

"You didn't have to," Luke says with a shrug. "I swear, that look on your face was enough."

"And then we kept almost knocking into each other," I say, gig-gling.

"Yes! And you seemed so flustered and frustrated with me, like I was doing it on purpose or something." He raises an eyebrow.

"Sorry," I say, covering my face with my hands. "I was a little, uh, edgy."

"Don't sweat it. It was kind of cute."

It's like everything stops as the word "cute" hangs in the air. What did he mean by that? That the situation was cute? That I was cute? His ears are suddenly red and he goes on with, "And now here we are enjoying a football game together."

"Amazing what a difference seven weeks makes," I say, though I'm still stuck on the cute thing.

"Indeed," Luke says. We're kind of staring at each other and then we both seem to realize this and look away at the same time. We're sitting with our hands resting on the bleacher, and if this was a TV show, and Luke was single, and I was interested in him, this would be the moment one of us reached over to take the other's hand. Instead, we both stare straight ahead and watch the band exit as the cheerleaders take the field.

"So much junk food, so little time," Jodie says, coming back with two Cokes and a bag of M&Ms. When she sits down, she shoves me, pushing me closer to Luke.

I shoot her a "seriously?" look, but she just bats her eyelashes. Luke can't slide over any farther because he's on the end, so now we're practically sitting shoulder to shoulder. It's extremely hard to put the cute comment out of my mind when we're in this position.

Thankfully, the football teams return to the field, and the RHHS team is visibly psyched up. The players sprint out, jumping and punching at the air. I see Rashad and a bunch of other players motioning for the crowd to get louder, and the roar that ensues gives me chills.

The game is really tight after that, but in the fourth quarter, Ringvale Heights manages to score a touchdown, putting them ahead 20–17. There are only three minutes left in the game, and that's when the rain starts.

"Uh-oh," Jodie says, noting the giant drops that are plopping on our ponchos. Umbrellas start popping up, and Luke raises his. "You guys want to get under?"

"Ooh la la. What will people think?" Jodie says.

"That I'm a very smart man who figured out how to get two lovely ladies close to me," Luke says, laughing. "Or that we're staying dry."

I'm more worried about what Greta would think, but the rain is starting to splatter on my glasses, so I scoot as close to Luke as possible. And Jodie scoots closer to me, which makes my right arm smash into Luke's left arm. Since he's holding the umbrella with his left hand, I can feel the muscles flexed under his long-sleeved shirt. A heat suddenly surges through my right side and I pray he can't feel it.

The rain starts falling in sheets then and the field is muddy in a matter of moments. No one in the crowd leaves, and as the rain falls harder, it just makes everyone louder. It's kind of awesome.

With about a minute left in the game, Lawndale gets very close to the RHHS end zone. At this point, everyone's standing and yelling and looking like drowned rats, but no one seems to care. Even Mrs. Gillroy and her husband are on their feet, drenched and screaming.

As the seconds are counting down, Lawndale has one last chance to score—they are now on the five-yard line. I wonder if the winds, now blowing the rain under Luke's umbrella, can somehow hold them back. There's an electricity coursing through the bleachers and everyone is screaming and I don't want to think about what might happen if this moment ends badly.

The Lawndale quarterback reaches back to throw and I see his target, this guy who is wide open in the end zone. *This is it*, I think, *this is where we lose the game and have to leave dejected and soaking wet in the rain*. But out of nowhere, just as the quarterback releases the ball, Rashad comes flying around, jumps up, and swats the ball down, just as the last second ticks off the clock.

The crowd leaps up as one and it seems like thousands of arms are flailing in the air. It's a wave of humanity and umbrellas.

"Rashad!" I scream, jumping in place. "Ohmygod!"

Luke is jumping too, and bellowing "Yeah!" in a way that makes him seem really dude-like. Jodie and the old guy behind her are high-fiving the bejesus out of each other. It's total mayhem in the bleachers with everyone celebrating. It's amazing. I'm soaking wet, I can barely see out of my fogged-up glasses, and yet this is the most thrilling thing I've ever been a part of.

Rashad was right. I should've done this a whole lot sooner.

"That was so much fun," Jodie says for the fourth or fifth time as we shrug off our ponchos in my bathroom. "Never in a million years did I think I'd be that into a football game for a school I don't even go to."

"We can totally go to another one, if you want."

"I'm in. Especially if Luke is there to be my love guru again," she says.

I feel my face grow hot at Luke's name, so I throw a towel at Jodie before I start peeling my socks off. They are so wet, they are stuck to my feet like a second skin. It's kind of funny that the game was so intense, I'd forgotten about my hatred for wet shoes and socks until this moment.

Jodie snaps her fingers. "I just realized who he looks like. That old picture of Almanzo Wilder you drew in fifth grade. For that *Little House* book report Mr. Irwin made you do!"

"Huh?"

"Stop feigning ignorance, Mary Ellen," Jodie says. "That thing hung on your wall for like four years."

"Because it was the best thing I've ever drawn," I say, hating the defensiveness that's creeping into my voice.

"No, it's because you deep down had a crush on the book version of him. And when you found out what he looked like in real life and that he didn't resemble your picture, you were legitimately pissed off. I remember it well," Jodie says, totally delighting in this.

I try to force a recollection of that picture into my mind. I'd thought Almanzo would be broad-shouldered, a little scruffy, but not too beard-y, with golden-brown hair and blue eyes. Okay, so maybe if you take away the suspender pants and add a tattoo you might get something close to Luke.

But I can't admit that to Jodie if I have any hope of moving this conversation along.

"Because it was how I pictured him," I say, forcing what I hope sounds like a casual chuckle. "You read a book, you have a certain idea of how things should be. Like how you thought Goron the Magnificent from *Enchanted Chasms* was supposed to be way more goth than the guy who played him on the TV show."

"Oh, don't even get me started about that," she says with a huff, and I think I've finally distracted her. But then she goes on. "Anyway, there's, like, a definite chemistry between you two."

"What's that supposed to mean?" I ask, my heart suddenly pounding.

"I'm just asking you to admit you think he's hot," Jodie says, folding her arms.

There's no getting out of this one, what with my face betraying me at every moment lately. "Fine, he's cute," I say, busying myself with yanking off my other sock. "But you can think someone's attractive and not, like, *want* them." There. That's logical.

Jodie rolls her eyes. "Come on, El, you guys definitely have a vibe going on."

"Well, vibe or not, he has a girlfriend," I say, becoming annoyed. "There's no reason for me to think of him beyond that."

Jodie stares at me for a moment, as if she's debating what she's about to say. "I'm just going to say this once: He only came to the game because he knew you were going to be there. Girlfriend or not, you're on that boy's mind."

I know Jodie's probably only saying this in the hopes that it'll put me over the Hunter hump for good, that she hopes I'll move on. But I'm suddenly horrified by something. If I am on Luke's mind, how does this make him any better than Hunter? And what if that makes me the Brynn in this situation?

It takes me a long time to fall asleep that night, but Jodie snoring on the air mattress next to my bed has nothing to do with it. All I can think about is if this makes Luke a bad person. If it makes me a bad person for enjoying his company and thinking he's . . . hot. So around 3:00 a.m. I make the decision to just not think of Luke like that anymore. He's strictly my classmate now. Satisfied with my new stance, I finally drift off to sleep.

So, of course, that's when I have my first Luke sex dream.

CHAPTER 15

It's kind of hilarious that I once thought the hardest part about home ec was having to see Brynn and Hunter grope each other. Because that has absolutely nothing on having to stand right next to the person you've been having sex dreams about.

Yes, dreams. Plural. As in, the harder I try to push Luke from my mind, the more he pops up shirtless and kissing me and, uh, doing other things in my dreams, which I've been having for over a week now, almost every night since the football game.

It's really, really uncomfortable. I mean, not during the dreams. That's surprisingly (and distressingly) fantastic. But seeing him in class? Total dilemma.

Today, for example, we're baking scones, and watching Luke's hands work at the dough is making me sweat a little. I'm on dish duty with A.J., so I turn the water on cold in an effort to cool off a little.

"Excuse me, I gotta get a little more flour," I hear Luke say, and before I know it, he's squeezing behind me to get to the pantry. His elbow grazes my back and I jump about ten feet.

"Holy crap, Agresti," Luke laughs. "You're seriously ticklish."

I just laugh nervously and leave it at that. Because all I can think about are his seriously defined pecs (at least they are in my dreams, and they look like they *could* be under his wrinkled Wawa T-shirt) and him kissing my shoulder like he had in the previous night's dream.

I wonder if it's odd for a virgin to be having sex dreams. I mean, I never had them about Hunter, which is strange considering he's the only guy I've ever kissed and, uh, done a few other things with. I also wonder if it's odd for me to be thinking of it as much as I have. And if this makes me some kind of tramp, considering Luke has a girlfriend.

But the dreams did give me comfort about one thing: It probably means I'm only attracted to Luke physically, and it should be easy to keep shallow feelings like that to myself and get over it quickly.

At least, I hope.

"Uh, Ellie, you've been rinsing that bowl for like five minutes," A.J. says.

I try not to turn red as I hand him the bowl. "Sorry, I'm out of it. I haven't been sleeping well."

"It could be the change in weather," Isaiah says as he lines a cookie sheet with parchment paper. "It's gotten pretty cold lately."

"True," I say, leaving out the part about my dreams being super, um, hot.

"You know what you need?" A.J. asks as he places the bowl in its cupboard.

"What?" I'm terrified he's going to say "sex" or something equally crude.

"Chamomile tea. Works like a charm."

I choke back a laugh and his brow furrows. "What's so funny?"

"Nothing. I just can't picture you getting cozy with a cup of tea is all."

"Laugh all you want. It works!"

"What works?" Luke asks, returning from the pantry with a cup of flour.

"I was just saying that chamomile tea is good for relaxing," A.J. says. "Ellie's having trouble sleeping."

"Is that so?" Luke says. Then he grins at me in a way that I swear to god makes me think he can read my mind. "Everything all right?"

"I'm a little stressed with classes and stuff, you know," I say, heat creeping into my face.

"Ah, don't let our in-class competition stress you out," Luke says. "We may be tied for second place, but that's not the end of the world."

We all kind of stare at the dry-erase board with the group rankings hung up at the front of the room. The Bukowskis are still leading everyone, followed by us and Synergy, then Jersey Strong, then the Bakers.

"But tied with Synergy isn't exactly beating them now, is it?" I say, and I know it comes out as snappish as it sounds in my head because Luke's eyes widen in surprise. I can't tell if it's fueled by my annoyance by the sex dreams or the frustration that somehow, no matter how hard we work in class, we can't seem to pull ahead of Hunter and Brynn for longer than a day or two.

"Sorry. I shouldn't have asked Mrs. Sanchez about the extra credit for our day at the races in front of everyone," I say. "We'd be ahead of them now if not for that."

"Yeah, but how were you supposed to know they'd do an activity, too?" Isaiah says.

I glance over at Synergy, where Brynn is lecturing Steve for brushing too much milk on top of their scones. "Oh, I totally should've known."

"We at least need Jared's group knocked out of first or I'll hurt someone," A.J. mutters as he sprinkles sugar on top of our scones.

"We're only ten points out of first," Isaiah says. "Totally catchable."

A.J. lifts our cookie sheet full of scones and places it in the oven. We survey the rest of the kitchens, and it looks as if we're the first ones to get our scones baking. "That ought to buy us a few points," A.J. says.

"That ought to buy us few points," a mocking voice parrots from nearby.

We swoop around to see Jared, sporting a paisley beret today, opening the refrigerator and shaking his head at us.

"You got a problem, jackass?" A.J. asks.

"No," Jared says, clutching a fist to his chest, and making a face like he's about to fake cry. "I'm just so touched that you guys have come together so well. You're like a Hallmark movie or something."

Out of the corner of my eye, I see Mrs. Sanchez watching us from her perch at the front of the room. I nudge A.J., in an effort to keep him from blowing up, but he ignores me.

"Dude, I swear to god, if you—"

"I have a question, Jared," I interject cheerfully. "Do you wear your beret to keep from getting cold when you're standing in front of the fridge for so long or are you just trying to hide premature male pattern baldness?"

Luke bursts out laughing, a funny, high-pitched cackle. I notice even the rest of Jared's group is fighting a smile. Jared, however, scowls at me. If Mrs. Sanchez notices this is going down, she doesn't say anything.

"Shut up, Ellie" is the only thing Jared can come up with. He fills a measuring cup with milk from the refrigerator, then storms off to his kitchen in a huff. I suspect I'll be the victim of some kind of mean-spirited blind item on The Buzz tonight as a result.

Isaiah is giggling and Luke is wiping tears from his eyes and patting me on the shoulder, making me all tingly. But A.J.'s face is stony.

"Why didn't you let me say what I needed to say?"

"Because Mrs. Sanchez was watching and I didn't want to lose any points. You want to beat Jared, right?"

"I don't need a babysitter," he says sulkily as he starts to clean off the counter.

Luke shakes his head as if to say, "Let him be." So I back off and return to the sink, where I wring out the sponge and watch A.J. scrub the counters so hard, his paper towels rip apart.

"Okay, everyone," Mrs. Sanchez says a few minutes later. "Since you've all got your scones in the ovens, I wanted to make an announcement."

For a moment, and I have no idea where this comes from, I'm terrified she's going to tell us we have to switch our groups. Like what she has just seen go down between my group and Jared has inspired her to shake things up a bit in the name of bonding.

"As you may know, the winter dance is scheduled for December fifth," she says, and I'm flooded with relief. "And every year at the dance, there's a refreshment table. This year, in the interest of saving money, the school has asked if my classes will provide homemade snacks. And they're going to need people to man the tables."

The whole class groans, but Mrs. Sanchez holds up her hands.

"But since I have six classes, I've figured out a way for this to work. Whichever group is last in points from each class will have to work the table for a half hour."

I check the dry-erase board. We're only twenty points ahead of Jersey Strong and thirty ahead of the Bakers, and there's four weeks of class left before the dance. We may be tied for second, but it's not a far fall to the bottom. I have no plans to go to the dance as it is and I'm certainly not looking forward to the prospect of being forced to watch Hunter and Brynn slow dance while I dole out cookies and brownies to the hungry masses.

Callie Gorman, one of the Bakers, who is always on the verge of making a grandstanding speech (she once told me she was a suffragette hooker in her past life), stands up. "We're being forced to partake in after-school activities because the school board is cheap?"

I can't argue with her there.

"You won't be forced into anything, Ms. Gorman, if your group doesn't finish in last place," Mrs. Sanchez says. "And for the record, any group in this class can finish in last, even those who appear to be front runners now. There's a long way to go till this term is over."

Luke smiles at us and nods as if to say, "See?"

And it makes me hot and flustered again. Ugh.

That night, I realize there's a reason I never go to parties: Dressing for the occasion makes me PMS-levels of grouchy. I am definitely not one of those girls who can put an outfit together effortlessly. I stand in front of my full-length mirror and my frowning reflection practically dares me to chuck it out the window.

I'm certain I don't have the right clothes for Alisha's party. Like, I'm sure the girls who do go out every weekend must get gussied up and look like something out of a Zara window. I will never be able to pull that off, and they'll stare at me and whisper about my lack of fashion sense.

I settle on a close-fitting brown V-neck sweater over a cream-colored camisole with lace trim. I've got my jeans and my favorite pair of brown leather boots. Basically, this would've been an outfit I'd wear if Hunter had said, "Let's go out, just the two of us," back when we were dating. But how am I supposed to know if this passes for high-school-party chic?

My phone rings then and it's Jodie, probably calling to run her outfit by me. Or maybe she worked up the nerve to ask Joaquin to come with us—they've been chatting a bit since the football game. We haven't really talked since Tuesday because her parents took her on a road trip to Georgetown, their alma mater, for a college visit.

"Hey, lady. Ready to observe your first keg stand?"

Jodie is silent for a moment, then clears her throat. "I can't go."

"Did your parents find out?" I say.

"No," she says, her voice flat and quiet. "I had a panic attack."

I'm so confused that I have to sit down on my bed. "When? Why? Are you okay?"

"I didn't tell you, but my parents and I wanted to test flying, in case I get into USC. We were going to fly down to DC since it's a short flight. Except I couldn't get on the plane because I had a panic attack at the gate. We didn't even end up going to Georgetown."

"Oh, Jodie, I'm so sorry," I say, my heart breaking for her.

"It's over. I can't go to USC."

"You can still apply, though," I say, trying to latch on to some sliver of hope. "Maybe you could drive or take the train there."

"Then I'd never really be able to come home. That takes too long. It's just not realistic."

I've never seen this side of Jodie. She's not the type to be melodramatic or feel sorry for herself. She must have truly come to a final decision about this, and there's no way around it.

"Forget the party," I say, looking for my bag. "I'll be right over."

"No, El, don't," she says quietly. "I really can't be around anyone right now."

"But—"

"Honestly, I just want to be alone. Besides, Alisha seemed to really want you there and she's so nice. Don't let her down."

"Well, I can—"

Jodie gives tight laugh. "No, you don't have to swing by after the party, either. Trust me, I really just want to be alone to process this."

"Okay," I say, still not wanting to believe that her entire college dream has just crashed down.

"Don't take it personally, okay?" she says. "I'll give you a call tomorrow. I promise. And please don't tell anyone."

"All right," I say. "I'm really, really sorry."

When we hang up, I just stare at my phone. I feel as if it's been decided *I'm* not going to USC, that's how hard I've been rooting for Jodie to get in. She's wanted to go there since I met her.

What little celebratory spirit I had has been sucked out by the phone call and I totally don't know if I can go to this party by myself. But then I remember Alisha and how excited she was for me to come. I allow myself a big sigh, then pull myself off the bed and grab my coat.

When I make my way downstairs, Mom is curled up on the living room couch, clipping coupons and watching what looks like a documentary on the Incas and Machu Picchu. Part of me aches to just climb in the recliner and pull the mothball-smelling afghan over me, and indulge my inner nerdiness with my mother.

"I'm gonna head over to Alisha's," I say. Mom thinks I'm going over there for a game night with a few classmates.

"Do you want a ride?" she asks, muting the TV.

It's cold and dark outside and the prospect of being transported to Alisha's house in a warm car is inviting. But it'll be obvious to my mom that there's more than a game night going on when she sees all the cars outside Alisha's house, so I'm going to have to suck this one up and tough it out.

"That's okay. Alisha lives over on Daffodil Lane, so it's close," I say.

"Well, if you need a ride back, call."

"Will do," I say, heading into the front hall.

"Have fun," Mom calls as I open the front door, and part of me wonders if she knows that there's going to be more than just Monopoly and Boggle at Alisha's.

Almost instantly, I regret not taking the ride. It's unseasonably cold for late October, and there's a sharp wind blowing, which makes my nose sting and my eyes water. I pull my hat down over my ears, then fold my arms and march headfirst into the wind.

Alisha's house is older, like mine, and it's set back from the street, with a long gravel driveway leading up to it. There are already a bunch of cars lining the driveway, and I can hear music thumping from her house, where it seems every single light is on. I remember Darpan once saying they're lucky because the house backs up to the woods, and if they have a party no one is in earshot to call the cops on them. I sincerely hope tonight isn't the night that goes by the wayside, as I'd like to not have a criminal record.

I climb the steps to the front door and see a couple totally making out on the porch swing next to it. I pray it's not Hunter and Brynn, then remember Alisha saying they'd be at Kim's. A combination of being freezing and feeling completely awkward makes me stride past them to the front door, which is open a crack.

The music becomes much louder when I open the door to let myself in. I wouldn't say the entire senior class is here, but the place is pretty packed. I scan the room for any RHHS TV people I can attach myself to, but I don't see anyone I know. Almost everyone is hanging out in the living room, drinking from red cups and beer cans. Some are passing around a joint and, instantly, I feel totally out of place. I step backward, thinking maybe I can make an escape before I'm spotted, when I hear someone yell, "Ellie! Thank god!"

I look to my right and see Alisha, wearing oven mitts and her walking cast, limping out of the kitchen. Her face is flushed, but she gives me a big smile, then grabs my hand in one of her mitts and leads me into the kitchen, which has a baby gate in the doorway.

"It's safer in here," she says as she opens the gate. "I want at least one room of the house to not get destroyed, so I told D if he kept everyone out of the kitchen, I'd make snacks."

There are a bunch of cookie sheets on the table and several boxes of frozen appetizers on the counter. This is how introverts cope with a raging party, right here.

"So, who else are you expecting?" I ask.

"Most of senior class, apparently," she says, blowing a stray lock of hair out of her face. "Like I said, we don't have to worry about Kim or any of them at least." Her eyes kind of sparkle when she says this and I laugh.

"Where's Jodie?" Alisha asks, frowning.

I remember how Jodie asked me not to tell anyone about USC, and I keep my word—even though I'd love to ask someone for advice on what I can do to help her right now. "She's not feeling well tonight."

Alisha nods. "Yeah, it's cold and flu season, it sucks. Oh, hey, you can help yourself to a drink out on the deck. We have soda. Hell, have a beer. We have enough to start our own bar out there."

I'm greeted by a gust of cold air when I step through the kitchen door onto the deck, and I'm glad my coat is still on. There's a group of fairly large guys gathered around a giant red cooler and a keg. I almost go back inside, because I'm not sure if I'm crashing some male-bonding moment right here.

Then I hear, "Hey, Rash, it's the girl who made you famous!" Rashad's head pokes up from the group and I'm flooded with relief. He waves me over.

"Hey, Mary Ellen. What are you drinking?" he says, throwing open the cooler as I approach. The guys are all looking at me and I realize they're all football players.

"A Coke, please," I say with a smile.

"Just a Coke?" asks Joey Santini, the tight end with, uh, the best tight end of any senior guy, if this year's underground senior super-latives are to be believed. "You helped Rashad land the girl of his dreams with that interview. You deserve a beer!"

Rashad nods and laughs. "The interview got Olivia McCoy to talk to me," he says.

Darren Perry, the quarterback, nods. "She said seeing how good he was with Montague made her go all gushy inside."

"I'm so glad!" I say. "Who knew psycho Montague could make a love connection?"

"Here, this Bud's for you," Joey says, opening a can and handing it to me.

"But I—" The words "just wanted a Coke" catch in my throat. I'm being kind of celebrated here and I don't want to seem rude, so I take the can. I don't have to drink the whole beer. Because this isn't going to be a "if this were a bad TV show" moment, where I get drunk and dance on tables and "come out of my shell."

"Thank you," I say, the can practically freezing to my hand.

"Cheers," Rashad says, clinking his can with mine.

"Uh, cheers," I reply. I bring the can to my lips and close my eyes. I've tasted beer before and I'm not a fan, so I take a tiny sip and try not to make a face.

Rashad tells me all about Olivia, whom he's had his eye on since sophomore year. "We have AP Calculus together, but she was always hanging out with her theater friends and I could never get her attention."

I take another sip of beer and it doesn't seem as bad as the first, but yeah, it's still nasty. "Sometimes all it takes is a smile," I say, repeating what the old guy sitting behind us at the football game told Jodie.

"Or, in this case, a dog," Rashad says. "She said she thought I was Mr. Serious before, but after she saw the interview, she sought me out for homework help."

"Well, I'm glad RHHS TV could be of service," I say, and we clink cans again.

We chat for a little bit longer and I guess I must be pretty much as lightweight as you can get because after a half a can of beer, I begin to feel at ease, but also a little woozy. I make my way back inside, shaking my head at Alisha. "The football team insisted on giving me a thank-you beer for helping Rashad get a date."

Alisha throws her head back and laughs. "You're one of them now!"

I dump the rest of the beer down the sink and throw the empty can in Alisha's specially marked bag. "Darpan swears he's taking it to the recycling center tomorrow, before our parents get home. But I'm going to bet that I'm the one who takes it because he's going to be too hungover."

"I'll help you collect bottles and cans tonight," I say, shrugging off my coat and laying it over a chair at the kitchen table. It's a lot hotter in the kitchen, and given my somewhat wobbly state, it's probably best if I get out of it for a little bit.

"Thanks, that would be so, so awesome," Alisha beams, as the timer goes off on the oven. "The less to do later, the better!"

I take a few grocery bags out into the living room, where a couple of people I recognize say hello to me. I take a moment to gauge what everyone else is wearing and realize I totally overthought my ensemble, since every other girl is also in jeans and boots.

I roll my eyes at my earlier angst and grab some cans and bottles off the floor. It seems like a lot of the crowd is gathered now in the dining room, where beer pong has been set up.

A group of four girls, cheerleaders, I think, are dancing all up on each other, and if they're doing it to make the guys salivate, they've succeeded. Jared, for example, is staring at them openmouthed from across the room. It's so rare to see him speechless about anything that I actually laugh.

That's when I hear it.

"Oh my god, Hunter, everyone's here!"

My hands twist around the top of the grocery bag as if on reflex. I don't even need to look to know it's Brynn. Perhaps I'm a glutton for punishment, because I turn to see Steve, Hunter, and Brynn coming through the front door. Or, should I say, Brynn staggering through the door.

"Someone's wasted already," Tasha Harrison, the captain of the softball team, says from the couch. Her boyfriend, Nate Yu, just kind of stares in disbelief.

"Yes, ma'am!" Brynn yells back, shoving her fist in the air. Kim's party must've been a dressier occasion because the guys are wearing ties under their sweaters and Brynn's in a black sheath dress with a purple cardigan.

"She, uh, had a little too much wine," Hunter says with what sounds like a forced laugh.

"I wanted to be loose," Brynn says loudly. "For this party!"

I am definitely not in the right headspace for this. Maybe I should have finished that beer after all.

Brynn plops down on the couch, pushing Tasha practically onto Nate's lap. "We almost didn't come, but then I was like, 'These are our classmates. We really should be bonding with them instead of scorning them.'" She doesn't seem to notice Tasha and Nate roll their eyes at each other when she says this.

Hunter smiles tightly and then seems to notice that I'm staring at them. *You're not supposed to be here* is probably the expression I'm wearing because he looks apologetic.

I scoot my way through the throngs, back to the kitchen, where Alisha is arranging some mini pizzas on a plate.

"Holy crap, are you okay?" she asks. "You look like your head's about to explode."

"Brynn and Hunter are here," I say, and Alisha's face falls.

"Oh god, I'm sorry," she says. "If you want to go . . ."

But suddenly, a flicker of defiance comes alive in me. I don't know if I drank enough beer for it to have been "liquid courage" but something is making me feel brave.

"No. I'm not letting them scare me away from a perfectly good party!"

"Rock on," Alisha says, giving me a high five.

I grab a plate of mini meatballs and march back out into the living room. If I can't bond with my classmates over alcohol, by god, I'll do it by feeding them.

And sure enough, everyone swarms around me the second I get back to the living room. They smile and say hello and, really, the alcohol hasn't made them mean or nasty like I feared. Instead, they're all just really hungry. I look for Hunter, as if to say, "See? I don't need you," but I don't see him or Brynn on the couch anymore. Probably off making out somewhere and messing up—

"Oh my god, she's totally going to vom!" someone yells.

I turn in time to see Brynn running into the living room, her hand over her mouth. Hunter is behind her, his hands full with a red cup and giant bottle of water. When Brynn stops suddenly by the fireplace, Hunter leans over her shoulder and whispers something, and that gets her to turn around . . . and puke all over his sweater.

"*Ugh*" is the general crowd consensus as everyone clears the vicinity. I feel like this should be a victorious moment for me, but I'm too grossed out to feel anything but skeeved.

Hunter stands there seemingly conflicted between wanting to help Brynn and wanting to take his sweater off.

"Dude, get her outside, now," Darpan yells. "She got some on the rug."

Everyone is just kind of staring at them, and some people start to laugh. Brynn is completely green, and Hunter looks like he wants to evaporate right there. Nope, the only victory I feel here is that this isn't my living room. Which makes me instantly feel for Alisha.

I step over to them, but stay a good few feet away. Hunter eyes me up and down, as if he's surprised I'm daring to be anywhere near them at the moment. "Go clean yourself up and then clean the rug," I say as briskly as possible. "I'll take her outside."

"Ellie, you don't—"

"No, I do. I don't want Alisha's house getting drenched in vomit."

Hunter nods. "Thanks."

Since I don't want to be thrown up on, I steer Brynn from behind by her shoulders out to the front porch. I grab a few of my grocery bags on the way out for good measure.

Thankfully, the cold air has driven the make-out couple inside, and it's just Brynn and me standing on the porch. I make the executive decision to sit us on the stairs since I don't want Brynn puking all over the porch swing cushion.

"What are we doing?" Brynn asks, her head lolling to the side.

"We're getting you some air," I say tightly.

"Why are you being nice to me?" she slurs. "You shouldn't be so nice to me."

"This isn't being nice, this is making sure you don't puke on Alisha's rug."

"Kay," Brynn says. "But you can hate me. I know you do. I would."

"It's okay." This is so not the response I ever thought I'd give her, but I fear if I told her it really sucks to have your boyfriend stolen from you, she'd start making a big scene out of it as only a drunk person can.

"Ellie, I'm not a bad person," she says, her face turning more red than green.

"I never said you were," I say. Then again, I did call her an asshole. And a "piece of work." But she's in no condition for logic at the moment, so I hope she lets that go by without argument.

"You need to know," Brynn says, and I see giant tears forming in her eyes . . .

This can't be good.

". . . I never meant to hurt you. It's just—"

"Agresti, hey!" We both look up and see Luke and Greta coming up the path to the house. They're both walking stiffly, with their hands in their pockets. I, however, am thankful to them for breaking up this extremely awkward and unwanted heart-to-heart.

"What are you guys doing outside?" Greta says, as Brynn's head flops to her knees. "Not enough action in there? I knew there wouldn't be."

Luke gives her an exasperated look that plainly says, "Come on," and I wonder if they're on the same page about being at this party.

"Brynn's, uh, a little sick," I say, and it's kind of funny to watch Luke and Greta both step back at once.

"Is this weird for you?" Luke asks, squinting at me.

"A little," I say, Brynn apparently not hearing. "But we can't have her pass out on the porch by herself now, can we?"

Greta shakes her head. "You're a better person than I am."

They both step past us. "See you inside," Luke says, with a wave over his shoulder.

I hope Brynn will just sit quietly—where *is* Hunter anyway?—but no such luck. She picks her head up and her face is totally tear-stained. "Ellie, I'm so sorry."

"We've addressed that already," I say, wondering what I have to do for her to stop bringing this up. "We're okay."

"But I don't want you thinking I'm a man stealer," she says, and I wonder if the tears are going to freeze to her face. "I didn't move in on him just to take him from you. I love Hunter. I've always loved him. Since we were kids. I never had the guts to tell him until . . ."

"You found out I was going to sleep with him," I finish. "And then you probably sent that info in to The Buzz, right?"

That's all I need to say. Brynn's flat-out sobbing. "I'm such a terrible person."

I don't respond with anything since nothing seems to appease her anyway, and suddenly, she's clutching my arm so I have to look right at her. "He said you guys were done and you knew it," she says between sobs.

I shake my head. Of course he'd lie about it.

"And even though I figured out he lied . . . I just can't help it. I really love Hunter. Like, truly love him. I wouldn't have tried to get between you guys if I didn't. You need to know that."

Two months ago, I probably would've yelled at her, "And I *didn't* love him?" But looking at her right here, wracked with shuddering sobs and her hair sticking to her face, I don't hate her. In fact, I almost feel sorry for her. And a little sorry for myself, too, since the cold air is cutting through my sweater right now.

I give her an awkward pat on the back and she rests her head on my shoulder. Okay, I wasn't going for that level of friendliness, but I don't push her off because it makes her stop talking. Instead, she's finally quiet. And by the time Hunter comes out, stripped down to his undershirt, my hands and face are completely numb, and Brynn's fast asleep.

"I think I cleaned it all up," he says. "Thank you for sitting with her."

"You're welcome," I say, steadying Brynn as I stand up.

Hunter puts his hands under her arms and lifts her up. "Come on, Brynn, I'm going to take you home."

Brynn makes some kind of unintelligible noise as Hunter wraps her arm around his shoulders.

I hand him a plastic bag. "Better safe than sorry," I say.

"Seriously, Ellie," Hunter says. "You really didn't have to do this."

"No, I didn't. But this seemed like the better option than cleaning up the puke."

"Well, you chose wisely," Hunter says, shaking his head. He leads Brynn down the stairs toward the driveway. "See you Monday."

"See you," I say.

It's strange, but as I watch them walk away, I realize that for the first time in a long time, I don't feel a pang of sadness or anger as they go. In fact, I don't feel much of anything.

But that could be because I'm frozen solid. With that, I head back into the fray.

CHAPTER 16

When I get inside, I check my phone, thinking three hours must have passed since I arrived, but no, I've only been here a little over an hour. How is that even possible? I mean, I've ingested half a beer with the football team, passed out food to the drunken masses, and helped out an undeserving ex in need. Surely that's way more than one night's worth of action for the average person.

"Agresti!"

I spin around and see Luke and Greta sitting on the stairs in the living room. Luke has a beer, but Greta is empty-handed, and they're also sitting a step apart, and not next to each other. There's a definite chilly vibe going on between them and I almost regret plopping down on the stair below Greta.

"I didn't take you for a partier," Luke says. I notice he's wearing a sweater instead of his usual T-shirt. It's navy and makes him seem more broad-shouldered than usual and makes his eyes look really blue.

Not that that means anything to me.

"I, uh, decided to branch out," I say, looking around the room and hoping Greta doesn't think I was just checking out her boyfriend.

"By helping the inebriated?" Greta laughs.

"I definitely didn't plan on that," I say, shaking my head. "But I will say seeing Brynn projectile vomit was a cautionary tale for the evening."

Luke leans back on the stair. "So you haven't been drinking?"

"No. The football team gifted me with a beer, but it started to make me feel a little, uh, not-so-good myself so I stopped."

"And you threw some grocery shopping in there?" Greta asks, pointing at my bag.

"Actually, I was helping Alisha out before that. You know, picking up empty bottles and cans and stuff."

"Hon," Greta says, patting my shoulder. "It's a party. You should have fun, not work your ass off. And you definitely shouldn't be sitting outside without a coat."

I'm surprised how warm she comes off when she says this, and not sarcastic. Then she stands up. "I'm gonna bail. I told Ginger I'd pick her up at five for Vermont tomorrow."

"Oh, right," Luke says, shaking the faraway look from his eyes. "Okay."

Greta merely squeezes his knee when she climbs down the stairs. I half expect Luke to stand up and grab her hand to kiss her goodbye or something, but he just stays where he is on the step.

We both watch Greta leave, and literally as she's walking out the door, A.J. comes in with a tall guy in a beanie who I'm pretty sure is his friend Patrick. I'm kind of relieved to see him, since I'm not really sure what I should say to Luke at the moment.

"Yo," A.J. says, spotting us on the stairs, as Patrick makes a beeline for the living room keg. "What'd I miss?"

I roll my eyes. "Some minor drama involving the result of too much wine, but nothing much aside from that."

A.J. looks confused, but doesn't say anything. "I smell something cooking. Where can I get some of that? I'm starving."

"Alisha's in the kitchen making appetizers and—"

"Great!" A.J. says, his face lighting up. With that, he practically sprints into the kitchen.

"Was it something I said?" I say.

Luke laughs and takes a sip of his beer. "Yeah, I think it was 'appetizers.'"

We sit in silence for a few minutes, surveying the scene. We can see the beer pong action from our perch, and Bryce and Anthony are apparently dominating, if their constant whooping is any indication.

"Want some help picking up empties?" Luke asks. He shakes his empty beer can and throws it in my bag.

"Uh, sure," I say.

We pick ourselves off the stairs and roam around the living room, which is now loud and crowded, grabbing cans and bottles.

"Did everything end up okay out there?" Luke asks. "I saw Hunter leave."

"It was fine," I say, thunking an empty beer bottle into my bag. "If you don't count the sobbing and begging to be forgiven stuff. Just a typical Friday night, you know?"

"Agresti," Luke says seriously, making me stop what I'm doing and look right at him. "We're at a party, right?"

"Well, it's certainly not home ec," I say, glancing around the boisterous room.

His face breaks into a broad grin, and he looks more like his old self than he has since he got here. "Then let's have some fun."

It's hard not to smile back, though I'm not exactly sure what he means by this. "Okay, but . . . Alisha. I told her I'd hang out with her."

Luke sets down an empty beer bottle on the fireplace mantel and surprises me by setting my garbage bag down and grabbing my hand. "Come on," he says, leading me toward the kitchen.

Alisha is arranging some mini pizza bagels on a cookie sheet, and she's surrounded by other plates full of hot appetizers. A.J. is leaning on the counter, practically drooling as he surveys the sea of hot goodies.

"Hey, guys!" Alisha says. "Want some snackage?"

Luke grabs a mini hot dog with one hand, his other still clasped around mine. I decide that if my face is red, it's because the kitchen is still overly warm from the oven being on. "Delicious," he declares as he munches down the hot dog in one bite. "Now, Alisha, don't you want to enjoy your party?"

Her brow furrows. "It would be nice to get out of this kitchen for a little bit, even if it's just to survey the damage."

"I'll totally watch the apps for you, yo!" A.J. says, popping off the counter. "Like, I can make sure no one gets more than me."

Alisha smiles at him, touching his arm. "You rock, A.J. I owe you one."

A.J.'s face turns bright red and I wonder if he maybe likes Alisha more than mini hot dogs.

Luke then takes Alisha's hand and leads us both out to the living room.

"Oh my god, it's a mess," Alisha says, scrunching her eyes shut.

"Don't worry about that now. We'll help you clean up," Luke says. "Now, who's up for beer pong?"

"Oh, I'm not drinking anymore," I say just as Alisha adds, "I have to stay sober in case the cops come."

"Not a problem," Luke says. "You guys can play with soda. We'll find someone else drinking beer, and we'll have an even match."

I expect Alisha to balk, but she suddenly brightens. "I know just the person," she says, pointing to Willow, who's just walked in. "Hey, Willow!" she says, waving her over.

Willow dances over in time to the rap song that's blasting over the speakers. "What's up, y'all?"

"Want to be my partner for beer pong?" Alisha asks.

Willow rips her coat off and throws it over a chair. "Bring it on!"

"This is hardly a fair fight," Luke says, his eyes twinkling.

"What, you think just because I'm small I can't keep up with a giant like you?" Willow says, pushing up her sleeves.

"Wellllll," Luke says with a shrug.

"She can totally hold her own," Alisha says, nodding enthusiastically.

"This I gotta see," Luke says as he sets to work clearing the cups off the table and Alisha replaces them with new ones. They then fill some of the cups with soda and others with beer. Luke and I stand at one end of the table and Alisha pretends to glare at us from the other end.

"You guys ready to get creamed?" Luke says.

"In your dreams, Burke," Alisha retorts, and Willow high-fives her.

Luke rests his hands on my shoulders and looks straight into my eyes. "Don't let me down, Agresti. I'm counting on you and your sobriety to anchor us. I had no idea Willow apparently drinks like a pirate, and now I'm scared."

I can't help but laugh.

"Look at you, all loosey-goosey," he says, shaking his head, but he winks at me.

I've never played beer pong and it shows in my first few attempts at landing a ball in a cup. Most bounce off the table. Or don't even hit the table and just whack people standing nearby.

"It's okay," Luke says, nudging me in the side with his elbow. "Sometimes it takes a while to become at one with the cups."

"All right, Buddha," I snort.

Alisha is, distressingly, awesome. She lands almost every one of her shots, and if she wasn't so damn nice, I'd have to hate her for it. And Willow comes as advertised. On the few shots Luke lands, she chugs her cups of beer defiantly and still maintains an air of sobriety. She's also a pretty good shot herself.

This, however, means Luke and I are drinking a lot. By the end of the first game, which Alisha and Willow of course win, I'm getting jittery from caffeine and sugar. Luke, probably because he's so tall, doesn't seem that buzzed.

"Rematch?" Luke yells across the table.

Willow points back at him with a determined "You're on!"

A.J. appears then with a tray of the appetizers and offers them to us.

"How's it going?" he wants to know as he scarfs down a pizza bagel.

"Pretty terrible," I sigh.

"Nonsense. Agresti is learning as she goes," Luke says, putting his arm around me. I try not to think about how nice this feels, and chalk up this gesture to the alcohol finally kicking in for him.

"Ooh, ooh!" A.J. says, placing the tray on the table. "Try throwing more on an upward angle and then aim down." He pantomimes throwing and I follow his lead, and amazingly, this seems to work. I fire at a cup and actually manage to get the ball in.

"Eeeeeee!" I say, jumping up and down. Luke gives me a double high five and even Alisha and Willow clap their hands delightedly.

Alisha's incredible aim still kills us, but at least I land two shots in the next game. Luke, exhibiting signs of buzzdom, collapses dramatically into a chair next to the table as Willow and Alisha do a victory dance to the Jay-Z song blaring from the living room.

"If you all will excuse me for a bit, I need to get my dance on," Willow says, boogying into the living room.

"I will never underestimate anyone's drinking ability again. Even if they are under five feet tall," Luke says, chugging a big cup of water. I stand in front of him and jokingly fan him with a place mat.

"Are we throwing in the towel?" I ask, and the weirdest thing happens. Luke looks up from his cup and his eyes lock on mine with such an intensity that I feel it—like I've been hit by a burning cattle prod on the inside. Then, ever so slightly, his knee brushes mine. And I think it's intentional. It catches me off guard so much that I stop fanning. I don't even know what to say or what to do, but I do know—

"You guys gotta stay," A.J. says, making me jump. "I wanna play you!"

"I'll be your partner!" Alisha pipes up with a big smile.

"Great," A.J. squeaks, his ears turning pink. He totally likes her.

So now we definitely have to keep playing. There's no way I can let my terrible aim and Luke's growing drunkenness stand in the way of a possible love connection. Especially since I'm glad it diverts from the cattle-prod feeling inside me because I don't even know what to do with that.

Luke raises his eyebrows at me and grins. "I guess we're gonna keep going."

"I guess we're gonna lose again," I laugh, as Alisha and A.J. bring in new cups on their side.

Luke stands up and his smile gets bigger. We're so close, our sweaters are trading static electricity. Like, if I were to touch him right now, we'd get zapped with a shock. "We're having fun, right?"

I nod.

"Good," he says. Then he leans his face a little closer to mine. "And I haven't told you this yet, but you, uh, look really nice tonight."

I feel the heat rising to my face and pretend to study my outfit so he can't see it. "Oh, thanks. So do you. Navy's, uh, your color."

"Is that so?" he says, straightening up and making his chest puff out. "Well then, I guess we make a good-looking pair, huh?"

My heart is racing. And I really don't think it's the caffeine.

Two hours later, Luke and I have finally won a game of beer pong (though I think Alisha and A.J., who seem to have a growing flirty vibe going on, took pity on us and let us win), the crowd has thinned out, and we've cleaned up and bagged most of the bottles and cans, which are now ready for the recycling facility. And all that soda I drank has made me majorly, majorly hyper.

"How can we be that bad at beer pong, Luke?" I squeal as we leave Alisha's house. "Oh my god, it's cold!" My heart is hammering and my hands are shaking, but I'm way giggly. There's no way I'm sleeping tonight, thanks to all that sugar. Maybe I should've stuck with the alcohol after all.

Luke cups his hands around his mouth and yells/sings, "Weeeeee aren't the champions, my friehennnd."

I whack him in the arm, unable to control my laughter. "You're going to wake the dead."

"Yeah, singing's not my specialty," Luke says. "Nor is throwing Ping-Pong balls into cups. But I kind of suck at basketball, too, so it makes sense. My little brother says that even though I'm tall, I don't look like a basketball player. What does that even mean?"

"Who needs to look like a basketball player anyway?" I say, skipping in front of him. "Especially when you're what Almanzo Wilder is supposed to look like!" What am I thinking? Oh, wait, I'm not. It's the overabundance of sweetened caffeine I ingested talking.

Luke stops in his tracks and laughs so hard that he doubles over, resting his hands on his knees. "Who is *that*?"

"You know, from the *Little House* books."

"And I look like this guy?" he says, wiping his eyes.

"No, you should."

"I am so confused right now," Luke says, and he starts laughing again. "I just hope it's a good thing."

"It is, I think," I say, giggling. "I had a crush on him. At least the one I had pictured in my mind." I realize what I've just said, and before Luke can register that, I babble on, "And then I got into my Weather Channel anchorman stage."

"You had crushes on anchormen?" he says, and it looks like he's on the verge of cracking up again.

"And reporters! Those guys who go out into the crazy weather and report from the middle of hurricanes and stuff? I found that really hot when I was twelve."

There's no hope now. Luke is doubled over again. "Man, Agresti, you're on fire tonight."

"Well, maybe not so much in the beer pong department," I say.

"We all have our talents. You and I just aren't going to take the beer pong circuit by storm in college is all," Luke says, wiping his eyes. Then he looks up. "So, weather expert. There's a ring around the moon. Does that mean anything?"

I study the almost-full moon. There's a giant halo surrounding it and it's quite gorgeous.

"It's ice crystals," I say, noticing I can see my breath in the moonlight. I can also see the natural highlights of Luke's hair. "It means it might warm up a bit, thank god."

"Damn, I was hoping for snow," Luke says. "But does it have any other meanings? Like, is it an omen?"

"That's my mom's territory, not mine. She's into all that new age stuff," I say. Then I cringe, remembering how that bothered Hunter so much.

But Luke surprises me when he replies, "That's so cool. Does she have crystals and stuff? My aunt has a whole bunch of those around her house."

"Oh, she has crystals, all right. And incense. And tarot cards."

"So, your mom likes to read into the future . . . and you like to predict the weather," he says. His eyes go wide like he's just discovered the theory of relativity or something.

He's pretty cute when he's drunk.

"You might be onto something. Oh my god, it's so friggin' cold!" I hug myself to try to retain some body heat.

"Come on, you're wearing like three layers of clothes—no way you're that cold. I'll race you to that stop sign," he says, pointing up ahead. "That can warm you up."

Then he takes off with no warning.

"No fair! You don't need a head start. Your legs are like an entire foot longer than mine," I yell, but do my best to catch up. The only problem is, I'm laughing so hard I start coughing and have to stop. Luke jogs back toward me and pounds me on the back, to aid with my coughing.

"You're such a gentleman," I cough-laugh.

"And don't you forget it," he says. His hand lingers on my back and even through I'm wearing "three layers of clothes," a charge goes through me, and it makes me nervous. So, when my coughing subsides, I skip ahead, and pretty soon we're at Luke's street. I stop, but Luke keeps walking. "Nope, I am walking you home."

"But it's freezing," I say, hopping up and down, but I feel the soda bubbles expanding in my stomach and I stop. "I can make it home fine by myself."

Luke looks at me over his shoulder. "I couldn't live with myself if something happened to you on the way home."

Now I burst out laughing. "Here? Yeah, I think the only thing I can be abducted by is aliens."

"Okay, I couldn't live with myself if you got abducted by aliens on the way home."

I'm kind of touched by this, but I'm still feeling silly. "The JAILE family would be down one person! The horrors!"

"Ah, you got me," he says, throwing his hands up. "I'd miss you too much. But then I'd just put a wig on Isaiah and pretend he was you."

I'm overtaken with cough-laughs again, and pretty soon Luke is laughing so hard he can't speak, either. I seriously can't remember the last time I had this much fun. By the time we get to my house,

I'm actually bummed. I never would've guessed that all those hours ago, when I was ready to hurl my mirror out the window.

I climb up the front porch stairs and look down at Luke. "If you ever want to be beer pong partners again, all you have to do is ask."

Luke laughs. "I'm flattered, especially since I, uh, let a four-foot-eleven girl out-drink me."

"Winning isn't everything, you know," I say, and mockingly wag my finger at him.

"Except in class, where we have to beat out Jared's group and Hunter's group," he says, stepping closer to the porch.

"Exactly." I smile at him and he steps up on the bottom stair of the porch, and we're almost even, height-wise. His eyes lock on mine, like they did at the party, and I'm suddenly nervous. I'm not sure what's going on here, if it's the giddiness of the night or the caffeine or the moonlight, but it feels like he's going to kiss me. And I'm surprised that I want him to kiss me. No, I'm not surprised, I get it. I like him.

There it is. I like him.

But he has a girlfriend. A girlfriend who, if I remember correctly, stated, "You're a better person than I am" earlier. And good people don't think about kissing another girl's boyfriend. Especially when they know how much it hurts to have another girl move in on your man.

"Agresti, can I—"

But I step back. "Don't."

Luke's brow furrows. "Don't what?"

"Don't say what I think you're going to say. Because I don't think I could say no."

"Damn, I guess I'm that transparent in wanting to kiss you, huh?" he says, running a hand through his hair and looking down.

The cattle-prod feeling comes rushing back, pulsating under my ribs, and my heart almost explodes right there.

"You have a girlfriend," I say. It practically makes my throat ache making that come out.

Luke smiles softly. "No, I don't. Greta and I broke up."

I blink hard. "When? At the party?"

"We came to the party as friends. We broke up a week ago," he says. "I've known for a while that I was having feelings for someone else, and I should've done it sooner." He tugs at the bottom of my coat when he says this.

I want to believe him. But this all just seems convenient. Why would Greta go to a party with her recent ex? I didn't even want to be in the same classroom as Hunter, let alone spend my free time with him.

Luke must take my silence for doubt because he sighs. "I was going to wait a little longer before I said anything to you, but I really had a great time with you tonight and I'd like more of that to happen. Sooner than later."

Why? Why is he saying all this and looking so damn good in the light of my front porch? But then I suddenly flash back to the pained expression on Brynn's face before. "He said you guys were done and you knew it."

But Luke isn't Hunter.

Luke steps up to the step below me and now I'm back to being shorter than him again. It's like the air between us is crackling with some unseen fire because I realize I'm not even cold anymore.

"Do you, uh, like me?" he asks quietly.

I bite my lip. My heart is hammering and I know if I deny it, I'm still going to die of a heart attack on these steps and it would give my feelings away anyway. "I like you. A lot." His face lights up when I say this.

"So, what do we do about that?" he asks, closing the gap of space between us by leaning in toward me slightly.

I can feel my pulse throbbing in my throat and I'm wondering if my blood ("Yes! Kiss him! Do thisssss!") is trying to override my brain ("Isn't it a little convenient that he's saying they just broke up?"). "Whatever we do, I think we have to give the breakup a little more breathing room, okay? I felt like shit seeing Hunter and Brynn together right after we broke up, and I don't want Greta to feel that way."

Luke nods, and stops leaning. There's still maybe, like, only a centimeter between us, though. "Okay, how long?"

He's so close I can see the porch sconce perfectly reflected in his eyes. "Well, I don't want Greta to go through what I did on The Buzz, either. Or you and me being made out to be a cheater and a home-wrecker or whatever BS Jared would concoct. So long enough for that to not be an issue."

"But we know that's not the case," Luke says, his brow furrowing. "And I'm pretty sure Jared's terrified of Greta, so he wouldn't go after her."

Luke isn't Hunter.

"Still. We should at least give it a few weeks."

"A few weeks, okay," he says, gently taking a lock of hair that's been trapped in front of my face by my knit hat. He expertly tucks it behind my ear, and I feel a rush of heat on that side of my face.

As if on reflex, I reach up and clutch Luke's hand. He squeezes my cold fingertips, then shoves each of my hands in the front pockets of my coat. He rubs my arms up and down, as if trying to warm me up, and I finally lean completely into him. One, because it feels nice. Two, because he's so warm and it's cold as hell.

"I'm always saving you from frostbite, Agresti," he says with a grin. Then he wrinkles his nose and looks so adorable that I feel my stomach get all warm, in a much better way than when the beer hit it before. "This is going to be a rough few weeks. I want to kiss you so bad right now."

He isn't Hunter. He isn't Hunter. He isn't Hunter.

I take a deep breath and look up at the sky, as if seeking permission from a higher power. I don't know that I get an answer, but I know my willpower is almost at nil. "I think maybe we can make a provision for that. You know, like a test-drive."

Luke's eyes twinkle and he lowers his face ever so closer to mine. "And when does this test-drive start?"

I can't take it anymore, I pull him by the open edges of his coat so now there's absolutely no space between us, and he takes that as his cue to cup my face in his hands. Then, his lips brush mine, gently at first, then a little more insistent.

Good lord, he's a wonderful kisser, not shoving his tongue down my throat in a slobbery fashion, like Hunter did the first time. And I may even enjoy the feeling of his stubble against my chin. It's sweet and warm and this is how first kisses are supposed to be. There's so much electricity zapping through me, I could probably power all of downtown Ringvale Heights right now.

"I don't know how I'm going to wait to do that again," he says when he pulls away.

"Are you kidding me? We're doing it again right now," I say, pulling him down by his coat collar and planting one on him. He wraps his arms around my waist and it feels so ridiculously right.

I suddenly hear footsteps approaching behind me in the house and I leap away from Luke just as the front door creaks open. Mom comes out with her car keys and purse, and I remember she has to pick up Dad from work. She jumps when she sees me standing there. "You just took ten years off my life," she gasps, clutching her hand to her chest. Then she notices Luke on the steps and her eyes go huge.

"ThisismyfriendLuke," I blabber, not knowing what else to say.

"Hey, Mrs. Agresti," Luke says, with a little wave.

"Nice to meet you," Mom says warmly, and I can tell from the sudden apologetic tone in her voice that she thinks something just happened between him and me.

"He walked me home from Alisha's," I say.

"Well, that was very nice of you," Mom says, giving Luke a big smile.

"It was no problem," Luke says, shifting his weight from one foot to another.

"He didn't want me to get abducted by aliens," I say, hoping that adding something funny might make my mom not think I was just engaging in serious smooching.

"Regardless," Mom says. "It's nice to know my daughter has friends who look out for her."

"Well," Luke says, stepping down off the stair and looking directly at me, "she is pretty awesome, you know?"

I pray my mom can't see how hard I'm blushing in the weak porch light.

"Yeah, she's all right," Mom says, patting my cheek.

Luke starts to back away, and, feeling bad that my mom broke this up, I blurt out, "I had a really good time tonight!"

"Me too," he says as he walks off. "See you Monday!"

See you Monday? After those kisses? Then I remember my "in a few weeks" rule. And then I have a sudden pang of longing because I don't know that I can wait that long to kiss him again.

I expect Mom to say something like, "So you're a total liar," but she merely yanks my hat off and ruffles my hair before she moves off the porch.

But just as she gets to the car she turns around and raises an eyebrow at me.

"That must've been some game night, huh?"

I try not to look too deer-in-the-headlights and just shrug while laughing nervously. Then I turn around quickly and let myself into the house, where I may or may not flop onto my bed and sigh the sigh of a girl who's just been kissed by the dreamiest guy she's ever met.

CHAPTER 17

My euphoria is short-lived, because it's kind of hard to sleep when you're not sure if you're a home-wrecker or not.

Like, Luke says he broke up with Greta to be with me. Isn't that what Hunter did to me to be with Brynn? Is Greta feeling all those horrible things that I felt right now? Because of me?

And then I think about how amazing it was kissing Luke last night and I don't want to care about being labeled a home-wrecker. But I still do.

I debate calling Jodie, but I know she's still in mourning over USC and that she's probably not feeling better about it today. When our favorite singer, T.J. Choi, left the boy band InSyte to become an organic dairy farmer, she was sad for weeks—and he was nowhere near as important to her as a degree from USC's School of Cinematic Arts.

Plus, I feel weird dangling this in front of her, like I'm being insensitive or something. "I know your college plans are all screwed up and you're depressed but look how much fun I'm having!"

So I get out of bed and stare into my mirror as I pull my hair into a ponytail. I certainly don't think I look like a home-wrecker, especially when my pajama pants have surfing cats on them. Surely an interloping harlot would have a more, uh, smutty wardrobe.

I check my phone and notice I have three texts: one from Alisha, thanking me for helping her clean up and saying she owes me a drink at Starbucks; one from Willow jokingly asking if I'm still sore from my beer pong "beatdown" (and admitting that she has a killer headache); and one from A.J. to the JAILE family, a photo of Jared passed out on Alisha's couch. Someone had replaced his beret with a lace doily, and Alisha's giving him bunny ears.

That none of them mentions anything about Luke and me is a good start. I must've kept my feelings off my face last night.

I'd texted Luke before I went to sleep, See you Monday? That's all??? with a wink-y face emoji.

So when I'm brushing my teeth and my phone dings, my heart does a little cartwheel when I see it's a text from him. His reply is the toothy-grin emoji, followed by a bike and flower emoji.

Use your words, Burke, I write back with a smiley face of my own.

Use your front door, Agresti, he replies.

I glance up in confusion, then quickly peer out the bathroom window, which overlooks the front yard. Luke is straddling his bike on the sidewalk, staring at his phone.

My stomach takes off in a flight of butterflies as I run down the stairs and grab my coat. My parents just left to sell some of our basement stuff at a flea market, so I don't have to worry about them seeing this. When I step outside, there's a single sunflower laid on the railing of the porch.

I narrow my eyes playfully at Luke, who's still on the sidewalk. I hope my face doesn't look as doofily delighted as I feel. "Is this like a floral version of ding-dong ditch?"

"More like a romantic gesture," he says.

"Then why are you all the way out there?" I ask.

"Just following the Agresti Rules. By my calculations we have, like, a few more weeks before we can, uh, give each other flowers in public."

I lean on the porch railing and glance up and down my street. No one else we go to school with lives on this block, so I think we're safe. "Well, maybe I'm going to add another provision that says Saturdays don't count when it comes to private kissing."

Luke leaps off his bike, tosses it on the lawn, and in seemingly one stride makes it to the porch. He's standing in front of me and I suddenly feel shy. I make a big show of smelling the sunflower and looking at him over its giant petals.

"Are you hungover at all?" is all I can think to say.

"Hell yes, but seeing you makes me feel a thousand times better."

"So I'm like Alka-Seltzer," I say, unable to contain my smile.

"Better," Luke says.

I peek up and down the street, then lower the sunflower. "We've only got thirteen kissing hours left in this Saturday. Maybe we should make the most of—"

I can't even get the "them" out, because Luke wraps his arms around me, lifts me up so we're eye level. Then he glances down at my pajama pants.

"Whoa, are those surfing cats?"

I kiss him in response.

Being secretly involved with someone is a lot harder than I thought. No one tells you that you're going to be thinking about this person all day, and yet you have to pretend like you're totally meh about them when you're in their presence. Especially when you just happen to be exiting a classroom together and his ex passes by and they say hi to each other and her eyes light up, happy to see him. Or when you sit in front of him at an assembly and can only smile at each other. Or when your school's resident gossip blogger has a front-row seat for the only class you share together.

For instance, when we're in class and making cinnamon pretzels, standing right next to each other at the counter, I want so badly for our arms to brush, but Luke is—maddeningly—keeping his elbows tucked into his side as he braids the dough.

I sigh involuntarily.

"What's wrong?" Isaiah says as he dries a freshly washed bowl.

I want to grab Luke and drag him into the pantry so I can run my hands through his hair and kiss him till I'm completely out of breath. What I say is, "This day is dragging."

"Not enough action for you, Agresti?" Luke says, not making eye contact with me.

"I've had more exciting afternoons," I say, as boredly as possible. Only after I've said it do I realize it sounds like I'm referring to the afternoons of the last few days where Luke and I find a quiet place and make out like there's no tomorrow. I decided we could see each other super secretly until it's safe to "go public" and Luke seems more than okay with it.

I see the dimple appear in Luke's left cheek and realize he's trying not to laugh.

I go to grab the dish soap, and as I do, my fingers accidentally brush the top of Luke's hand, which is resting on the counter. His mouth drops open, as if he's jokingly scandalized by this action, but then his eyes soften and he gives me a small, incredibly hot smile, and I can't help it when a giggle escapes.

Of course, that little moment somehow caught Jared's attention, and his face is scrunched up in concentration, as if trying to figure out what he just saw.

Crap.

Quickly, I contort my face into something I hope doesn't scream "flirty." And I make sure to ignore Luke the rest of class.

I'm still thinking about that an hour later while proofreading tomorrow's RHHS TV script. According to Luke, Greta is heading out for some kind of training for a week so if Jared does sniff something out, she'll at least be in Canada and won't have to see Luke and me for a few days. My phone buzzes then, and it's a text from Luke: Risking your phone's battery life to see if you want to meet at 4:30 at the skate park.

Worth the risk. See you there, I text back. I don't realize I'm grinning till I hear Alisha say, "Someone's happy the day's over!"

I quickly stash my phone in my hoodie's pocket. "Yeah, it's been dragging."

Alisha crouches down next to me, smiling excitedly. "Well, this is top secret, but I've got to tell you. The weather reporter position is opening up! Chris and Mia are going to ask you if you want the job."

My eyes must bug out in alarm because Alisha squeezes my arm. "Only if you want the gig. They won't pressure you. And you'll have some time to think about it because you wouldn't start till Thanksgiving week."

I slump back in my chair. Doing reports every now and then is one thing, but a daily gig? That's live? That just seems . . . absolutely terrifying. But Alisha is looking at me so hopefully that I can't bear to let her down. And I can't deny that taking the job would probably make Brynn and Kim and Hunter's heads explode. "I will. Think about it, that is. And thank you for warning me and giving me time to prepare."

She smiles at me, but then her brow furrows. She glances over her shoulder, as if making sure no one's in earshot. "There's something else I wanted to ask."

"You're not going to ask me to be an anchorperson, I hope," I say with a nervous laugh.

"No, uh, is something happening between you and Luke? I mean, if so, I think that's awesome, and you don't have to, like, tell me anything. But a post just went up on The Buzz you might want to know about. It makes it sound like Luke cheated on Greta with you."

Good lord, Jared works fast. I feel myself force maybe the fakest smile in the history of fake smiles. "No, we're just friends. Jared's probably just still pissed at me from a couple weeks ago when I insinuated that he's balding."

Alisha nods. "Well, maybe he needs to get better at making up his stupid lies, too. Anyway, I thought I'd warn you, just in case."

"Thanks," I say. Then I have to fake a few minutes of enthusiastic conversation about our history class before I can't take it anymore and pretend to check the time on my phone. "Oh, crap, I have to meet my mom." I bid Alisha a quick farewell, gather my stuff, and hightail it out of the studio, then duck into an empty stairwell to load up The Buzz. And there it is, the latest post.

Cheaters Never Win

Was this snow bunny done dirty by her beau? Sources say a new lady love might have blown up their *amore*, resulting in an out-of-nowhere dumping. Sounds Fish-y to us.

A full-on garden of thorny angst blooms in my stomach then, to the point that I have to sit on the stairs and catch my breath. This has to be made up. Luke wouldn't lie about this.

Then I have another momentary freak out: What if Greta's already looking for me to tell me off? Or worse? How is this even happening?

When I've gotten my heart rate down, I creep out the back exit, and as I round the corner of the building toward the street that leads to the skate park, I see two girls sitting on the curb. One has her head on her knees and the other is rubbing her back as if she's comforting her. I'm briefly worried that a stomach bug has hit campus, but then the one girl lifts her head, and I almost do a double take. It's Greta, her blonde hair free from its braids, all wild and curly today. Her face is tear-stained and her eyes swollen from crying. It's so jarring to see her this beaten down and vulnerable that my first instinct when seeing her is pity, not out-and-out fear.

"But why would he do this to me?" she says in gasping sobs. "Doesn't he know what I did for him? Why would he lie?"

My heart sinks all the way down to my ankles as the words from The Buzz post practically float in front of me. *Done dirty.*

"He's an asshole, that's why," her friend says, rubbing her back. "And a stupid one, clearly. Like he didn't think you'd find out."

Greta wipes her eyes with the back of her hand and shakes her head. "I mean, he's with *her*? And then lies to me about it? What the actual fuck?"

"We could kill her," her friend says with a snort.

"I'm not going to rule it out. I wish I wasn't going away because I'd kill him first."

Greta may say more, but all I can hear is the pounding of my own pulse in my ears. I don't know if it's fear that Greta's going to slaughter me, or knowing that I'm about to start crying myself, but my feet seem to realize this is a situation I don't need to be part of and steer me back the way I came.

The back of my throat starts to burn and I can't tell if I'm about to start crying or scream or both. How could he? Luke Burke, the one who is supposed to be nice, is just like every other dude out there with a dream to get with as many girls as humanly possible.

This is exactly what I didn't want. And now I'm in it. And I'm the Brynn in this scenario. And I'm probably going to get murdered by Greta.

I get a few blocks from school when tears start burning my eyes.

I promptly blink them back. I'm not going to be sad about this. Been there, done that, got the T-shirt. No, I'm not going to be the depressed victim again.

I stomp to the skate park, my eyes darting around as I head to the back of the building, to a maple tree that's brimming with burning red leaves. We just kissed under this tree yesterday—and all I could think then was how perfect it all was.

The door creaks open and Luke saunters out, his eyes meeting mine in a way that on other days I'd describe as "flirty" but today it makes my stomach turn.

"Couldn't stay away, huh?" Luke says, smiling devilishly.

"You lied to me."

He wiggles his eye brows suggestively. "Okay, you got me. I don't like the smell of your shampoo. I *love* it. Drives me crazy."

He thinks I'm kidding.

"Knock it off," I snap, and his face sobers. "Did you think I wouldn't find out? That I'm stupid or something?"

"Find out what?" He folds his arms, which I know is body language for guilt.

"I saw Greta today. Crying. And from the sounds of it, you guys weren't exactly as broken up as you made it out to be."

Now Luke's eyes narrow. "I don't know what you heard today, but I can almost bet it's not what you think."

The fact that he'd try to gaslight me on this is amazing. Are all guys my age completely deceitful jerks? Or just the ones I'm attracted to? "I've done this once, and I am sure as hell not going to be on the other side of it," I say.

Luke's face turns a deep shade of red and his jaw clenches. "Why do you think I'm lying?"

"Because it came straight from Greta's mouth," I say, throwing my hands up. "And I saw the way she was looking at you when we were walking in the hall yesterday."

Now Luke's eyes bug out. "The way she was *looking* at me? Seriously?"

"And then there was today's fantastic Buzz item about Greta being done dirty."

"Done dirty? We broke up mutually."

"Or so *you* think," I say.

If it's possible, Luke's face has grown even redder. "Why do you care so much about what that stupid site says? You know Jared's an asshole."

"Maybe because the last time I was the subject of it, all the information was true," I say through clenched teeth.

"Jesus, so you think I'm a liar now?" Luke says, shaking his head. "Listen, Ellie, I know you've been burned before, but I don't know how to make you believe me just because you can't move on."

The fact that he calls me Ellie surprisingly stings. And how can he possibly be turning this around on me? "I'm not apologizing for looking out for myself after what happened with Hunter."

Luke throws his hands up. "Well, maybe that's your problem. You're still living in your last relationship. And I guess maybe we shouldn't do this anymore because I really don't feel like paying for all the bullshit he dumped on you. If you don't trust me, I don't know what more I can do." With that, he turns on his heel, flings the door open, and stomps back inside.

Five days. Is that a new record for a broken heart?

CHAPTER 18

I manage to fake normalcy pretty well the next day. I hang out with Alisha and the TV crew in the morning, eat lunch with Isaiah, and get through a group project in English without anyone being like, "Ellie, are you all right?" Probably because I now basically hold a PhD in not crying in public.

I guess some life skills you don't learn in home ec.

I desperately wanted to tell Jodie about this last night, but she had Chinese class, then said she had to go to some dinner with her parents. So at lunch, I finally text her, Any chance you want to meet up at Starbucks later?

A few minutes later, she replies. Sorry, I have to work today.

And that's it. No rain check. No "come meet me while I'm on my break," which I've done before. Ever since the USC thing, it's felt like she doesn't want to deal with anything—including me. Like, we haven't even seen each other in person since the football game. I'm about to reply with a sad-face emoji and "I miss you," but wonder if that would make her feel guilty. I don't want to do that, so I don't reply.

To ignore the growing feeling of agitation in my stomach, I scroll through The Buzz several times, and there are no more thinly veiled mentions of me being a home-wrecker or Luke being a lying lothario or Greta being tragic and unbraided on the curb. Greta hasn't sent anyone to kill me, either, so that's a bonus.

But I know home ec is going to be a challenge because I'm not sure how Luke is going to act. I don't even know how I'm supposed to act, but as angry as I am, and as many dagger-eyes I want to give him, I have to keep it bottled up. And that just makes me angry with myself. I mean, I'd just gotten to a place where this class was tolerable—likeable, even—and now I've gone and screwed it all up *and* I can't act any differently because I don't want Isaiah and A.J. to catch on. Because I'm not going to jeopardize our position in the class rankings, especially when we're so close to first place.

"What's with all the canned goods?" Isaiah says, noting that our table is stacked with cans of beans and vegetables and tuna. The Bukowskis' table has a bunch of cleaning supplies on it. The Bakers' table is stacked with toothpaste and moisturizer.

Before I can answer, Luke comes in and takes a seat with a neutral "hey" to everyone. I don't make eye contact when I say it back. I do, however, make the mistake of noticing that he's wearing a royal-blue, long-sleeve shirt that probably brings out his eyes to a crazy degree, the fabric hugging his arms and chest in all the right places.

He probably did this on purpose to torture me. To show me what I'm missing. As if I'm the one who masqueraded as a nice guy and lied about not breaking up with their significant other. I force myself to stare at my hands.

And then Mrs. Sanchez saves my life.

"Okay, everyone, today we're going to organize all the PTA donations for the St. Mark's homeless shelter." She gestures at our tables and then at several large boxes on the floor next to her. "Since this isn't our usual class assignment, I'm going to break up the routine a bit and put you in different groups. There won't be any points for this."

A.J. and Isaiah both slump in their seats. Luke stares at the boxes, so I have no idea what he's thinking. I fight really hard to not look relieved, but seriously, this is fantastic news.

"I'll give you a slip with a category on it, and then you'll join everyone else who draws that category," Mrs. Sanchez says, extending a small brown bag toward my table.

Isaiah and A.J. both pull out slips marked "toiletries." Luke gets canned goods. I hold my breath as I pull out a slip marked "cleaning products." I'm so relieved I smile at Mrs. Sanchez, a silent thank-you for sparing me an afternoon of awkwardness.

"All right, cleaning products!" Hunter whoops from behind me.

No.

I spin around in my seat to confirm that we're in the same group, and, sure enough, Hunter is waving around a slip identical to mine. Brynn is frowning at hers, so I'm guessing that means she's not in our group.

Before I have a chance to ask Isaiah or A.J. to switch with me, they've wandered over to the table that has the stacks of tooth-paste. Brynn shuffles over to them, along with Bryce.

I probably shuffle just as slowly to the table that's piled with paper towels, bleach, and laundry detergent . . . where Jared is already standing. We're joined by Hannah, who hasn't said two words to me since Hunter dumped me. I inhale deeply and close my eyes, and when I open them, I see that Luke has landed himself with a girl from Jersey Strong and two girls from the Bakers, and they're already laughing about something.

"Of course," I mutter to myself, trying to ignore the twinge in my stomach.

On our table, there's a clipboard with a chart on it, which we have to fill in with the products we have. It seems like it'll be a good distraction, so I grab it. We work silently for a few minutes, until Jared seemingly gets bored and leans on the table, resting his chin on his hand. Then he grins devilishly, his eyes flitting between Hunter and me. "Is this weird for you guys, working together?"

"No, is it weird for you?" Hunter says with an amount of sarcasm I didn't know he had in him.

"Oh, right, you guys were simpatico at the party," Jared says, tossing a roll of paper towels like a football. "Although I think that might be because *someone* has moved on."

I feel my cheeks flush and I hope the alarm I feel in my gut doesn't register in my eyes. I just glare at him, maddeningly unable to come up with anything to say.

Thankfully, Mrs. Sanchez leaves two boxes next to our table and we can start packing things into them.

I notice that Brynn is bossing her group around, clipboard in hand, pen over her ear. I can hear her condescendingly explaining why she should be in charge of the chart. I lock eyes with A.J., who gestures like he's strangling himself, which gets me to chuckle. But I can't even hear myself over the loud peals of laughter coming from the canned goods table. Luke is pretending a box is so heavy that he can't lift it, delighting his female partners. I exhale through my nose slowly.

"What's the matter, Ellie? Missing certain family members?" Jared asks and sticks out his lower lip in an exaggerated pout.

"Do you, like, even have a life outside of trying to start shit?" Hannah says, narrowing her eyes at Jared, surprising me.

But he's still staring at me.

"Jared, I don't know what your problem—"

"And how's it going here?" Mrs. Sanchez says before I can finish.

"Fantastic!" Jared says.

"Looks like you've got a full box already. Ms. Chow and Mr. Curtis, why don't you follow me and I'll get you situated with some packing tape and labels," Mrs. Sanchez says, waving them toward the front of the room.

"Can we tape Jared's mouth shut, too?" I mutter before I can stop myself, which makes Hunter snort so loud that he clamps a hand over his mouth.

"He's such a dick," Hunter says.

"The biggest," I say.

There's another burst of laughter then from Luke's table—they're all doubled over, giggling about something. Like, who knew canned goods could be so hilarious?

"So, have you gotten your Penn State application in?" Hunter asks as he piles paper towels into another box.

"Last week," I say, grateful for the distraction. "What about you?"

I could be imagining it, but Hunter shifts uncomfortably. He bites his lip and nods. "Princeton, of course. And a couple of other safety schools."

He must be worried he's not going to get accepted to Princeton, and that his family will kill him if he ruins the family legacy and doesn't get in. It's the only thing that would explain that look on his face. But, since I'm not his girlfriend anymore, it's not my business to ask, so I don't say anything.

"I noticed you were late to class yesterday—was that something to do with your other applications? Because I know Ellie Agresti doesn't cut class."

A flicker of annoyance burns through me. We aren't close anymore, and yet he's under the impression that he knows me so well. Even if he is kinda right in this instance, it's irritating that he thinks I'm still the same person I was two months ago.

"Actually, I was interviewing someone for a segment on RHHS TV. And I think they're going to ask me to be the weather forecaster," I say and I look directly at him when I say this, because I know his jaw is going to drop. And it does. Because I guess *I* still know *him*.

"Wow, that's awesome," he says when he recovers. I wait for him to add something vaguely undermine-y like, "I can't believe you're actually working *there*." So I'm shocked when he's like, "You seem really at ease in front of the camera. I bet you'll be great."

"Thanks," I say, almost a little disappointed I can't fight him on this.

"Are you going to have a funny sign-off or anything at the end?"

I wrinkle my nose. "I hadn't really thought about it."

"Oh, come on, you have to!" Hunter says. "Like, 'That's the forecast. I'm Ellie, don't be jelly.'"

It's so bad, I actually can't help it when I chuckle. "Well, I'm definitely not going with that."

Now Hunter laughs. "You're right, it's terrible."

Our laughter has caught the attention of Luke, who's peering at us over his clipboard. When our eyes meet, he quickly diverts his gaze back to his chart. I wish I could say I feel smug in having caught him, but I just feel sort of hollow inside.

Jared, apparently having witnessed this exchange of glances, gives me a smirk from the front of the room, and my feelings of hollowness are replaced with simmering disgust. I don't hurl the roll of paper towels in my hand at him, and I consider that a small victory.

I have to take these wins where I can.

CHAPTER 19

Over the next couple of weeks, Luke and I only speak when necessary, and he's as cool with me as I am with him. It's not easy, but I go out of my way to joke around and be as easygoing as possible with Isaiah and A.J. to try and keep our group dynamic intact. We've even managed to hang on to second place while Synergy has dropped behind us by ten points. It's my one small joy right now.

But apparently, I'm not getting an Oscar anytime soon, because my mom's asked if I'm okay at least three times, and then, one day at lunch, Isaiah looks up from the book he's reading about the race-horse Seabiscuit and fixes me with a solemn stare.

"Are you and Luke fighting or something?" he asks.

I squeeze my eyes shut. Crap. I know I can't deny it because Isaiah has clearly seen the tension between us and he's not dumb. But I don't want to make it anymore soap opera than it already is. "I'm sorry, is it making things awkward for you and A.J.?"

Isaiah wrinkles his nose. "We're big boys, we can handle it. I just wondered if, you know, you were okay. You've seemed sad."

I give him my most hopeful smile. "Without getting into it, I'm okay, and thanks for asking. And if it does make things weird for you guys, tell me, okay? I don't want to mess up our group. I'm trying to keep it normal."

"Like I said, we can handle it. It's just that you guys . . . oh, never mind." He looks back down at his book and I'm not sure if I'm supposed to prod him about finishing his thought. Since it's Isaiah, I decide to let it go. But I do wonder what he was going to say.

I pretend to be deeply interested in my French homework, but I'm distracted. Have I really seemed sad? I've tried to make a point to not wallow, but I guess I'm not that great at hiding my emotions. Though, I thought if anything, I'd probably come across angry or at the very least peeved. But, somehow, I'm projecting sadness? To the point where the quietest person in my life feels the need to ask if I'm okay?

I . . . don't know that I want to think about that.

I *do* know it can't help that I haven't even been able to talk to Jodie about it. I've only seen her once, at a bowling birthday party for our St. Catherine's friend Audra, and she was weirdly in this super-enthusiastic state, which, after having known her the last nine years, I knew was totally put-on.

"You hanging in there?" I'd asked. "I know you're not that jazzed about bowling-alley pizza."

"Should I not be okay?" she'd shot back. It was confusing because it looked like she was blinking back tears, but her voice was totally angry. So I dropped it.

I silently cursed the fact that USC is a plane ride away, because I'm terrified she's never going to be the same again and I'm about to lose my best friend.

This all means I need to toe the line for the people who are still speaking to me, so when I get to the school laundry room for that day's home ec lesson, I try to smile and be as chipper as possible. Even if I still can't really look Luke in the eye, I make a point to stand next to him as we fold freshly washed towels. He's wearing a T-shirt today, and I notice he's got a sizeable bandage wrapped around his left elbow. I wonder if he got it while training, but I don't have it in me to direct a question to him.

It helps that A.J. is unbelievably grouchy today, grunting responses to questions and downright snarling at Jared, who keeps "accidentally" bumping into our table.

"If he does that one more time, I swear to god," he grumbles.

"Whoa," Luke says, holding his hands up. "Don't give him the satisfaction."

A.J.'s face gets more snarly. "He's being more of a prick than usual."

Jared is on the opposite side of our table, holding court with his group. He's too busy pretending to do a striptease with dish towels to hear A.J.'s comment.

I don't get to think about that too long because Mrs. Sanchez claps her hands together. "Everyone, I have an announcement! The Monday after Thanksgiving, we're going to be doing an in-class Feast-Off. This means you will be responsible for creating your own special occasion menu and those menus have to stick to your budgets."

Luke and Isaiah both sigh deeply. I know what they're thinking, that all we can afford on our budget is macaroni and cheese from a box.

"Whoever is the most creative and puts together the best meal for their budget gets up to fifty points."

The whole room starts buzzing. Fifty points could catapult anyone to the top. And given our limited budget, that would mean anyone behind us could leapfrog us. Like Synergy.

"There are ways to be creative about spending, so don't think your group can't compete if your budget is tight." She doesn't have to look our way when she says this, but I know that comment is directed at us. "Think about what kind of meal you want to prepare. The more challenging the meal, the more points you're likely to get."

I look at my group members and they're all wearing the same deep-in-thought expression.

"Yo, like, maybe we could do this?" A.J. says suddenly. "Fifty points would put us, like, solidly in first place."

I don't know if it's because that line of thinking is crazy or because grouchy A.J.'s being the optimist here, but we all kind of stare at him blankly.

"But with our budget?" Isaiah says. "Maybe we can get some points but those other groups are going to have the money to make rack of lamb and stuff. Jeez, even the Bakers have more money than we do, and they're only just behind us."

"It doesn't have to be super-fancy. She said 'the best meal for our budget,'" A.J. says.

"And the most challenging," Luke says, sounding tired.

A.J. exhales through his nose. "You guys aren't looking at this the right way. My grandma's supermarket gives out free turkeys if you spend a certain amount of money. I think our fake class supermarket would too, especially if we asked Mrs. Sanchez about it."

"You're right. That's exactly the kind of creativity she's looking for," I say. Then I peek over my shoulder to make sure Jared's group isn't listening. Luckily, Jared's too consumed resuming his striptease via dish towels to be paying attention.

"We can probably throw together some affordable side dishes," Luke says, rubbing his chin.

"And my grandma has a recipe for turkey seasoning and stuffing that's awesome," A.J. says.

At that precise moment, Jared, now flinging his towels around like propellers, whacks Isaiah in the back with one. Mrs. Sanchez is too busy showing Jersey Strong how to clean out a dryer's lint filter to see this.

"Jesus, watch out," Isaiah snaps.

Jared bats his eyelashes. "I'm just working on my new stripper routine."

"Yeah, well, you kind of suck at it," Luke says.

"Perhaps," Jared says, lowering his towels. "But then maybe I should seek out A.J.'s mother for advice."

A.J.'s head flicks up from his folding. "What did you just say?"

Jared shrugs. "Oh, come on, A.J. I know she ditched you when you were young, but wasn't she a stripper?"

I'm alarmed at how red A.J.'s face is growing. In fact, Luke and I lock eyes at that moment, like our concern for him overrides whatever chasm is between us. He takes a step forward, as if anticipating A.J. throwing a punch or something, but A.J. stays rooted in place. "She was a cocktail waitress," he says through clenched teeth. "There's a big difference."

Jared tilts his head and taps his chin with his finger. "Is there, though?"

In one instant, A.J. is glowering at Jared. In the next, he grabs the bottle of detergent sitting next to him and I know what's going to happen next.

"Don't!" I gasp, reaching forward to try and grab A.J., but he doesn't seem to hear me, because he rears back and it looks like the bottle is going to hit me in the face in that movement, but two hands yank me back before the bottle can clonk me.

"A.J., dude!" Luke cries from behind me, his hands firmly on my shoulders.

A.J. turns around and his arm drops. A look of recognition crosses his face, like he realizes what could've just happened and, for just a moment, his face crumples slightly, like he might cry. But then his color goes bright red. "Fuck!" he yells, and, instead of throwing the detergent at Jared, he hurls it across the room, where it slams into the white cinder-block wall, leaving a big blue splotch of soap that trails down to the floor.

"A.J. Johnson!" Mrs. Sanchez booms, pointing at the door. "Principal's office. Now!"

A.J.'s face has gone pale, but his jaw is clenched. I expect him to try and take Jared down with him by saying he was taunted, but for some reason, he doesn't. Without a word, he storms out of the room.

Most of the class is just watching shocked and openmouthed. Bryce and Anthony, however, are laughing hysterically, like a pair of overly gelled hyenas, and I see Brynn whispering something to Hannah, both with judgmental looks on their faces. Hunter, though, is staring at me, his eyes full of concern.

Luke's hands are still on my shoulders and he's breathing heavy.

"You all right?" he asks.

"Fine," I say, though I know I'm shaking slightly.

"I saw that happening in slow motion," he says wearily, and his hands finally drop off my shoulders. Jared is next to us, so I take a huge step away from Luke.

"You grabbed her just in time," Isaiah says, shaking his head.

Mrs. Sanchez comes over to our group and squeezes my shoulder.

"Are you okay, Ms. Agresti?" she asks.

"Her?" Jared yelps. "What about me? He was going to throw it at me!"

Mrs. Sanchez turns and fixes him with a cold stare. "But he didn't, did he?"

Jared blanches like he's tasted something sour, but he doesn't say anything.

"I'm fine," I say to Mrs. Sanchez, and she pats my arm. As she walks away, Jared makes a face behind her back and his group-mates wear a collective bitchface, as Jodie would say. "That guy's a thug who belongs in juvie. She has no idea what she's talking about," Jared mutters, just loud enough to hear.

I'm shocked when, Isaiah—sweet, quiet Isaiah—takes a step in Jared's direction, but Luke moves in front of him. "Dude, don't," he says under his breath.

"We can't let him talk about A.J. like that," Isaiah whispers harshly.

"No, we can't," Luke says. "But we can't give in to Jared, either. It's what he wants."

"So we're just supposed to sit and take it?" Isaiah says, his shoulders sagging.

I glance around the room. The meatheads are playing a mock game of basketball with a rolled-up towel and cackling. The stoners appear to be studying a bottle of detergent to see if it could work as a bong. Jared is mocking Mrs. Sanchez behind her back as she evaluates the folding capabilities of Hunter and Brynn's group. "Excellent job, Synergy. Ten points for you," she says, and Brynn squeals and jumps up and down, linking arms with Hunter as Mrs. Sanchez walks away. It all makes my blood rush into my ears and my heart pound, and I turn to face the guys.

"No," I hear myself say. "We're going to beat them all and get into first place with the best damn Feast-Off meal Mrs. Sanchez has ever seen."

CHAPTER 20

I try to find A.J. after class, but I don't spot him anywhere.
I'm not sure what I can say to him, but I want him to know I'm not
mad. I can't bear for him to think I'm pissed at him the entire weekend. I'm pretty sure he's not working today, but I reroute myself
past the deli where he works on my way home anyway.

And that's where I run into Luke, who's coming out the front door.
He spots me right away, but doesn't seem surprised or upset by my
presence.

"Oh, hey!" he says.

It's too late for me to back away and run, and that would look
super crazy of me, so I offer a "hey" back and tuck my hair behind
my ears uncomfortably.

"I'm actually glad I ran into you," he says, his face serious. "Are
you okay? From before?"

Something inside me seizes. We haven't really spoken in weeks,
but his eyes are filled with concern. For me.

He lied to you. Stop it, Mary Ellen.

"I'm okay," I say. "I'm more worried about A.J., to be honest."

"Same. It's why I'm here," he says. "Him throwing that bottle . . . It just seems like something isn't right."

There's a strange tug in my gut, like my body's trying to be like, *Luke cares about A.J., isn't that sweet?* I try to ignore it. "So he's not working today?"

"Nope, he must've went straight home," Luke says. "He's seemed stressed out a lot lately. I'm wondering if he has something going on at home. Has he said anything to you?"

I shake my head. "No, but then he doesn't seem like the type to open up."

"True." Luke shoves his hands in his pockets. "I just hate seeing him so angry."

"I think the only thing we can do is let him know we're here to talk if he needs it. I mean, he has his friend Patrick, but . . ."

". . . It can't hurt to let him know his fake family has his back, too," Luke says with a small smile.

I feel myself starting to smile back, but bite my lip to stop it. "What if we both text him tonight? We can stagger it, so he doesn't think we're ganging up on him or anything."

"Good call. He doesn't seem like he's going to want anyone to feel sorry for him."

"I'll make sure to add a GIF of, like, a girl in a bikini to throw him off the scent."

"Look at us, teaming up," Luke says. And then he smiles bigger and my heart gets all fluttery and now I know the real reason I've been avoiding him: my hormones are not to be trusted.

We both just kind of stand there awkwardly, I guess waiting for the other to leave. I finally adjust my backpack on my shoulders and start to say, "See you Monday," but Luke interjects with a "How are you?"

"Good?" I say, unable to keep the uncertainty out of my voice. If Isaiah can see that I haven't been myself, I wonder if Luke has noticed, too. And that's the absolute last thing I'd want.

"I liked your RHHS TV report on the new band uniforms."

I almost laugh because that report was only thrown together for filler on a slow news day, but Luke's face is so sincere that I choke it back. "Thanks. They, uh, asked me to do the weather."

Luke's eyes light up and he starts to step forward to shake my hand or hug me or something, but he stops just short and drops his arms to his sides. "Dude, that's awesome! You're going to kick ass."

"Thanks," I say. I finally point at his bandaged arm. "Did that happen on the ramps?"

Luke's face flushes and he laughs as if he's embarrassed. My stomach clenches when I have this awful feeling he's going to admit he got this injury hooking up with another girl or something, and I swallow hard.

"I tripped over a pile of clothes in my room and came down on the edge of my dresser. Didn't realize it was that sharp until then. This is what I get for being a closet slob."

I can't help it when I let out a laugh that's fueled by a massive wave of relief. "Closet? Your shirts are always in a perpetual state of wrinkledom, Luke."

He looks like he's about to laugh, but throws his hands up dramatically instead. "Ironing is boring! And annoying! And my mom refuses to do it for me. Like, I can throw my clothes in the washer and dryer, but ironing is just . . . no."

"A bridge too far," I say.

His eyes are twinkling and he finally grins. "I like it better when we're on speaking terms, even if you're giving me crap for my, uh, laundry habits."

I feel my face flush and look at my feet. "Yeah, speaking does make that whole 'communication' thing a little easier, I guess."

"Good. Let's keep it that way." He climbs back on his bike and gives me a wave. "See you on Monday."

"See you," I say, feeling something welling up inside me but unsure what it is. Regret? Relief?

No. It's disappointment. Like, did I expect him to end that conversation by begging for a second chance? Why would I want that? I shake my head as I walk.

This is not a road we're going down again, Mary Ellen. There can be a thaw, for the sake of peace in class, but feelings? No. He lied to you.

I guess I just can't look at him from the neck up.

That won't be hard for the next seven months.

CHAPTER 21

A.J. doesn't respond to my texts by Saturday afternoon. In fact, last night, Luke started a text chain between our whole group to discuss what we should make for the Feast-Off, but he doesn't respond to that, either. Luke and Isaiah are chock-full of suggestions, though, and I have a hard time keeping up, even though it's a rainy day and therefore crazy slow at Cityscape Shoes.

"Mashed red potatoes?" I say out loud after reading Isaiah's suggestion. "But mashed sweet potatoes are so much better."

"No," Richard says, looking up from his crossword puzzle. "Sweet potatoes are a bitch to cut. Go with the red potatoes. It'll save you time and fingertips."

"See, this is why it's good to have a coworker who cooks," I say.

"I just know my carbs, what can I say?" Richard says with a laugh. He sobers quickly when something out the window catches his eye. "There are some people standing outside getting soaked. I think they're waiting for the bus."

I move over to the window, behind the display of snow boots, and under the faint light of a parking lot streetlamp, I can make out three figures huddled close together, their jacket hoods up. One appears to be a little girl in a bright-pink coat, and she's wearing a skirt and tights.

"It's coming down pretty heavy," I say. "I bet they were at the pharmacy . . ."

". . . and they closed five minutes ago," Richard says, checking his watch. "Tell them they can come inside here."

I push through the front door, which is kind of tough considering the wind is blowing back on it pretty hard.

"Excuse me," I call, poking my head out. All three turn around and when I squint I can see the person in the middle is an old woman with an oxygen tank at her side. "If you want to wait in here, you totally can!"

"Oh, thank you," the old lady calls back, and they make their way into the store.

The little girl comes in first and pushes her hood off. "Brrr!" she says, shaking a head of dirty-blonde curls. "It's much nicer in here."

"We lost our umbrella," the old woman says with a smile. "And we didn't think the bus would drive away without us!"

"What a terrible night for that!" Richard says.

"We have to wait for the next one, but it's not for another twenty minutes," the little girl says.

I notice the third figure, apparently a guy in a dark jacket, is lingering outside. The old woman notices, too, because she backpedals and leans out the door. "A.J., get in here or you'll catch your death."

I kind of freeze in place when she says this. I feel it even more when I hear a very familiar voice reply, "I want to make sure the driver sees us."

"Nonsense," the woman says back. "You can track the bus on that app on your phone. We'll know when to go out."

Very slowly, the black-coated figure trudges inside. It takes him a moment to push his hood back, but when he does, it's totally the A.J. I spend last period with.

"Hey," I say, wondering why he won't look me in the eye.

"Hi," he says, focusing on the snow boots display by the door.

"Do you two know each other?" the woman says, looking from A.J. to me.

"Yes," I say, hoping I sound friendly, even though I'm a bit taken aback by A.J.'s coldness. Maybe he still feels bad about yesterday or he's afraid I'm going to bring it up. "We have home ec together."

The woman's eyes light up. "Oh, you should see how much A.J. is applying that class at home! I've never seen my grandson so taken with something. He cooks for us all the time now, right, Sammi?"

The little girl nods vigorously and I'm struck by how she and A.J. have exactly the same pale-blue eyes.

"And the budgeting!" A.J.'s grandma says, nodding to Richard. "They're learning so much. A.J. set up a chart for us and—"

"Gran," A.J. interrupts, annoyance in his voice. "I don't think they care about our budget."

"Tsk, tsk," she says, waving him off. "If I'm proud of you, I'm going to say it, dear. Besides, you know how much that budget helped us, what with the rent going up and my emphysema making me work less."

I stare at him as he acts all interested in the wall full of boxes containing kids' sneakers. Obviously, a member of his home ec family interacting with his real family isn't exactly his idea of a spectacular Saturday.

"You should see A.J. decorate cupcakes!" I say, figuring a little praise from my end will show I'm not pissed off at him for yesterday. "Our teacher couldn't believe how good he is. She said he should—"

"Maybe we should splurge for an Uber," A.J. says, looking flustered, but A.J.'s grandma, her face beaming, ignores him.

"What does his teacher say, hon? I like it when I hear good things from them and not 'A.J. doesn't apply himself.'"

"She told him he's good enough for pastry school," I say, keeping an eye on A.J.'s reaction to this. He seems to be biting the inside of his cheek, which I don't understand.

A.J.'s grandma shakes her head at him. "You're always so close-mouthed about these things. Why wouldn't you tell me that?"

A.J. just stares out the window and shrugs in response.

"I bet he's too busy figuring out how to cart me around," she says. "Our car had to go and die last week and we've been taking the bus everywhere. He doesn't seem to trust his old gran by herself, though."

"Well, that's a good grandson in my book," Richard says.

A.J. just continues to stare out the window.

"Normally we go to the Drugfair in our neighborhood, but we were out at the mall today and figured we'd stop here because it's on our way. Little did we know they close earlier than our Drugfair!" A.J.'s grandma taps her oxygen tank. "Don't ever smoke. It'll cost you in more ways than one."

"Where do you live?" Richard wants to know.

"In the Southvale Apartments in Ringvale Heights, over on Columbus Avenue."

"Gran!" A.J. barks. "Why do you always have to be so specific?"

"Because we live there," A.J.'s grandma says. "I doubt these two are going to come rob us blind."

So that's why A.J. had me pick him up at the dentist's office. The Southvale Apartments are considered the "shady" part of Ringvale Heights, if a mostly upper-middle-class suburb could have a shady part of town. Hunter would always hit the automatic locks on his car when we'd drive up Columbus. "There are probably hundreds of meth heads and junkies on this block alone," he'd say.

While it's true there are always some incidents listed in the *Ringvale Heights Gazette*'s crime blotter from Columbus Avenue, there are enough DUI reports and domestic disputes from the rest of town to kind of even it out. I think Hunter was going by urban legend more than anything.

A.J.'s face is totally red and I suddenly feel sorry for him, which is exactly the reaction he probably didn't want me to have and why he hasn't said anything. But still. He's ashamed of where he lives, and his grandmother, who looks to be his only guardian, is in poor health. I wonder if this has anything to do with his mood lately and if Jared was just what put him over the edge.

It's kind of awkward as we wait for the moments to pass, and A.J.'s grandma and sister do all the talking. Finally, the bus is shown to be a few blocks away on the app, and Sammi cheers and runs out the door.

A.J.'s grandma waves as she heads for the door. "So lovely to meet you both, and thank you so much for the shelter!"

"No problem," Richard says. "Get home safely."

A.J. kind of lingers and slowly heads for the door. He pulls his hood back over his head and starts to push out the door, but then stops and turns around. I'm startled by how stressed he looks and I know exactly what he's telling me: *Please don't tell anyone about me.* What he says out loud, though, is, "Thanks. See you Monday." He heads out the door, but then, at the last second, dashes back in. "Oh, and my aunt has a great corn casserole recipe that's really cheap to make. I'll hit her up for it. And I can get the turkey and stuffing recipe, of course."

"Awesome." I smile. He doesn't smile back, but he does give me a double thumbs-up before he heads toward the approaching bus.

"What was that about?" Richard says.

"Our home ec project," I say.

"Good thing he's not graded on his conversation skills," Richard says. "He's not exactly chatty, is he?"

"No," I say, watching the bus pull away. "But he's family."

CHAPTER 22

"**. . . And looking ahead to tomorrow, the Thanksgiving** forecast is pretty much perfect. Plenty of sunshine and highs in the low-fifties for the RHHS/Bollingwood football game or for anyone who signed up for the Ringvale Heights Turkey Trot."

I get all this out, ignoring the nagging voice in my brain that says I sound like I have absolutely no breath control and that I'm probably smiling like a lunatic.

"And that's the forecast. Back to you, Mia and Chris," I say and have to stop myself from exhaling loudly and slumping against the green screen.

Willow gives me a thumbs-up from behind the camera as Mia throws to Alisha with the sports report. I give an exhausted smile back. I survived day three of TV weather forecasting. Even my looming physics test today seems like a walk in the park in comparison.

When the show ends, Alisha high-fives me. "If you felt nervous today, it didn't show at all."

"My breathless projection was that good, huh?" I say drily.

"Stop. Seriously, for someone on their third day, that was awesome."

"Holy shit," Chris says from behind us, making both Alisha and me turn around. He's staring at his phone and he starts to laugh. "I think The Buzz got hacked. You guys need to see this post."

Everyone in the room whips out their phones. I huddle close to Alisha as she loads up The Buzz, and there it is: what looks like a video screen shot of a horrified-looking Jared holding a balled-up pair of socks, with the headline:

Stuffing for the Turkey?

Which asshole who just so happens to run this gossip site got caught packing his pecker checker? We'll just say it rhymes with Mared Burtis.

There's then a video. It looks like a dress rehearsal for the school play, *Julius Caesar*, which Jared's starring in. He's dressed in an ancient-Roman-looking tunic and carrying a sword. He's about to deliver his line, when he steps forward and a balled-up pair of socks falls out from between his legs. He goes completely pale and picks it up, and for the briefest second, I feel bad for him. Everyone on stage behind him starts to laugh. But he continues with his lines, tossing the socks into the wings of the stage.

The amount of gasps and hysterical giggles going around the room is something to behold.

"It's about damn time someone gave him a taste of his own medicine," Willow says, coming over to Alisha and me.

"Seriously," Alisha says. "Although, he's such a sociopath that this could just make him worse."

I wrinkle my nose. "Is that even possible? Wait, don't answer that."

Unsurprisingly, The Buzz post is the most talked-about thing all day. Jared just kind of glowers through home ec, and while no one in the JAILE family addresses him directly, we have a great time snickering about it as we head over to Luke's house that afternoon to work on our meal strategy for the Feast-Off and finish our monthly budget.

"Socks," A.J. says, shaking his head. "He keeps socks stuffed in his jock."

"'Socks in His Jock' sounds like a lost Dr. Seuss book," I say, which makes Luke laugh so hard, he almost falls off his bike.

"Now, now," Luke says when he's recovered. "We have to give Jared credit for holding his head high today."

"Yeah, looks like he really grew a pair," Isaiah says before dissolving into giggles, and that sets us off again.

We're still cackling as we approach Luke's house, which is as homey and inviting as the last time I saw it, the day of the interview. A sudden wave of sadness extinguishes my Jared-related schadenfreude, and I wish we could go back to that day, when nothing had yet been ruined by lies and reckless kissing.

Luke unlocks the front door. "Welcome to my humble abode."

"This place could be on HGTV," A.J. says when we step inside. "My grandma watches enough of it, I should know."

He's not wrong. The living room is perfectly decorated and charming, with a stone fireplace and built-in bookshelves flanking it, and cozy overstuffed couches, where Luke motions for us to sit down.

"My mom and stepdad had it restored last year. It's an original Craftsman, whatever that means," Luke says as he plunks down on one of the couches.

"Well, they have good taste," I say, thinking of the mismatched furniture in my own living room.

We throw all of our recipe cards and a couple of cookbooks onto the coffee table, and Luke pulls out an iPad.

"Okay, so we've got you guys prepping the turkey on Sunday," Luke says, pointing at A.J. and me, and we nod. "Isaiah and I are going in early Monday to peel the potatoes and prep the green beans and corn casserole."

"I wonder if any of the other groups are going in early?" I say, chewing my pen cap.

"Let's not worry about any of them," Luke says. "Our destiny is in our hands."

"There's only twenty points separating us from the Bakers. And Synergy—"

Luke holds up his hand with what looks like an annoyed scowl on his face. "We've got this. Unless we completely burn everything, we'll get those fifty points."

I'm about to argue that I want to be ahead of Synergy, not tied with them—like, they could get fifty points, too. And if Jared's team gets fifty points, they'll still be twenty points ahead of us—when A.J. points at something over my shoulder.

"Yo, is that you? What happened to your tooth?"

I turn around and see what A.J. is pointing at, a photo on the shelf behind me. There's a tall guy with a kid, and I assume it's Luke and his little brother until I look closer and see that the kid, is in fact, Luke, complete with freckles and a chipped front tooth.

"Yeah, and that's my dad. You can see where I get the height from," Luke says.

"And you have his smile, even with the chipped tooth," I say almost involuntarily.

He laughs. "That's the photo from my first communion. My dad told me I couldn't skateboard that morning, but I didn't listen, and so of course I fell off my board right before I had to be at church and broke my front tooth on the curb. My dad was, like, the nicest person alive but he was really pissed about that. You can't tell in that picture, though."

"When did he pass away?" Isaiah asks, then he shakes his head. "Sorry, you don't have to talk about him if you don't want to."

"No, it's okay," Luke says. "He had liver cancer. He was first diagnosed like three years after that picture. We thought he beat it, but it came back a year after that and it was really aggressive. He died four days after my brother Ryan's third birthday."

The sadness in his voice gives me such a strong urge to lean over and squeeze his arm supportively, but I force myself to stay put.

"That's really rough, I'm sorry," Isaiah says. "That must've been hard."

Luke shakes his head. "It was. I was having trouble in school and was such a dick to him and my mom right before he found out the cancer was back. And then it was like I was terrified of him when he got sick again. I feel like his last few months alive I was a total shit to him, just because I didn't know how to act."

"You were twelve," I say softly. "I bet your dad knew it was coming from fear and not because you hated him or something."

"I know," Luke say. "I just feel like you read all these books and see all these movies where people are sick and everyone just rallies around the sick person. Everyone else in his life did. Except me. I think it's why I focused so much on the biking after that, because he knew I loved that and encouraged it."

"It's like you were finding a way to, like, connect with him," A.J. says.

"Yes, exactly. I . . . I do wish he'd gotten to see me do so well with the bike stuff." Then he glances at the three of us, and we all must be wearing expressions of total sadness because Luke laughs lightly. "Now that we've made this a therapy session, is there anything you guys want to get off your chests?"

"I have to get laughing gas every time I go to the dentist, or I freak out," Isaiah says.

"I used to eat Play-Doh," A.J. says

I think I'm feeling something for you right now and that worries me. What I say is, "I told all my friends in third grade that my cousin was Christina Hemmings from *California Cowgirl* and that she was coming to my birthday party, but of course she didn't and half those girls never spoke to me again."

Luke smiles. "Go big or go home with those childhood lies, huh?" The front door creaks open then, followed by a gravelly voiced "Luke, I'm home."

"In the living room, Mom," Luke calls back.

My heart suddenly begins to pound. It's like one side of my brain is all, *You're going to meet Luke's mother!* and the other is, *Except it means nothing because you're not dating, Mary Ellen.*

A short woman with golden-brown, feathered hair steps into the living room. She grins as she peels off her black leather jacket, and in a raspy voice declares, "This must be the other family you're always talking about!"

"The family that doesn't nag me about cleaning my room," Luke deadpans.

She throws back her head and cackles and my heart squeezes momentarily realizing they have the same laugh.

She leans over and smooths Luke's hair, then smiles at all of us. "How are you guys?"

"Good," Isaiah and A.J. say in unison.

"Great, how are you!" I chirp with a big toothy grin, and it's only then that I realize I'm suddenly sitting ramrod straight.

"I'm lovely, thanks for asking, honey," she says, beaming at me. She has kind eyes. Luke's eyes.

Luke bites his lip in what I assume is amusement, and it hits me then: That was me using my "mom cred."

"Well, I know you guys have a lot of work, so I'll leave you to it. But if you need anything, just yell. My name's Casey. I'll be in my room catching up on my DVR."

"Well, now that *that's* over with . . ." Luke says after she walks away, and I notice he's blushing slightly.

"Dude, your mom's great," A.J. says.

"Yeah, she's cool," Isaiah agrees.

"You look like her. You both have—" I stop myself before I say "kind eyes" because that could get misconstrued. "—the same hair."

Now Luke bursts out laughing. "The same hair? She's stuck in the eighties!"

"The same hair color," I clarify. Then I clamp my mouth shut before I dig myself any deeper.

We settle back into strategizing our cooking times then, and I think we're only halfway through when I notice how dark it is outside. And also how much I have to pee.

I stand up and stretch. "Um, where's the bathroom?"

"Straight that way, on the left," Luke says, pointing down a hallway behind him. I make my way in that direction, passing a room with a door that's open a crack and Luke's mom must be watching a soap opera in there because I hear her say, "Why would you do that, Jenna? He's never going to leave her for you. They're the supercouple of the show, for crying out loud."

I suppress a smile as I continue down the hall. I see two doors to the left and one is wide open. It must be Luke's room because there's an enormous poster of a guy upside down in midair on a BMX bike. Also, the room is a mess. The bed is unmade and there are clothes all over the floor. Luke's elbow injury makes a ton of sense now.

A red-faced Luke swoops by then and shuts the door. "Heh-heh, nothing to see there."

I can't help but laugh. "That was an eyeful."

Luke's mom emerges from her room then. "Oh, sweetie, did you just have to see that mess? I hope you aren't scarred for life."

"It's not that bad, Mom," Luke says, his face even redder now. "Besides, Ellie wants to be a meteorologist. She's seen worse on those weather disaster shows."

Casey nods approvingly and winks at me. "Smart and pretty, that's a good family member to have."

Now my ears get hot. I drop my eyes to the floor and focus on the beautiful dark-brown inlay of the hardwood floor below me.

"Why don't you guys take a break and use that foosball table downstairs you begged me to get," she asks.

"We've still got a lot of work to do," Luke says. "We're probably going to be here late."

Casey seems to consider this. "Well, okay, then why don't I heat up that lasagna and some meatballs for you guys? Joe and Ryan are at that Devils game tonight and someone's got to eat it, right?"

My stomach growls as if on cue, and they both hear it. Casey smiles at me, her blue eyes sparkling. "I'm going to take that as a yes. Sit tight, sweetheart, we're gonna get you fed."

Maybe I *could* be friends with Luke. Just for his mother.

Casey sets the dining room table and eats with us, telling stories about Luke that make us laugh and make Luke's face grow redder and redder.

"If I'd known all my deepest secrets were going to be spilled tonight, I'd have suggested we work at the library," Luke says, shaking his head.

"But then we wouldn't have gotten this feast," A.J. says, his mouth full.

"Yeah, thank you, Casey," Isaiah says. "I wasn't expecting to get fed!"

Casey winks at him. "Any family of Luke's is a family of mine."

"I assume this means we should be in charge of kitchen cleanup," Luke says.

"Of course we should," I say, standing up and gathering my plate. "It's only fair."

"I approve of this other family of yours, Luke," Casey says, ruffling his hair.

Much like we do in class, we station ourselves by the sink and kitchen cabinets, basically forming a human dish-washing chain. A.J. washes, Isaiah and I dry, and Luke puts everything back where it belongs.

"I'm sorry that even out of class, we're cleaning a kitchen together," Luke says with a laugh.

"Please," Isaiah says. "It's the least we could do for your mom getting us—"

He's cut off by a loud burst of music with the words, "Here's my story, sad but true, it's about a girl that I once knew . . ."

Luke closes his eyes. "Mom, come on, please!" he groans.

"She took my love and ran around, with every single guy in town," Casey's voice intermingles with the music. Then she pops her head into the kitchen. "'Runaround Sue' is a classic, honey. Your friends should know it."

Now Luke shakes his head at us apologetically as his mom dances out of the room. "Sorry, this is my mom's after-dinner routine. Cleaning the house to the oldies."

A.J. bops his head along as he washes a glass. "I dig it."

I move in time to the beat as I dry a plate and Luke's face softens. "Looks like Agresti likes it, too."

An unexpected explosion of delight cuts through me, hearing him call me Agresti again. "It's catchy," I say.

And then it happens. We're all dancing, moving in rhythm to the music as we dry plates and utensils. Luke extends a hand out and I take it, and he expertly twirls me around, then spins me back toward Isaiah, who catches me. I lose my footing, though, and we stumble backwards into the counter and laugh so hard that we both start crying.

A feeling of warmth grips me then, the act of dorking out and just enjoying my fake family. Even Luke. It's the happiest I've been . . . in a while.

When we get back to work, Casey lowers the volume, but continues with the oldies playlist, which is the soundtrack to the rest of our budgeting. We're either super reinvigorated from the food or our dorky dancing or both, and we manage to finish up our meal-prep discussion and do our budget in an hour.

My mom, who's been driving for Lyft to make some extra money on her days off, texts that she's on her way home and can pick me up. Isaiah's mother arrives first, then Patrick rolls up for A.J., leaving me waiting on the porch with Luke.

"I'm really sorry about my mom," Luke says, digging his hands into the pockets of his jeans.

"Stop it," I say. "Your mom's great. She's friendly and she fed us. She's basically a goddess."

"If I tell her you said that, she'll"—Luke pauses and looks down—"well, I can tell she already really likes you."

"I'm hard not to like," I joke. I say it because I feel the need to defuse something here, something that feels like Luke is saying *he* really likes me.

I keep my hands shoved in the pockets of my coat, as if that will stop me from doing something I'll regret, should it come to that. There's about six inches between Luke and me, and he's not wearing a coat, so I can still smell the dish soap on him. A slow song is playing from inside, something about smoke getting in your eyes. We're both slightly swaying in place to it, trying to stay warm.

"You're really good at the weather reporting," he says. "You sound just like the weather people on TV, I'm not even kidding."

A feeling of warmth blooms inside me and I can't help but smile. "Thanks. It's stressful, but I think I'm slowly getting the hang of it. Any tournaments coming up?"

"Not till after the holidays, so it's all training till then."

"Well, that just gives you more time to nerd out about Christmas, then," I say.

Luke gives a small chuckle, but his smile doesn't quite meet his eyes. "I didn't think of that. I almost forgot it's December next week. I've been preoccupied, I guess."

It hits me then: Has Luke been sad, too, and he's just better than me at hiding it?

A swath of headlights illuminate the street, and my mom pulls up alongside the curb. She waves to us from the driver's seat and Luke waves back.

"Have a good Thanksgiving tomorrow. And thank your mom again for dinner," I say, which makes Luke smile a little bigger.

"She's going to adopt you if you're not careful," he says. "Happy Thanksgiving."

When I climb in the car, there's an overwhelming scent of pine trees and I make a gagging noise.

"Sorry, the last passenger went a little overboard with his cologne," Mom says.

I instantly feel bad, because I know Mom doesn't love driving people around. "Was he at least nice?" I ask.

"He was going on a date and he was nervous. I didn't have the heart to tell him he overdid it with the, uh, scent," my mom says, cringing.

As we drive home, Mom asks how everything went and I brace myself for her to ask me about Luke again, like that morning before the races, but she doesn't. Still, I'm reminded of that sad look on Luke's face.

He's a liar. He doesn't get to be unhappy, the rational part of my brain argues.

But the other, ridiculously empathetic part of my brain is like, *Maybe he misses you.*

My phone buzzes then, and my heart starts to race, thinking it might be Luke. But it's actually a text from Alisha.

Jared went nuclear.

There's a link to The Buzz and there's one massive entry. And unlike all the other posts, no one's mentioned in veiled blind items. No, their names are outright used. I skim posts about a girl's alleged nose job and one about Bryce Pratt's family giving him an intervention over steroid use. There's one about Greta struggling in her training runs because "she's not getting any vitamin 'D.'" And then I see it.

A.J. Johnson is so poor, he was spotted dumpster diving in the Gardner's Deli parking lot. Hope he found some good meals. I mean, deals!

"I'm going to kill him," I say through clenched teeth.

"Yikes, what's going on?" my mom says.

"Nothing," I say, squeezing my phone so tight I'm shocked it doesn't shatter in my hands. "Nothing at all."

CHAPTER 23

Mrs. Sanchez has given us permission to come in the Sunday before the Feast-Off to prepare our turkey, since it has a very specific marinating time of "overnight." In fact, Mrs. Sanchez looked pretty impressed when we said we wanted to do it on a weekend, even though it meant she had to come in and unlock the school and classroom door for us. "You're a very resourceful group. The rest of the class should be watching out for you."

"I think she wants us to win," A.J. says when Mrs. Sanchez retreats to the teacher's lounge while we work on our turkey. Our job is to follow A.J.'s grandma's recipe for soaking the turkey in a "brine" and leaving it until tomorrow morning.

It also means it's the first time I've seen him since The Buzz's post—which was deleted about an hour later, but still survived via screenshots—went live.

"I just want you to know, I never said anything to anyone about the day at the shoe store," I say as we take the turkey out of its packaging.

"I know you didn't," he says with a shrug. "And I was trying to fish out a plastic milk crate I accidentally threw in the dumpster during my shift. So what Jared said was a complete lie. I'm not that bothered."

He's chewing his inner cheek, so I know he *is* bothered. I have to wonder if any of Jared's other stories were out-and-out lies, too—I keep thinking of Greta doing poorly in her training and can't help but feel guilty over that.

"I'm sorry Jared takes all of his BS out on you, though," I say.

A.J. sighs. "He's still pissed at me for laughing at him in eighth grade when he was doing this monologue in English. He was doing this whole thing about his mom cheating on his dad, and I thought he was acting out a scene from a play or something and that he was being over the top on purpose. Like, I thought I was supposed to laugh. And then my laughing made the whole class laugh. But it turns out he was actually talking about his real-life parents."

"Oh my god," I say.

"Yeah, I felt like shit when I found that out. But that wasn't till, like, two weeks later. I tried to apologize to him, but I don't think he believed me. He's pretty much taken it out on me ever since."

"Well, he's gone above and beyond what you did," I say.

"Whatever. It is what it is."

What it is is bullying, I want to say, but A.J.'s jaw is set and I don't want to push him on it. I turn my attention back to our task.

"This is the weirdest thing I've ever heard involving a turkey," I say as we clean out a big white bucket that once held cement mix.

"Trust me, it works. We used it the other day and it was perfect," A.J. says, handing over a recipe card.

I study the card, which has been written out in a very neat script. "So, Isaiah will take it out of the brine and put it in a pan before homeroom. And you're coming down later to put it in the oven?"

A.J. nods. "And then it'll be ready just in time for class."

"Sounds easy enough," I say.

We set to work dumping vegetable stock, salt, and various spices into our biggest pot. We have to simmer these for twenty minutes, so we start cleaning out the turkey while this is happening.

"Ugh, gross," I say when I realize we have to take out its innards.

"Allow me," A.J. laughs, and sets about removing them while I gather my stomach.

"So," A.J. says, not looking at me. "You're, like, friends with Alisha, right?"

I so know where this is going, but I play along. "Yes."

"Is she, uh, seeing anybody?"

"Not as far as I know. Why? Do you like her?"

"A little," he says. "But I don't know. I mean, I don't know if she'd ever go out with me."

"Stop it. You guys looked like you were having a great time together at the party."

"It's just that she's so smart and I'm like a C student," he says, staring at his hands.

"One, I don't know what grades have to do with a good relationship. Two, I do think Alisha would be receptive if you asked her out. She seemed pretty into you at the party," I say. "It can't hurt to ask."

A.J. shrugs and mumbles an "Okay, maybe," but the worry lines are gone from his forehead. Then he clears his throat. "At the risk of sounding like my grandma, what's going on with you and Luke?"

I freeze mid-stir. "Huh?"

"Yo, I know something's happening there," A.J. says. "Or happened. You were all flirty and shit at the party and I actually made a bet with Alisha that you guys would be a thing by Thanksgiving."

I give my fakest laugh, hoping it will cloak any hysteria in my voice. "Well, sorry to say you lost."

A.J. narrows his eyes. "So when you guys weren't, like, even speaking or looking at each other a few weeks ago, that was over nothing?"

I just shrug, hoping I seem as blasé as possible. "That's in the past. We're fine now."

A.J. blows out his cheeks. "Except he's still totally into you. He doesn't even have to say it. He looks at you like you're a giant chocolate cake or something."

My head whips up involuntarily. And my expression must be a dead giveaway because his eyes light up. "I knew it!"

"A.J., please. If you need to win the bet, win the bet, but don't ask me to talk about this," I say. "Also, I don't want to put you in the middle. I've been trying super hard to avoid that."

"I, uh, put myself there," A.J. says. "And this isn't about the bet. I just thought . . . you guys, you know, seemed to really like each other."

That A.J. would actually be invested in Luke and me makes a tiny part of me soften. If you'd told me three months ago that the crass kid would be rooting for me in a romantic relationship, I would've laughed so, so hard. But it also stings at the same time, knowing why this can't happen.

"Anyway," he goes on, "if it means anything, I'm just saying I'm pretty sure he likes you, so, just, like, keep that in your pocket or whatever."

"I'll take that under advisement," I grumble. Then I tap the spoon on the pot. "I think this has simmered long enough."

We turn our attention back to the turkey and don't bring it up for the rest of the afternoon.

When we're finished, A.J. catches the bus to his neighborhood, and I grab a hot chocolate from the Starbucks down the road and sit there for a while, thinking. It's like the turkey and its bucket of brine are resting on my chest and I'm not sure what to do about it. Luke appears to still have feelings for me, and I have clearly not moved on if I'm actually worrying about this.

How can I possibly still be feeling something for someone who lied to me? Did I learn nothing from Hunter?

I ponder this and literally feel my heart palpitate as I walk home. I decide I need to talk to Jodie about this. Funk or not, I've given her more than enough time to mourn USC and I need her and her no-nonsenseness right now. Perhaps admitting what's going on will give her something to be mildly happy about, since she can be all, "I told you so."

I pull my phone out from my backpack and I groan when I see the battery's dead. I'm returning my phone to my backpack's front pocket when a car honks from behind me. Since I'm walking in the middle of the street, I move to the side to let it pass, but I hear it creeping up next to me.

"Ellie, hey!"

I turn and see Hunter smiling at me. What the hell is he doing over here on a Sunday?

"Oh, hey," I say, hoping my lack of enthusiasm conveys that I want to be alone.

"Want a ride?"

"I'm two blocks from my house," I tell him, taking a long sip of my drink, even though it's barely warm, to keep this conversation from going further.

"I know. I was coming to see you," Hunter says and his smile disappears. "I could really use your advice right now about something."

"I don't know. I really need to get a jump on my homework." Total lie, but I mean, come on.

"Please, El," Hunter says. "I need to talk to someone, and you're the only one who will get it."

"Fine." I try to keep from rolling my eyes. He pulls over to the side of the street so I can get in, and then starts fiddling with the radio.

"Um, I don't have all day," I say.

"I know, I know. It's just . . . I'm thinking I don't want to go to Princeton anymore," he says.

"Whoa," I say slowly. Seriously, now, I get why he needed to talk.

"In fact, I know I don't want to go there. I applied to Tufts, and if I get in, that's where I'm going."

"Damn, your family is going to flip."

"And I think Brynn might, too. She applied early decision to Princeton and I have, like, no doubt she'll get in."

I have to clench my jaw to keep it from falling into my lap. Brynn—studious, driven-to-the-point-of-snobbery Brynn, who could probably get into most Ivy League schools—based her college decision on where Hunter was going? Yikes.

"She's a big girl" is what I actually say. "And if she loves you, she'll get over it."

"I tried hinting to her the other night why Tufts would be a better school for me, since it has a good music program and their a cappella groups are so well regarded and stuff, but she kind of just laughed me off."

Is it weird that I know exactly why Brynn laughed him off? Because she must now realize how winning the talent show last year has gone to Hunter's head if he thinks he's ready for an award-winning collegiate-level group.

"My family is never going to understand this," he says, shaking his head.

"Well, you're just going to have to tell them and let the chips fall where they may. It is your choice, after all."

Hunter's silent for a minute. "That's it? That's all you can tell me?"

I narrow my eyes at him. "What do you want me to say? It'll be okay? I don't know that. I'm not psychic, you know."

"I thought you'd tell me how I should follow my dreams and that everyone else needs to get off my ass."

"No," I say, losing my patience. "You wanted me to tell you what you wanted to hear."

"Jesus, Ellie. You used to have all the answers."

"That's the thing," I say, and for some reason tears start burning in my eyes. "I don't have a vested interest in your life anymore. I mean, I'm sorry you're in such a tight spot right now. But you just expect me to be here for you and have all the answers because I did in the past?"

He doesn't have a reply for this, and the fact that he's that oblivious makes me even more annoyed. Then he's all, "You've changed."

That's. It. "Hunter, you dumped me for another girl you apparently had feelings for long before we met, hooked up with her before you broke up with me, treated me like that was somehow my fault, and now I'm supposed to be the same old Ellie? Do you know how much you hurt me?"

"You're just being a hypocrite," he snaps.

"Excuse me?" How is he possibly turning this on me?

"I heard how you and Luke were all over each other at Alisha's. And didn't he have a girlfriend then? You're not any better than me."

I feel my throat constricting. I want so badly to scream and I start shaking. "And who told you that?"

"Steve saw you guys. Which means the whole class probably saw you, so don't deny it."

"We were not all over each other," I say, my face going all hot. I don't want to lie, but I don't want to give him any satisfaction right now. "We played beer pong together and that's it."

"See, you're even drinking now because of him," he says, shaking his head.

I'm fairly sure I've never been part of a more ridiculous conversation, but I can't seem to extricate myself from it. "I was playing with soda. But even if I was drinking, what's the big deal? Everyone else drinks. Jesus Christ, you drink. And your girlfriend puked all over you from drinking too much. When the hell did you start"—I struggle for the word—"idealizing me so much?"

"I just think you've changed a lot and it bothers me. And I think it's Luke's influence."

I actually burst out laughing. Like, I don't know what else to do right now. "Hunter, you really have lost the right to judge how I have or haven't changed. Honestly, if I have changed, it's a result of how you treated me and that's that."

His face goes bright red. "I just don't appreciate you going off on my sense of morals when you're not doing too well with them yourself."

I'm so done. I feel my blood pulsating in my temples and I clutch my Starbucks cup so hard I almost crush it.

"Whatever you think is going on between Luke and me is none of your damn business," I growl. "Now stop projecting all your defensive shit on me."

He shakes his head and a forced laugh comes out, and I know I've hit a nerve. "You know what, Ellie? Good for you for moving on. Because I guess if Luke's so damn great he'll finally be the one to get you to chill out and devirginize you!"

Without even thinking, I rip the lid off my drink and launch its contents into Hunter's face. Well, not quite, because he moves his face when he sees the cup coming and the now-cold hot chocolate mostly lands on his shoulder. But still.

Before he can react, I yank the car door open and grab my backpack in one motion. That makes the open front pouch of my backpack tip forward and everything in it spill on the seat. I don't care. I slam the door shut, glaring at Hunter through the window with a rage I've never known. He stares at me for a second with a look that resembles regret, but then I shake my head disgustedly at him, and he peels off into the growing darkness.

I stomp the rest of the way home and I'm glad to see that my parents aren't there. I need to be able to vent to Jodie without them hearing it. I reach for my backpack, and when I see the open front pouch hanging down with nothing in it, a sense of dread wells up inside me. My phone was in there, with my pens, eye drops, and lip balm. All of which are now on the passenger's seat of Hunter's car.

Luckily, Jodie's number is one of the few I know by heart, and I use the upstairs cordless phone to make my call.

"Hello?" Jodie asks, sounding annoyed. Normally, she's all, "Yo, El, what's up?"

"Hey, it's Ellie. I'm on my landline."

"Oh," Jodie says, sounding less annoyed but still not like herself. "I thought you were a telemarketer or something. Did your phone finally die?"

"No, you're not going to believe this," I say. "It fell out in Hunter's car while I was—"

"Hunter's car?" Jodie repeats, her tone changing back to annoyed. "What were you doing in Hunter's car?"

"It's seriously the most—"

"Jesus, Ellie, you still haven't gotten him out of your life yet? Is that why we've barely spoken the last few weeks?"

Seriously? She's making this my fault? "We've barely spoken because you're in a perpetual funk these days."

"Nope, you've been super evasive lately and now I know why, since you apparently think hanging out with Hunter again is acceptable behavior. Why can't you just get over him already?"

I take a deep breath, wondering if it's possible to strangle my phone. "Jodie, I'm very, very sorry you're not going to USC, but you don't need to take it out on me and—"

"Excuse me? You know how much USC meant to me. Do not throw that in my face."

"Yeah, I do. And I know that your life isn't over because there are other colleges that you don't have to fly to, which you seem to have conveniently forgot during this stupid extended pity party." I feel my eyes bugging out and I suck in my breath. Did I really just say that?

But before I can take it back, Jodie makes a strange noise between a laugh and a yelp. "You're going to lecture me? Oh, that's rich, Miss Avoid Everything That Makes You Feel Bad."

Whatever bit of regret I just had evaporates instantly. "What's that supposed to mean?"

"You stick with what's safe because you can't bear to have your feelings hurt. You don't want to experience anything new and just stay in your little shell, so you stick with the familiar, even if the familiar is an asshole like Hunter. God, even your obsession with beating his group is like a weird, sick way of keeping him in your life."

I suck in my breath. "Newsflash, Jodie, I hooked up with Luke last month, but I haven't told you since you've been so busy feeling sorry for yourself and I felt bad. And I told Hunter off today for good. I actually dumped my drink on him, but since you're too busy being a raging, reactionary bitch right now, maybe we can have this conversation another day."

With that, I slam down the phone.

Seriously, what did I do to deserve today?

CHAPTER 24

It might sound crazy but the Feast-Off is the only thing keeping me focused at the moment. It's like all of my anger and angst and fed-upness is funneled into creating the perfect meal.

And this is fine with me because I don't want to think about yesterday. At all. Like, if I remember my fight with Hunter, I'm liable to punch someone. If I think about my fight with Jodie, I feel like I might start crying and never be able to stop. I mean, this is a pretty epic moment in our friendship. Aside from a minor tiff in the sixth grade over who was the bigger T.J. Choi fan, we've never really fought. I've always tolerated Jodie's pushiness and sometimes opinionated advice because it's a minor part of who she is. But our argument took that to a whole other level, and since neither of us has apologized, I'm terrified this might be a permanent thing.

"Are you okay?" Isaiah asks at lunch that day. He's staring at me with a deeply furrowed brow over a book Mariana gave him about horse care. He's been working at the equine therapy center on Friday afternoons and Saturdays, the only two days his mother would concede. But it seems to be enough for Isaiah, who has been practically glowing since he started working there, and every lunch period he devours the reading material Mariana gives him.

"I'll be all right," I say.

"You sure?" he asks. "You look upset."

"I just had kind of a late night last night is all." Okay, that's kind of true. I kept waiting to see if Jodie would call me and simultaneously fought the urge to call her. That went on until about 1:00 a.m., when I finally fell asleep.

Isaiah doesn't look like he believes me, but he stops the line of questioning.

I'm digging half-heartedly at my pudding cup when a shadow falls over our table.

There's a loud thwack as a heavy Ziploc bag is dropped on the table between Isaiah and me, startling the both of us. I look up to see Brynn standing there, scowling.

"Hunter said to give this to you." It's more of an accusation than a declarative statement.

I examine the bag, which contains my phone and all the stuff that fell out in Hunter's car. I don't know if Hunter is still too pissed at me to have brought it himself or if he knew Brynn's path would cross with me before his.

Or maybe he thinks I'm liable to throw another drink in his face.

"Thanks," I say.

"What were you doing in Hunter's car yesterday?" Brynn asks, her eyes bright, her nostrils flaring.

"He saw me walking and offered me a ride home," I say slowly. Approaching this like you would a possibly rabid animal caught in a trap seems the best track here.

Isaiah's eyes are darting back and forth between us, his mouth slightly agape. I'd laugh if I didn't think Brynn was about to pounce on me for any sudden moves.

"And what happened that all your shit fell out in the car and you didn't even realize it?"

Uh, did Hunter not tell her we fought? Oh, wait, of course he didn't. Then he'd have to admit how it all started, with him not wanting to go to Princeton. I let out a deep, exhausted sigh. "You'll have to ask him that."

Brynn's face has now lit up an alarming shade of red. Before her head can full-on explode, I give her my most exasperated look. "I can assure you, it's not what you think it is."

"It better not be. Seriously."

I don't know what's firing up this level of snark in me right now, but I flutter my eyelashes at her in what I hope is the most dismissive way possible. "If I were you, I'd be more worried about the Feast-Off. Hope you don't mind working the dance because Synergy is, like, totally going down."

Isaiah's jaw drops even lower.

But Brynn doesn't have a comeback for that. Instead, she makes this annoyed snorting noise and stomps off.

I pull the phone out of the bag, and much like yesterday afternoon, it's still dead. When I look up, Isaiah's completely wide-eyed.

"What was that all about?"

"Let's just say I gave Hunter a good telling off yesterday. That's none of her business, though."

Isaiah narrows his eyes. "So you're not sneaking around with him?" The rising angst in his voice makes me smile.

"Isaiah, do you think if I was having an affair with Hunter, I'd have toyed with Brynn like that? Hell no, I'd rub it in her face after what she did to me."

He seems to ponder this for a moment. "And you would've been right. Good point," he says finally, picking up his book again.

Too bad when he drops his head down to read, I can see Brynn scowling at me from her table.

I resume concentrating on my pudding. In roughly two hours, my group is winning the Feast-Off. Then she'll really have something to scowl about.

It's probably a little ridiculous that I'm daydreaming about our presumed victory during my next two classes. Even though I've eaten my lunch, my stomach growls at the thought of the hot, brined turkey and deliciously carb-loaded side dishes we're preparing. I picture Mrs. Sanchez smiling beatifically at us, telling the whole class to see what a good job we did, Brynn scowling even more, and then, by some twist of fate, Jared's team falls out of first place into dead last and has to work the dance.

When the bell rings at the end of French, I spring out of my seat and am the first one to the door. I hustle my way through the crowded hallway, dreaming of victory and tryptophan-induced contentment. The meatheads will scoff in grand meathead fashion, Jared will have to shove his beret in his mouth to keep from screaming, and Hunter, Steve, and Brynn will rue the day they laughed at my accidentally salty chocolate chip cookies. I don't have any issues with the stoners, but I do hope they are at least a tiny bit envious of our feat.

By the time I get to the home ec room, I'm bordering on giddy. I scan the room for my family members, to share a psyched-up look with them, but they're not at our table. In fact, they're all gathered in our kitchen, staring into the refrigerator, their faces ranging between tense (Isaiah) and flat-out pissed off (A.J.).

"What is it?" I ask, feeling my smile evaporate.

Luke wordlessly points in the refrigerator, and there, on the bottom shelf, is our uncooked turkey sitting its roasting pan.

No. This is not happening.

That's when I hear giggling behind me and when I look over my shoulder, I see Steve and Hannah watching this go down as if it's a sitcom.

"What the hell?" I say, turning back to my group. "There's no way we're winning now. Like, seriously, what. The. Hell?"

"Agresti, it's not that big a deal—"

My cheeks get all hot as I spin around to face Luke. "Not that big a deal? We've been working toward this all marking period. But clearly, I'm the only one who gives a shit."

Luke flinches, and even Isaiah recoils, suddenly frowning.

I turn to A.J., who's been mysteriously silent. "Why didn't you put it in?"

He stares at me hard. "I had to take my grandma to the hospital because she fell this morning."

My stomach drops, as if I'm on an emotional elevator that's free-falling from the complete and total anger penthouse to the "oh crap, how can I be that stupid?" basement of embarrassment.

I find my voice. "Oh my god, is she okay?"

"She's fine, she just had to get a few stitches," he says, his eyes boring through me. "If you'd have checked your texts, you would've known that—and we might be eating turkey right now instead of staring at it in the refrigerator."

"Texts?" I repeat, feeling my shoulders sag.

"Yeah, I asked if you could run down and put the turkey in the oven since, you know, I was indisposed."

"I lost my phone and didn't have it until lunch, and even then the battery was dead," I say, becoming more than a little annoyed at his accusatory tone. "Why didn't you text anyone else?"

"Because I figured you'd see it!" he says, practically yelling.

"And that's my fault?"

"I thought you'd have your phone on you!"

"She didn't have her phone because she was hanging out with Hunter yesterday and he had it," I hear someone hiss.

I turn around and see Brynn leaning toward our kitchen, her face red and screwed up.

"What's that supposed to mean?" Luke asks, looking between the two of us.

"She left her phone in Hunter's car," Brynn says, her voice going up an octave, and attracting the attention of her group. "God knows what they were doing in there for her to forget it."

I shake my head, not even believing any of this. "For the last time: Nothing happened."

"What's going on?" Hunter asks, tugging at the collar of his sweater nervously.

"Just talking with Ellie over here about what a great, fabulous boyfriend you are," Brynn snits. "Did you think you guys could hook up again and that no one would find out?"

With that, Hunter shakes his head, grabs Brynn by the hand and marches her into the pantry, where we can hear his muffled voice talking sternly and hers sounding basically hysterical.

The guys are all staring at me wide-eyed.

"Seriously," I say, feeling my blood start to boil. "Nothing happened."

"Sounds to me like the lady doth protest too much," a smarmy voice pipes up. I turn around to see Jared leaning on his counter, looking like he's mentally composing a salacious blind item in his head.

"Shut up, Jared," I say. "You have no idea what's going on here."

"Oh, but I think I do," Jared says, grinning devilishly. "You and your merry group of losers are going to finish in last place, but it seems like you're actually a winner for finally slutting it up lately. Not bad for a former cold fish."

In that moment, everything weirdly slows down. It's like there's an explosion inside me, and it bursts out to my feet, which makes me jump out of my kitchen. Then the explosion travels into my hands, which reach for Jared's neck. I'm suddenly off the ground, tackling Jared to the floor, and his beret goes flying across the room. I feel my knee meet the tile with a hard thunk and pain registers in my brain, but I'm too busy intermittently pummeling Jared's chest with my fists, then shaking him by the shirt collar to care.

"Get! Off!" he gasps, and I realize I've knocked the wind out of him. He reaches up to swat me away, but I knock his hand back with significant slap. I feel a hand on my back, like someone is trying to pull me off of him, but I somehow manage to roll Jared and me into the bottom of a nearby kitchen counter, which we knock into with such force that an entire tray of deviled eggs comes crashing down on top of us.

"Ms. Agresti! Mr. Curtis!" Mrs. Sanchez yells, and I'm vaguely aware of her running over, as I grab at deviled eggs and pelt Jared's face and head with them. "We're not losers, I'm not a slut, and you're a jackass! A complete and total jackass . . . who . . . wears berets!" I scream, as he squirms underneath me. Even over the blood rushing in my ears and Jared's yelling, I hear various noises around the classroom, from hysterical laughter (I assume the stoners), hollering something about the eggs (the meatheads) to ohmygod-ing (Steve and Hannah).

I'm in mid-throw, when someone grabs me under my arms and pulls me off of Jared, who quickly crawls away.

"You're crazy!" he screams, his voice cracking, as he pulls himself to his feet. His group mates step away from him, as if he's carrying some kind of disease.

My heart's pounding so hard that I almost feel like I can't catch my breath.

"Aw, that was pretty awesome. You've had that coming for a long time, dude," Callie laughs from the Bakers' kitchen. If I wasn't in such a state, I think I'd probably hug her right now for saying that.

"What's come over you, Ms. Agresti?" Mrs. Sanchez says, her eyes wide with horror.

"I've had it with him," I manage to say as I shake myself free from the grasp of the person who grabbed me, and realize it's Bryce. We'd rolled all the way into Jersey Strong's kitchen and it was their deviled eggs I'd destroyed. I instantly feel even worse.

"Well, both your groups aren't getting any points for this lesson, and both you and Mr. Curtis can pack your things and head to the office." Mrs. Sanchez looks so disappointed that I want to cry.

I notice the collective shocked expression of my group changes to total annoyance. A.J. even hurls an oven mitt at the floor in disgust.

"Please," I say, "Don't penalize my whole group."

"Now, Ms. Agresti," Mrs. Sanchez says, wearily pointing to the door. "You too, Mr. Curtis."

Jared, who has pieces of egg flecked in his hair and stuck to his forehead, swipes up his backpack and storms out. I gather my things slowly so I can give him a head start to the office.

"I'm sorry I ruined your eggs," I whisper to Bryce. I brace myself for him to yell at me, but he surprises me by merely patting me on the shoulder. The rest of his group doesn't look so pleased with me, but they don't bitch at me either, and it almost makes me feel worse.

The rest of my classmates are all staring at me, some whispering and others tittering. I know I have egg in my hair, but I'm too embarrassed to shake it out. I can't even look back at my group, seeing as how I just ruined everything for them. Tears start burning my eyes as I leave, and they thankfully don't start falling until I get to the hall.

When I get to the principal's office, I'm shaking as well as crying. I've never even gotten a detention before and I'm terrified of what's to come.

"Oh, please, don't try to get sympathy by being a girl and crying,"

Jared says. He's sitting in a chair closest to the principal's door, so I take a seat four chairs away from him, lest I have any more urges to hit him.

Ms. Ahmed, the school secretary, is staring at me openmouthed. It's probably the egg, but maybe it's the fact that a girl and guy got in a fistfight. "And your name is?" she asks.

"Mary Ellen Agresti," I say.

She nods, then disappears into the principal's office.

"We're totally going to get suspended, you know," Jared says.

"Yeah, well, maybe you'll think of that the next time you mock me or my group," I whisper harshly. "Or anyone else for that matter on your stupid gossip page. You're lucky I'm a girl with no upper body strength and not any of the guys you mention who could do some actual damage."

He doesn't have an answer for that, and it's not like he can respond anyway. The door to the principal's office opens, and Ms. Ahmed ushers us in, closing the door behind us with an ominous click.

Three days' suspension. Yes, I got the maximum penalty because, as Mr. Golding reminded us, there's a zero-tolerance policy at RHHS for fistfights.

Amazingly, Jared didn't argue it. Probably because he realized we have witnesses to his constant harassment of our group, which I was quick to bring up. But also, I never mentioned The Buzz, and I think he was waiting for me to talk about it. He probably figured a three-day suspension for fighting is a whole lot better than the trouble he'd get into for his pet project.

We're dismissed long after the bell rings (because of our clean records and because it's the end of the day, Mr. Golding let us go without our parents having to come pick us up. But he made it clear he was calling them), and after I go to the bathroom to get the egg out of my hair, I head to my locker. Basically, I do anything possible to delay going home, where I'm sure my mom is going to freak out on me after Mr. Golding's phone call.

I can see a light on in the home ec room, and I peer inside to see Mrs. Sanchez surrounded by cleaning supplies, trying to get up the mess from the eggs.

"Mrs. Sanchez?" I say, putting my backpack down. "I'm so sorry for disrupting class like that and making such a mess. I swear to god, it'll never happen again."

Mrs. Sanchez studies me for a minute, then sighs and stands up. "I must say, in all my years of teaching, no one has ever used food as a weapon."

I don't know if she means this as a joke or not, but since she's not chewing me out for my lack of conduct, I figure she doesn't hate me. "Let me help you," I say, grabbing some paper towels and Windex. "I just want you to know, I'm not a violent person. I have no idea where that came from."

Mrs. Sanchez bites her lip as I start to scrub the floor. "I think I know where it came from. I know Jared isn't the easiest to get along with."

"Still," I say, slightly relieved she knows I'm not a raging psycho, or at least thinks I'm a raging psycho who has her reasons. "I could've handled it better."

"Well, I will say your group was very disappointed today," Mrs. Sanchez says, and it's like I've been stabbed in the heart. "I felt worse for them as a whole than for anything else."

Not worse than me, I guarantee that.

"What happened to the turkey?" I ask.

"It's still in your refrigerator," she says, pointing to our kitchen. "I told the boys I'd take it by the church down the street for their soup kitchen."

"I can take it over to the church now, if that's okay," I say, wiping the last of the egg from the floor.

"That would be lovely. I'll call them to let them know you're on your way," Mrs. Sanchez says.

I march over to our refrigerator and carefully grab the roasting pan, which is now covered in tinfoil. Even though the pan is sturdy and has handles, it's a bit awkward to carry because of the weight of the turkey, plus the weight of the books in my backpack. I pretend like it's super easy to walk as I make my way out of the room.

I turn to Mrs. Sanchez before I walk out the door. "Were the guys really pissed at me?"

"I wouldn't say that. But like I said, they did seem disappointed."

I must look as pained as I feel because Mrs. Sanchez gives me a reassuring smile. "Don't worry. They'll forgive you."

I can only hope she's right. Because I'm not exactly sure I'd forgive me if I were them.

I carry the turkey through the main hall and am glad there isn't anyone left at school to see me. I'm sure I'd get some quizzical looks carrying this massive tin-foiled thing down the halls.

It's starting to snow when I get out to the nearly empty parking lot, big, fat dry flakes, the kind that will totally stick and give us a nice few inches before it lets up. Unfortunately, since my hands are full, I can't pull my hood up, and flakes start smacking me in the face as I walk.

"Agresti!" I turn around and am totally shocked to see Luke leaning on the bike rack. He looks as if he's been waiting outside for a while, if his red cheeks are any indication. I try not to think about how ridiculously cute he is, all rosy-cheeked and windblown.

"Hey," I say, unable to look him in the eye.

"I was hoping I might run into you. Are you all right?"

I nod, feeling a little relieved that he at least doesn't hate me. "My knee's a little banged up, but I'll live."

"And what was the verdict from Golding?"

I shake my head and sigh. "I got my first suspension. That'll be something I'll proudly tell my grandkids about, I'm sure."

Luke throws his head back and laughs, which delights me. "Man, I always thought there was a little fire in you, but I never thought that would happen."

"Yeah, well, that makes two of us," I say, giggling. It feels good to laugh after everything that's happened today.

"Are you taking the turkey to the church?" he asks.

"Yeah, I told Mrs. Sanchez I'd take it over for her."

"Here, let me carry it."

"No," I say, stepping away from him. "I was such an asshole to you guys and I'm the one who messed everything up, so I need to do this."

"Jeez, don't feel that bad about it. Jared totally deserved it, especially after what he said to you."

"But I let you guys down," I say, my voice cracking. "We may not have won today, but if our side dishes were good enough we could've pulled ahead a little."

"You're still worried about the points?" Luke says, his eyes narrowing.

"Of course. Did you end up making the side dishes?"

He shakes his head. "We knew we were getting a zero already, what would the point have been?"

"Ugh. If I'd have just kept myself in check . . ."

"Agresti," Luke says, stepping closer and surprising me by tilting up my chin with his finger. "If you didn't hit him, I would have."

I look at Luke through the snowflakes. The way he's staring at me right now is so intense, it makes my heart rate speed up and I have to catch my breath. Then a big flake smacks just below my eye and I shake my head to get it off but it doesn't budge.

Wordlessly, Luke reaches toward my face, and with his thumb, gently wipes the snowflake from my cheek. A rush of heat goes through me, and I'm surprised the turkey doesn't start cooking right there in my hands.

I gaze into his eyes, his thumb now caressing my cheek, and I know if he tries to kiss me out here I won't—

"Arrr, arrr, arrrrrrrr!"

I jump and almost drop the turkey, but Luke laughs. "Way to ruin the moment, Montague," he says over his shoulder.

Sure enough, beyond the chain-link fence, Montague is terrorizing one of his cinder blocks. And I have to thank him for that, because it completely snaps me out of this dreamy, snow-globe-y moment and back to reality.

Luke's face falls. "What?"

It takes everything in me to say it. "I can't."

His brow furrows and there's a wounded look in his eyes. "You were just about to kiss me."

"I don't know," I say. "I miss you. I'm attracted to you. I just can't get over the fact that you lied to me."

"Oh my god," Luke says, turning around and storming back toward his bike.

"Luke, come on," I say. "Put yourself in my position."

He hops off the bike, lets it fall and stomps back, coming toe-to-toe with me, and for a second I think he's going to grab me in a passionate kiss like in the movies. But instead he throws his hands up.

"You can't ask me to see something from your point of view when you're wrong, dead wrong," Luke says, his face red, his eyes bright. "I've told you Greta and I were broken up, but, no, you want to believe a stupid gossip blog over me. But then, you're still so damn obsessed with beating Hunter, maybe you're still hung up on him or something, and that's where this is coming from."

He doesn't wait for me to react. Instead, he stomps back to his bike, gets on, and speeds away, his tires leaving a fine black line through the dusting of snow on the pavement.

When he's gone, it's so quiet that I can hear the snowflakes lightly hitting the tin foil on the turkey. I look around dazedly and realize that I'm in the parking lot, the same place Hunter dumped me in horrific fashion. Which means it's the second time in three months I've had a guy tell me off right here.

I really hate this parking lot.

CHAPTER 25

I'm numb as I walk home, and I'm not certain it has to do with the blustery breeze and thousands of snowflakes attacking me, nor the fact that I've been walking really, really slow. I think my brain may be shutting down and going on strike, considering all the emotions it has had to process in the last twenty-four hours.

I try to count my blessings, like my grandma used to say. I have my health (aside from the inevitable cold I'm going to catch from wandering around outside in the snow for so long). I have three days away from school, so I won't have to deal with the rumor mill, which, by Friday, will probably have twisted the story into me using clubs and nunchucks to put Jared in a coma.

But if my brain somehow voted to secede from my body, I don't think I could blame it. Especially since we are going to have to face my parents over the whole suspension thing and that in itself makes me want to crawl into the fetal position in a closet somewhere and not come out till I'm forty-six.

Just as I climb the steps to the porch, the door flies open and my mom is staring down at me, her face flushed, her mouth hanging open.

"What has gotten into you, Mary Ellen?" she asks when she can finally speak, and I can see the veins popping in her neck.

I can turn and run. I'm still not technically in the house and she'd have trouble catching me since she's not wearing shoes right now.

"And where have you been? We've been trying to get you on your phone for over an hour."

The reminder of my dead phone makes me realize I'd have no means of communication if I did run away, so my only choice is to go inside.

"My battery died," I say quietly as I walk inside, and I stop short when I see my father sitting on the bottom step of the staircase. Oh my god, he left work early, too.

"You attacked your classmate?" he asks, not even trying to hide the disappointment on his face.

"It was provoked," I say, dropping eye contact. "He said I was a slut and he called my group losers."

"Your principal made us very aware of that," Mom says. "But since when do you go around tackling people and throwing things at them?"

"Um, one fight doesn't exactly make me the bad seed," I say, my fear suddenly replaced with crankiness. I mean, I've never given them any issues before. Ever.

"What we're worried about is that you've never resorted to violence," Dad says sternly.

"Yeah, Mary Ellen," Mom says. "What kind of person does something like what you pulled today?"

That's when something in me snaps. "Maybe the kind of person who didn't want to sleep with her boyfriend! Because that's where this whole damn mess started in the first place!"

Both my parents' faces go from stern to OMG, and it would probably be amusing if I wasn't the one in the hot seat here.

"Or if you want to take it further back, it's because we had to move here. Because then I never would've met Hunter and he never would've dumped me for Brynn—"

"He dumped you for Brynn?" Mom says, her voice going up a few octaves. "Why didn't you tell us that?"

"Because you already didn't like him and then I would've had to tell you I was partially dumped over lack of sex and I really didn't want to get into that with my parents," I say.

Dad has a look on his face like, "Yeah, ain't that the truth," but Mom frowns sadly, as if she's hurt. "Well, you could have told us. But how does that lead into you getting in a fight with this Jared boy? That isn't like you at all, El."

"I know it's not like me!" I yell, unable to stop myself. "But when you get dumped for being a frigid bitch or whatever, and then you have to share a class with your ex and his new girlfriend and when you're finally getting over him, you start liking another guy who turns out to be another liar and then your best friend can't go to her dream school and she takes it out on you and you tell her off even though you know she's really hurting," I gasp for air, "and then you get in another fight with your ex-boyfriend because of all your pent-up anger and his new girlfriend starts accusing you of sleeping with him and you stupidly take all your anger out on your group and that Jared guy overhears and accuses you of being a slut, well, yeah, I kind of had had it."

I catch my breath and feel a little dizzy, as if getting all that off my chest was like getting thirty vials of blood drawn.

Mom and Dad gape at me, their mouths literally hanging open.

"I felt humiliated by a lot of it and because I know you never liked Hunter and he's what triggered everything. I guess I didn't want to get an 'I Told You So.'"

"Oh, El," Mom says, and sighs. "I know I wasn't great with Hunter and I apologize. But never in a million years would I have said 'I told you so.'"

"Me neither," Dad says.

"Well, then I'm sorry for assuming," I say quietly, and sit down on the step next to my dad. We're silent for a few minutes and I hold my breath waiting for my punishment.

"The boy who turned out to be a liar, is that Luke?" Mom says, her brow furrowed.

I nod sadly.

"What did he lie to you about?" my dad says, clenching his jaw.

I almost burst out laughing at his paternal side getting triggered. "It's fine, I handled it."

Mom's eyes are narrowed like she doesn't believe me, and I have to clench my own jaw so I don't melt down over that. It's not something I want to go into now.

"It sounds like you've had a lot on your plate, El. And I'm worried this has a lot to do with what happened to you in middle school, and maybe we didn't do enough to help you stick up for yourself then, and it's rearing its ugly head now."

I sigh deeply. "I hadn't even thought of that. But it kind of makes sense. I didn't ever tell off the people who made fun of me, and I think, deep down, I always wish I'd had. I've never really gotten over that. But that's not on you guys."

Mom tucks my hair behind my ears. "I really want you to know you can talk to us instead of keeping everything bottled up inside."

I nod, feeling the slightest bit relieved. "I will. I thought I could handle it all, but clearly I reached a breaking point. I won't let that happen again."

"Good, I believe you," Mom says, caressing my cheek. The phone rings then, and Mom goes to answer it. Dad pats my back. "I've been dying to know what happened with the Feast-Off. Did you get to do it before the fight?"

I can't help but laugh.

"What? You were looking forward to this for weeks. I want to know if you brought down all your classmates with that amazing menu you were planning."

Tears sting my eyes over realizing how that never got to happen. "No, I got us disqualified because of the fight. But I was really flipping out on the guys before that. I took the class competition way too far. I think they hate me."

"Aw, El," Dad says. "I bet they're over it already."

I can only shake my head regretfully in response.

"Next time?" Dad says, lowering his voice. "You throw raw eggs at a boy who insults you like that. Deviled eggs are too good for him."

I laugh. "The deviled eggs made a nice mess, too."

"Well, any boy who makes comments like that deserves what's coming to him and I'm glad you did it. And I think your friends will forgive it, too."

My friends. I'd never thought of them as that and yet . . . it's true. I like being in class with them. I like hanging out with them. We give each other advice. We laugh a lot (or at least we did before today). Sure, I'm not going to invite them over for a sleepover or go prom-dress shopping, but they're kind of like my school . . . family.

And here I am, three months after dreading the sight of them, hoping that they feel the same way about me.

My parents may be pretty cool in that they're not grounding me, but they're more than making up for it by leaving me lists of things to do during my suspension. Like cleaning the toilet. And dusting everything from the shelves to the molding on the floor to behind the radiators.

"This isn't a vacation, sweetie," Mom says when she wakes me up at 6:00 a.m. the next day.

I can't argue with her, seeing as how great she and Dad were about my meltdown, so I wait until she's out of the room to groan into my pillow.

But by 11:00 a.m., I'm kind of glad to have the long list stuck to the fridge with a "Whistle While You Work" magnet because it lets me ruminate things as I go, especially how to make things up to the guys.

I'm pondering this as I vacuum the blinds in the dining room, with Earth, Wind & Fire blasting on the record player. One of my epic moments of procrastination this morning was thumbing through my mom's old records and deciding which would add the perfect soundtrack for household duties, and I'm humming along when there's pounding on the front door.

Instinctively, I drop to the ground and kill the vacuum. I'm worried it's either a kidnapper or a religious group.

Bangbangbangbangbang!

I crawl along the floor on my stomach, wondering if I can peek through the curtains without being seen.

"Ellie!" a voice calls out. "It's me. I know you're home because the music is blowing your cover."

I throw open the door and Jodie is standing there in her coat and backpack and St. Catherine's uniform.

"How did you—"

"I cut class," Jodie says, brushing past me.

"You cut school?" Chinese class is one thing, but high school is another animal entirely.

Jodie raises an eyebrow at me. "You got suspended?"

I squint at her. "How did you know?"

"I stopped by the shoe store and Richard told me. He thought I knew."

I slap my hand to my forehead. I'd been texting last night with Richard and told him about the suspension, and that my parents were still allowing me to work.

"Did you really throw scrambled eggs at that Jared guy for calling you a whore?" Jodie's eyes are kind of hopeful and it makes me laugh.

"It was deviled eggs and he said I was 'slutting it up lately,' if we're being specific," I say.

"No!"

"Yes! And before this convo continues, can I just say I'm really sorry for yelling at you about USC?"

Jodie waves her hand. "Thank you, but I know I've been an über-bitch lately. Even my guidance counselor yelled at me. And I really shouldn't have gone off on you about Hunter like that. Especially since you hooked up with Luke. Spill."

We plunk down on the couch and I launch into the whole story of the party and the secret kisses, the lying, and the fallout.

Jodie frowns. "I really wish you'd told me."

"I wanted to, but you were so bummed about USC," I say. "And for what it's worth, no one knew, and that's probably for the best considering what happ—"

I can't get the rest out because a sudden torrent of tears grips me and Jodie has to swoop in and smooth my hair from my face.

"Ugh, I thought I was over this."

"You really liked him," Jodie says sympathetically. "Knowing you, you've been sitting on this and it's eaten away at you."

"You're not wrong," I say. "I've tried being friends with him, but the feelings just keep coming to the surface."

Jodie scrunches up her face in thought. "You're a hundred per-cent sure he was lying to you?"

"The way Greta was crying, I don't think there's any way Jared made it up."

Jodie shakes her head. "I know I only met him that one time, but, for what it's worth, I wouldn't have seen this coming, either, so don't beat yourself up. I'm really sorry he turned out to be such a dude."

"I guess that's what I get for taking a risk," I say, forcing a laugh. "You were right about that, though. I run away from things."

"I'm so sorry I ever said that. I mean—"

"No. I ran away from middle school, which was probably valid, but after that I just kept avoiding anything tough. It's half the reason I was probably with Hunter in the first place. I didn't have to meet anyone and make an effort if I just took on his friends. I mean, I tried to drop home ec to avoid him. What kind of person does that?"

"Someone who's looking out for themselves?" Jodie says. "Don't be so hard on yourself, El. You'll take risks when you're ready."

I smile at her, my number one cheerleader since the fourth grade. "I can't believe you actually cut school."

Jodie shakes her head. "Well, let's just say I've done some reprioritizing."

I picture her cutting all of her classes from here to graduation and giving up on college all together. I must have a freaked-out look on my face because Jodie throws her head back and laughs. "I just mean that I'm trying to not be so concerned about school right now and more about myself. You're right about the college thing."

I start to apologize again, but she holds up her hand. "I know I'm terrified to fly, but if I'm serious about this TV writing thing, I think I really have to give a long hard think about my options."

"Could you do NYU or something? Don't they have a good dramatic arts program?"

"I applied there, Columbia, and Emerson. I'm not going to lie, it's an adjustment not thinking about USC anymore." She smiles, but it doesn't quite meet her eyes.

"You'll do great no matter where you go," I say, squeezing her arm.

Jodie blows out her cheeks, then glances around the room and spots the vacuum next to the drapes. "Are you doing housework?"

"That's my punishment. It could be worse, I guess."

Jodie taps her chin thoughtfully. "What if I help you out with that and we make some grilled cheeses for lunch and then watch terrible daytime TV together, like we used to during our middle school vacations?"

"Best. Day. Ever," I say, clapping my hands.

"You know, if this were an old TV show, we'd totally hug right now and the studio audience would go 'awww,'" Jodie says.

"I don't need a studio audience," I say, and throw my arms around her.

"Aww," Jodie coos, and we both double over laughing.

CHAPTER 26

On the third day of my suspension, I'm tasked with heading over to the Shop & Save to do the food shopping. I decide to go early enough that I don't run into any of my classmates—surely they won't be hanging out in the produce aisle at nine thirty in the morning.

I'm hit with a sudden wistfulness as I enter through the automatic doors, thinking of my group expedition here back in September, and how wary I was of all the guys at that point.

Now I'm just hoping they'll speak to me again.

The wistfulness hits its full peak when I steer the cart through the frozen food section. In my winter coat, I'm nowhere near as cold as I was that day, but the memory of the smell of Luke's sweatshirt hits me like the world's saddest cannonball to my stomach. It doesn't help that Christmas carols are playing, and I wonder what Christmas nerd Luke would think about that.

I really can't think about him like this. It's not good for anyone.

I manage to finish shopping without losing myself further down Memory Lane, and for that I'm grateful. As I'm pushing my full cart out the door, my eyes fall on someone sitting on the bench outside the Shop & Save entrance.

Someone with blonde braids, snapping blue eyes, and a snow-board across her lap.

Stop looking, stop looking, stop looking, my brain implores me, but it's too late. Greta must feel my gaze because she turns her head, her eyes instantly locking on mine.

"Hey! Mary Ellen!"

Oh crap. Oh crap. Oh crap.

I squeeze my eyes shut and am filled with silent regret for never making a will. I'm just going to have to hope Jodie knows she can have all my old InSyte merchandise.

I finally manage to lift my hand in a weak wave and hope I can fix my expression into something other than guilt.

Greta moves off the bench and walks over to me, hugging herself against the cold. If she's going to bludgeon me with her snowboard, I hope it's quick.

But it's not beating the crap out of *me* that's she interested in.

Her eyes sparkle and she grins. "Did you seriously take down Jared?"

Then, I swear to god, she lifts up her hand and instead of punching me, she makes a motion to high-five. So I do. She gives my hand a robust thwack. "Bad. Ass. And thank you."

I'm still ready to run. I'm not convinced this isn't going to be an ambush of some kind. "He had it coming," I say.

She rolls her eyes dramatically. "Understatement of the year. That guy didn't even learn from being called out, no, he had to turn it up a notch."

"Yeah, I suspect I'm not the only one who wanted to flatten him after that last post."

"What did he say to make you blow?"

"We were in class and he called my group losers, then implied I'd made my way from cold fish to raging slut, basically," I say. "I was having a bad day already and that was enough to set me over the edge."

"Typical dude, thinking he gets to label us to fit his narrative," Greta says. "Should've punched him myself for the stuff he said about me."

I squeeze my eyes shut, waiting for her to call me out. But when I open them, she's shaking her head. "Like, he had to tell the whole world about Evan Fishman and drag Luke into it."

It's as if the chilly temperature has somehow breeched my coat and frozen my insides. I don't even get to say anything because Greta keeps going. "I swear to god, he was the biggest mistake of my life. What was I even thinking? Still wasn't any of Jared's business, though."

"Evan Fishman?" I blurt out when I finally have the capacity to speak.

Greta blinks. "Yeah, he and I were hooking up. I thought it was more but it was only 'messing around' to him—direct quote there—so when he went off with that girl he works with . . . wait, I thought you read The Buzz?"

I'm suddenly sweating in spite of the cold air. "I thought it was Luke who'd, uh, done you dirty."

"Luke?" Greta says with a snort. "He can be a stubborn ass sometimes, but no. It was Evan who quote, unquote, did me dirty, though I guess I deserved it for being dumb enough to fall for his lying ass."

I remember Evan driving Greta to Luke's that day of the interview, and how she looked at him when she said goodbye. And then it hits me: "Fish-y." It wasn't referring to me, the cold fish. It was referring to Evan.

Fishman.

Oh my god.

Now Greta shakes her head. "I mean, we had issues, Luke and

me, but it's all because we broke up over the summer and got back together when we shouldn't have. Then I had to start falling for another guy? I was really confused. Luke finally was like, 'This isn't really working, is it?'"

It's like someone's taken a wrench and clamped down on my stomach and started twisting, to the point that I feel nauseated. It's actually worse than anticipating getting beaten up.

"So, when you came to the party together, you were already broken up?"

"The party. . . ." Greta bites her lip and scrunches her nose in thought, then her eyes brighten. "Yeah, we'd been split for about a week at that point, but we were trying to stay friends. I was in a bad mood that night because Evan blew me off. I didn't tell Luke that, of course, but I shouldn't have gone. But I'm kind of glad I did, because I got to see that Luke was at least moving on."

She raises an eyebrow at me pointedly and I feel my face flush. I try to make a noise of apology but it's lodged in my throat.

"I thought something was brewing between you guys. He was trying to act all closed off when he saw you, and I knew."

"Nothing happened while you guys were together," I manage to say.

Now she laughs, a hearty, musical chortle. "Oh, I know. I thought if something *was* going to happen between you guys, at least Luke would be happy and I'd feel a little less guilty about, like, emotionally cheating on him. So I left that night, hoping it would nudge something between you two, I guess. My reasons were completely selfish, I can't lie."

Oh my god. Oh my god. Oh my god. How am I such a colossal idiot?

I must look completely stricken because Greta pats my arm. "Seriously, it's okay, I know you didn't move in on him while we were—" She pauses. "But wait, that would imply that something did happen eventually, but it doesn't look like you're together now."

I close my eyes and shake my head. "Long story. Very long, very stupid story. Pretty much all my fault."

A tall older woman who resembles Greta and has to be her mother comes out of the store then. "Ready to hit the road? We've got six hours of driving ahead of us."

Greta nods and gathers her snowboard, then she turns back to me. "Listen, I don't really want to talk up my ex because he's, like, still my ex and that's just weird, but he's a good dude. And he's not really great at holding grudges. Just in case that means anything to you."

"Thanks. And, uh, good luck training," I croak as she and her mom walk away.

I can only stare at my cart full of groceries. I just wasted the last few weeks being angry and self-righteous over something that didn't even happen. That Luke had even kept speaking to me is crazy. *I* wouldn't speak to me.

How can you make an apology big enough for that?

CHAPTER 27

On Friday morning I have three agendas:

One: Return to school and keep my head held high if anyone makes fun of me for my fight with Jared. We have an early dismissal today, so at least any snarky asides will be confined between the hours of seven thirty and noon.

But it's easier than I thought, considering when I walk in, I get a literal ovation from the stoners who hang out outside the cafeteria. Callie Gorman even shakes my hand and cheers, "That fight was the most righteous thing I've seen. Give 'em hell, Ellie."

And it's not an isolated incident. In the short time I'm in the building, I get high fives, salutes, and thumbs-ups from anyone passing me. I guess I underestimated how many peoples' lives have been made hell because of The Buzz.

Speaking of, Jared didn't write up our brawl, but I knew there was no way he'd post about himself being beaten up by a girl. He must have had an appointed proxy in his absence, however, because while The Buzz's posts have been scant, there was one about some kind of huge fight between Brynn and Hunter that seemed to span all the days I was out.

Destiny Done?

This formerly destined pair is apparently on the verge of a breakup, if their constant public spats are any indication. A classroom confrontation over alleged cheating has led to more arguments, culminating in a very audible fight over lies surrounding one's college choice. Sources whisper it may be over between them.

So I guess Hunter came clean about Tufts. Still, after I read that, I make a point to delete The Buzz from my phone's search history, and vow not to visit it anymore. It's the start of the "Ellie doesn't care what you say about her anymore" era, and that means killing gossip sources at their root.

Number two on the agenda: Start the road to reconciliation with Luke.

I labored all yesterday over an apology email—which I sent to Jodie for approval as I was writing, to which she replied this is great. JUST CALL HIM THO—which I intend to send after I make a total fool of myself on the morning TV broadcast.

My palms sweat as I wait for Mia to throw it to me for the forecast. She finishes a story about tryouts for the spring musical, then grins at me.

"And now back from her well-earned hiatus, here's Ellie Agresti with the weather."

I force my perkiest smile. "Thanks, Mia. This weekend's forecast looks great, with clear skies and highs in the forties. We're watching a potential nor'easter that may give us some snow Tuesday into Wednesday, but it's too early to say what track it's going to take and how much snow it would give us, so don't go making any snow day plans just yet. But fear not, tonight, we'll be enjoying clear conditions for the winter dance, with lows around thirty-two."

I basically spit that out at lightning speed, causing Chris and Mia to exchange a nervous glance, probably freaking out there's going to be a huge time gap to fill. So I quickly add, "If I can, there's something I want to say about, uh, recent events."

Mia nods vigorously, though Chris is frowning apprehensively. He eventually nods, though, and I pull out the index card I carefully filled out last night. My hand is shaking, so I try holding it with both hands.

"As many of you know, I've been the center of some, uh, hot gossip this year. I think a lot of us have been, actually. So let me do this in a way you may understand: Which senior is neither a cold fish nor slutting it up? She's a weather nerd who likes tacos and lilacs and just wanted to fly under the radar when she transferred here. She may have stuck it out in the wrong relationship just to keep it that way. The irony, then, is that relationship basically shoved her into the spotlight."

I can't help but shoot an exasperated look to the camera then, and I hear people in the studio and the nearby classrooms laugh. It's all I need to keep going.

"But losing that relationship forced her to take a different approach to things. She still prefers to stay under the radar, but she's now better at being in the spotlight. She used to be afraid to speak her mind, but now she can . . . for the most part. She wouldn't have had the guts to do this three months ago and she thanks the friends she's made for helping her get to this point, the friends who have accepted her as she is: Isaiah, A.J., and Alisha, you're the best." At the other end of the table, Alisha clutches a hand to her heart and mouths "Aww," at me.

I smile before swallowing hard and forcing myself to stare directly into the camera. "She is also as flawed as anyone else. Like, when she snaps at her home ec group because she's taken a class assignment way, way, way too seriously in the name of proving something that never really needed to be proved—I'm beyond sorry, guys. Or when she finds out she's been incredibly wrong about something for a very long time. And she really wants to tell Luke Burke that she really likes him, that she's sorry more than she can say, and that she hopes he saves her a dance tonight. And she doesn't care who knows it."

There's a collective "oooooooh" and wolf whistles that erupt from the classrooms by the TV studio.

"Anyway, that's all I wanted to say."

I glance back sheepishly at Mia and Chris, who are staring at me with their mouths hanging open. "Back to you, Mia and Chris!"

They carry on with the broadcast as if what I just did was totally normal, but Willow's eyes are bugging out of her head from behind the camera as she mouths an exaggerated "Oh my god" at me.

I quietly wait for the broadcast to end, and the second we're clear, I practically sprint toward my backpack to grab my phone and hit send on the email to Luke. Alisha jumps out in front of me, her face giddy. "I knew you were into Luke! Why didn't you say anything?"

I grin widely. "I just did, didn't I?"

She laughs. Willow joins us and pokes me in the arm. "I'm shocked it took you as long as this. It was obvious back in that interview you did with him."

"Well, uh, we kind of started seeing each other in secret after the party . . ."

"Since the party?" Willow says, her eyes huge. "Jesus, I need to give Luke crap. I saw him at Target a couple days after the party and I was like, 'Are you and Ellie secretly dating or something?' and he was like 'That's the craziest thing I've ever heard.'"

"Well, it wasn't really a lie because we broke up pretty soon after. I got mad at him and it ended up that I was totally wrong."

I must look distraught because Alisha squeezes my elbow. "He'll forgive you. I know he will."

"For real," Willow says. "That boy is cuh-razy for you. It's all over his face."

Their optimism buoys me for a bit, but then I check my phone. Nothing.

I'm on edge the rest of the day, to the point I'm glad for the early dismissal because my concentration is nonexistent. By the time we're released at noon, with no texts or in-person appearances from Luke, I'm ready to sink into the nearest crevice for the next decade or six.

"I bet he just wants to talk to you in person tonight," Alisha says as we walk out of school together.

I offer a weak smile and pray I don't start crying. "We'll see."

I can't break down because I have to focus on my third agenda for today: Make it up to my home ec group that we have to be at the dance tonight. My plan is kind of complex and will require every bit of concentration. I've already reached out to Mrs. Sanchez on the matter and she's agreed to help me, so at least there's that.

It would just be whole lot easier to concentrate if Luke were speaking to me.

CHAPTER 28

"Are you sure about this?"

Mrs. Sanchez is looking at me with what I think is a mixture of admiration and "this girl is completely nuts."

"I'm pretty good at multitasking," I say with a shrug. That's a total lie, but I at least need to try. If I don't, I might burst into tears over not hearing from Luke.

She consults her phone. "Well, your shift doesn't start until nine thirty, so you have a good two and a half hours to finish."

"Oh, it won't take that long," I assure her. "Thank you again for opening the classroom for me."

Mrs. Sanchez opens her mouth, like she's about to say something, then stops herself and smiles. "You're welcome. And good luck to you. I'm sure your group members will be very pleased to have a decent meal in their stomachs before your shift begins."

"I hope so," I say. And I also hope it helps to make them forgive me.

When Mrs. Sanchez exits the home ec room, I dash to my kitchen and throw open the refrigerator and study the contents inside. Mrs. Sanchez is completely right to be doubtful of my abilities, because I have two hours to cook five side dishes. By myself. While wearing a black velvet cocktail dress and heels.

I yank my shoes off, since they're only going to slow me down. I then tie on an apron, knowing that my mom will be less than pleased if her dress gets stained with potatoes and cream of mushroom soup.

Then I set to work—I'm a whirlwind of filling pots with water, then placing them on the stove and starting the oven. I raid the pantry and the refrigerator for our ingredients. I'm moving around so much, I feel my hair starting to pop out of the French twist I'd tried to do by myself.

I attempt to tuck in the offending loose tendrils when all the water on the stove starts to boil at once, sending water sloshing over the sides of the pots.

"Eeeep!" I squeal, reaching for the burners and lowering them, praying the water doesn't jump out onto me.

"Jeez, Agresti, you trying to out-do Martha Stewart or something?"

After I jump about ten feet, I blow a stray lock of my hair out of my face and see Luke in the doorway. He's out of breath, as if he's been running, but he's grinning.

Utter relief and a fluttery feeling fill my stomach at the sight of him in a navy-blue suit, white shirt and red tie. He's here, and he doesn't seem like he hates me. And he looks totally hot.

Then a wave of disappointment hits me. "This was supposed to be a surprise," I groan.

Luke makes his way into the room, peeling off his suit jacket as he gets to our kitchen. As he tosses the jacket over the corner of a nearby chair, I notice his tie is printed with little reindeer.

"Well, I *am* surprised. Because I have no idea what you're doing."

"I wanted to make all of our side dishes tonight. Like, I wanted to make it up to you guys."

"Make up what?" Luke says, wrinkling his nose.

"The fact that I was such an überbitch and we're here tonight as a result of that," I sigh.

Luke shakes his head and laughs. "The points thing sucks but we definitely didn't hold this against you at all. We heard what Jared said."

I gaze at the array of pots and pans and food spread on our counter and start to laugh. "I knew I should've just sent a group text apologizing."

"I would've preferred a GIF with a kitten or bear cub saying 'I'm sorry,' instead of, you know, a home-cooked meal," Luke sniffs, but he can't keep a straight face.

"Well, I can at least use this to make up for the fact that we have to be here tonight," I say, feeling almost dizzy with relief that he's being himself.

"Fair enough," Luke replies, and starts rolling up his sleeves. "Where do we start?"

"Oh no," I say, wagging a wooden spoon at him. "You shouldn't have to help. This is all me."

Luke bites his lip like he's trying not to laugh. "And you were doing so well before I walked in here?"

"All right. You can do one thing. But just one thing."

"Then I better make it an important thing!" Luke smiles again, and tosses his tie over his shoulder. Then he starts digging around our apron drawer and pulls out the green flowered one, which he ties around his waist. He notices me staring at him, and I realize I'm smiling when he's like, "What?"

"Oh," I say, trying not to giggle. "I just enjoy it when you wear the girly apron."

"I knew it! You always get this little smile on your face when I put it on."

"So you wear it for my pleasure, then?" I say, clearing my throat and hoping I sound jokey and not all cocky and "I know you want me."

"I aim to please," he responds, which doesn't tell me much, but I'll take it.

"How did you know I was in here?" I ask, as I hand him some potatoes to peel.

"Mrs. Sanchez said you were up to something and I put two and two together and sprinted on down here. I, uh, read your email. And I heard you may or may not have given me a shout-out while doing the weather this morning?"

I finally look at him directly. "You heard? Were you not here?"

"I had a dentist appointment, so I never came in today. But let's just say everyone who has my phone number let me know."

I slump against the sink. "I do my version of a grand gesture, and the grand gesture receiver wasn't even here. I knew I should've just called you to apologize."

Luke turns toward me fully. "I definitely appreciate it."

"Seriously. I was horrible to you. For no reason. I'm so sorry I let Jared and my own stupid imagination make me doubt you. Like, I don't even know what I can do to make up for that. And you were right about me taking the competition too far—it was for all the wrong reasons. I really don't give a crap about what Hunter or Brynn think anymore."

"I probably could've explained things better to you," he says, and I feel sort of melty inside that he's trying to make me feel less bad when really, yeah, this was all on me.

"Anyway, I'm glad we're okay now because I've been holding onto this for a while," he says, a mischievous smile spreading across his face. He then opens our utensil drawer, reaching pretty far into it, then pulls something out with a triumphant smile on his face.

"For you, my lady," he says with a bow. In his extended hand is a spatula—with rhinestones and red and green gemstones glued onto the handle.

"Oh my god, a real-deal bejeweled spatula!" I say, delight coursing through my whole body.

"Courtesy of my mom's hot glue gun," Luke says. "I wasn't sure how to make a gold-plated pancake turner, unfortunately."

"My birthday is in February," I say. "I'd love—"

There's a hissing sound as one of the pots starts to boil over and Luke reaches for the knob to turn down the flame. As he does, water spits out from the pot and onto his wrist.

"Damn it!" He winces as he yanks his arm back.

"Oh no," I say, and without thinking, grab a wad of paper towels and run cold water from the sink over them. I wring them out quickly and grab Luke's hand, then press the damp pile of towels onto the underside of his wrist.

"It's not that bad," Luke laughs. "It just surprised me."

"Still," I say, taking the towels off and examining his wrist. "You don't want to take any chances. I'll feel really bad if I scarred you. Especially after you've gifted me with the world's most fabulous spatula."

The ice-cold paper towels are making my hand numb, but I notice Luke isn't exactly complaining. In fact, he isn't saying anything, so I glance up and he's staring down at me, his expression at once soft and intense, if that's possible. It makes my heart catch in my throat and I don't feel like I can speak.

"You don't know how badly I want to kiss you right now," he finally says.

"You don't know how badly I want you to," I say.

With my hand still pressing the paper towels to his arm, he leans down and very gently kisses me. It's like I touched the hot stove, such is the surge that runs through me, and I'm kissing him back in a matter of seconds.

"Wait," I say, pulling back. "I just want you to know, I'm all in on us, okay? No more worrying about Hunter and Brynn's group. No more reading The Buzz or giving a crap about what anyone says. No hiding or being on the down-low."

"I think Jared knows better than to cross you again," Luke says.

"But I'm glad I can say out loud that the total badass who put him in his place is my gal."

I laugh. "So, you're only into me for my intimidating physical strength. Nice."

Luke smiles and shakes his head and wraps his arms around me. "I've been into you since the day at the grocery store. You looked so cute in my sweatshirt. And I didn't wash it for weeks because I liked the way it smelled."

I wrinkle my nose in thought. "Funny, I think it was you juggling the oranges that, uh, did it for me."

"So the Shop & Save is where romance is born, huh?" Luke says, reaching over and tucking part of my failed French twist behind my ear.

"And people think grocery stores are boring," I say. Then I surprise him by pulling him down by his tie and kissing him like a guy who wears ugly aprons for my benefit deserves to be kissed.

An hour and a half, five side dishes, one dessert, and four more kisses later, I head down to the gym to find Isaiah and A.J. The gym is pretty packed with my schoolmates, who are either slow dancing or standing on the sidelines. I spot the snack table, which is being manned by one of Mrs. Sanchez's other classes.

And almost instantly, my eyes fall on Hunter and Brynn, who are swaying to the music. I guess The Buzz item was wrong, seeing as how they're here together, but they're not really looking at each other as they dance, as they both seem to be staring off into space. Hunter must feel me staring because he suddenly meets my gaze over Brynn's shoulder. I prepare for him to shoot daggers at me with his eyes, but he surprises me by giving me a small smile and nodding. An acknowledgement of me taking out Jared? An apology for the other day? I don't know. And, refreshingly, I don't even care. But I nod back with a smile of my own, then keep on moving.

Isaiah and A.J. have ensconced themselves in the corner, and they don't exactly seem like they're too thrilled to be there, if the looks of boredom (Isaiah) and yawning (A.J.) are any indication. But I can't help but smile at how handsome they are in their suits and ties.

I give them a big wave, which catches their attention, but before I can say anything, A.J.'s all, "What happened to you?"

"I was suspended?" I say slowly.

"No, your hair," A.J. says, pointing at my head. "It looks like you were fighting a tornado."

"Oh!" I say, touching the sprung-free strands. "Well, I didn't do such a good job of styling it." And I was kind of too busy making out with Luke to have time to stop in front of a mirror, but that seems better left unsaid.

"Mrs. Sanchez said you were doing some kind of top-secret thing," Isaiah says.

I nod. "It's a peace offering. I feel terrible about what happened the other day."

"Why?" Isaiah says, and it almost looks like he's grown an inch or two in the three days I was out. "You had to do what you had to do."

"Still, I didn't have to be so awful to you guys and I know none of us are thrilled to be here," I say. "So I need you to follow—"

"Ellie! There you are!" I turn around to see Alisha walking toward us in a cute black strapless cocktail dress with a royal-blue pashmina thrown over her shoulders. "You look great!"

"So do you!" I say. I notice A.J. is nervously tugging at his suit jacket and adjusting his tie. I suddenly feel bad that I'm taking him away from a chance at alone time with Alisha.

"I need you to come with us," I say to Alisha.

"Me?" she says, blinking in confusion. "Where are we going?"

"It's a surprise. Follow me."

"Are we going to get in trouble for leaving?" A.J. asks.

"Nope, we have Mrs. Sanchez's permission to be gone until nine thirty."

"What about Luke?" Isaiah asks.

"He, uh, helped out a little," I say, knowing I'm blushing.

Isaiah grins, giving me a knowing look. "Oh, right, he's your boyfriend now."

"Yeah, that was a great weather report, yo," A.J. says, batting his eyelashes. "Sunny with a chance of looooove."

"Yeah, yeah, yeah," I say, waving them off as we walk. "It won't affect our work, I promise."

I lead the group to the home ec room. The lights have been turned out and there are candles lit on our table, which has been set with plates and utensils.

"What the . . ." A.J. says, squinting in confusion.

"It's all of our side dishes," I say. "Happy Feast-Off, four days late."

"You're kidding," Isaiah says, his eyes wide. "How did you do all this alone?"

"I had a little help making the potatoes," I say, winking at Luke.

"Jeez. What made you go to all the trouble?" Isaiah says.

I shrug. "You guys. I just wanted to let you know I, uh, appreciate you."

"Oh, I'm so beyond touched," A.J. says, fake sniffling. Then he gives me a light punch in the arm, which I know is his way of saying "thank you."

I turn to Alisha. "And I want you here because you're the only person from Hunter's group to not throw me aside and I'm really, really glad for it."

"And we're glad to have you here, too," A.J. says, making a show of grabbing an extra plate and utensils, then adding an extra chair to our table.

"Unless you plan to outdo us in cooking like you did in beer pong," Luke jokes. "Then you can go right back to the dance."

Alisha laughs. "All right, then, what are we eating?"

"I think the question is 'what aren't we eating?'" Isaiah says, surveying the food all lined up in serving dishes on the kitchen counter.

"You made the corn casserole!" A.J. says, and I swear to god, he actually claps.

"It's the least I could do for making us so far behind in points," I say, helping myself to mashed potatoes.

"Well, it was kind of worth it," A.J. says, as he sits down. "You beating the crap out of Jared with deviled eggs is the awesomest thing I've ever seen. And I'm sorry for not saying it sooner."

"You should've seen it," Isaiah says to Alisha as they sit down. "She tackled him and he couldn't get up. His beret went flying halfway across the room!"

Alisha throws her head back and laughs. "Mild-mannered Ellie. I can't picture it!"

"I was kind of surprised no one jumped in to stop me," I say, taking a seat next to Luke.

"Hey, it was a fair fight," Luke says. "You were holding your own quite well." He nudges my knee with his, and I fight the urge to swoon.

"That, and we were living vicariously through you," A.J. says between mouthfuls.

"Yeah, and then Bryce had to take pity on Jared and stop you," Isaiah says, laughing.

"Was Jersey Strong all bitching about me after I left?" I ask.

A.J. nods. "But then you missed it—the Bakers made this crazy standing rib roast thing, so of course they won and—"

"Wait, the stoners won?" I say.

"Yup," A.J. says. "And Jersey Strong was pissed because they finished in second and accused the Bakers of cheating because they were thinking like us and put their roast in the oven earlier in the day . . ."

". . . And Mrs. Sanchez flipped out on them," Isaiah says. "And then she took most of their points for the day because of lack of sportsmanlike conduct."

"Insane. So that means only Synergy and the Bakers got a lot of points?"

"Yup," Luke says. "And then, as you know, some members of Synergy were having a meltdown all day—"

"That's Hunter and Brynn's group," I tell Alisha.

"Oh, lord," Alisha says, rolling her eyes. "I can only imagine that the 'who' melting down was Brynn, then."

"And their meal came out all half-assed, so they didn't get that many points," A.J. finishes.

I think about this for a minute. "So, basically, we still have a good shot at being in first place by June . . . and I mean that in the least competitive way possible."

"Of course we can win," A.J. says. "We're learning sewing in January. I mean, can you picture Bryce and Anthony with a needle and thread?"

With that, we all bust out laughing and it's awesome and I take a moment to soak it all in. There's the "thuggish juvenile delinquent" who's now telling us about his new job at a bakery in downtown Ringvale Heights, which will help him decide if he wants to "go to pastry school, if I'm still into that in the fall." There's the "solemn, silent guy" who is laughing so hard at A.J.'s description of his new boss that he starts pounding the table with glee. And there's "the tat-tooed goliath bad boy" looking disappointed as he dabs at a stain on his reindeer-festooned necktie. He feels my gaze and his eyes soften as they meet mine. Under the table, I rest my knee against his and he smiles.

They say if you can't take the heat, get out of the kitchen.

I'm glad I stayed.

ACKNOWLEDGMENTS

The journey from *Home Ick* to *The Secret Recipe for Moving On* literally spanned a decade, and over those ten years, you pick up a lot of gratefulness for the people who made this dream a very tangible thing. The hugest of thank-yous to:

The beyond wonderful editorial team at Swoon Reads: Jean Feiwel and Lauren Scobell, who took a chance on me, and allowed Ellie, Luke, A.J., and Isaiah to have life beyond a Word document saved on my laptop; Kat Brzozowski, for putting me at ease with the very first phone call we had about this book, and for being a guiding force and nurturing it from first draft to actual, polished novel; Holly Ingraham, for her invaluable first-pass edits that helped reshape this story and bring out its best aspects; Erin Siu, whose enthusiastic comments and sharp edits helped keep me focused through the more challenging changes; Starr Baer, Maddy Newquist, and Emily Heddleson, for catching all the errors that would most definitely haunt my dreams if they made it into print; Trisha Previte, for creating such a delightfully adorable cover that captures the spirt of this book perfectly; Emily Settle, for walking me through all-things Swoon Reads blog-related; and Brittany Pearlman, for all your help and hard work with marketing and publicity.

Janet and Bob Bischer, my parents, who very kindly bought their then-broke-ish daughter the laptop the first draft of this book was originally written on. I'm glad it churned out something more meaningful than salty Yankees tweets and cat-photo-centric Facebook posts.

Kenneth Wert, a genius plotter and the very first believer in this book, who, upon hearing the plot for it back in 2009 was like, "That's going to get published!" It took longer than we thought, but it happened, and that confidence gave me confidence to keep going. Long live our "Newport Days"!

Micol Ostow and my fellow writers in her spring 2010 YA novel-writing workshop, where this story officially began on page. And the biggest of thanks to the critique group that grew out of that class—"The Rogues," a wise, witty, incredibly talented group of writers who are essentially this book's godmothers and have been there every step of this saga: Linda Blum, Joanne Donovan, Nancy Lambert, Danielle Rumore Lundquist, and Fiona Taylor.

Alyssa Reuben, whose insights helped the first draft become a solid foundation for what exists now.

My very first "readers": Laura Carney, Rachel Chang, Aimee Leinhardt, and Courtney Pressler, whose requests to see my first draft made me feel like a "real" writer.

My friends and coworkers who have been have been stalwart champions of this book, my unofficial therapists when working through book-related challenges, and also so understanding when socializing has to take a backseat to writing/editing/rewriting: Erica Brown, Amy Dolan, Dexter Gasque, Claire Goncalves, Rana Meyer, Vicki Obe, Stephanie Sloane, and Tonya Trudo.

The Swoon Squad, who have been an absolutely vital source of useful information and support. I'm so glad we have each other!

And, finally, the Swoon Readers who vocalized their love for this book with votes or comments. This book doesn't get to the point of needing an acknowledgements section without you, and I'm not sure I'll ever be able to convey my thanks for that enough.